I0819240

U N D E R L A K E

UNDERLAKE

A Novel

Erin L. McCoy

Doubleday / New York

FIRST DOUBLEDAY HARDCOVER EDITION 2026

Published by Doubleday, a division of Penguin Random House LLC,
1745 Broadway, New York, NY 10019.

Doubleday and the portrayal of an anchor with a dolphin are
registered trademarks of Penguin Random House LLC.

Book design by Anna B. Knighton

Library of Congress Cataloging-in-Publication Data
Names: McCoy, Erin L., author
Title: Underlake : a novel / Erin L. McCoy.
Description: First Doubleday hardcover edition. | New York : Doubleday, 2026.
Identifiers: LCCN 2025024426 | ISBN 9780385552073 hardcover |
ISBN 9798217008391 trade paperback | ISBN 9780385552080 ebook
Subjects: LCGFT: Fiction | Detective and mystery fiction | Novels
Classification: LCC PS3613.C38375 U53 2026 | DDC 813.6—dc23/eng/20250529
LC record available at https://lccn.loc.gov/2025024426

penguinrandomhouse.com | doubleday.com

Printed in the United States of America
1st Printing

The authorized representative in the EU for product safety and
compliance is Penguin Random House Ireland, Morrison Chambers,
32 Nassau Street, Dublin D02 YH68, Ireland, https://eu-contact.penguin.ie.

For my mother, Paula

I

Otta

When the last sod was laid on the south slope of Paintsville Dam in the spring of 1979, the valley to its north filled up with water, and two hundred and forty people drowned.

All that remained of Paintsville was a five-thousand-acre lake, sterile and glassy in the shadow of the hills. The dam's two slopes—one of rubble, one of grass—met in a spine of road. Beneath this were two million cubic yards of rock fill and earth, and beneath this, a concrete tunnel through which the lake water, with the sluice gates' permission, passed. The tunnel carved through ribbons of red clay, beneath which a layer of limestone clasped Paleozoic coral in its teeth. Caves wound their way through the stone, and a long tongue of aquifer, slick with beetles and milky salamanders, shuddered with the groans and slips of the mantle, which bore it all.

Two hundred and forty people dead. It became the defining tragedy of Steels, a one-stoplight town and former neighbor to

Paintsville due northeast along a state road flanked by goldenrod. The city council mounted a bronze placard by the lakeshore, then left it to oxidize.

Once, Allie and I took a boat out on the lake and I fell overboard, and while I was suspended under the water—in shock and not knowing how to swim—I thought I saw a chimney winding up through the silt. A chimney under the lake, just like the stories we had heard. The town didn't like to talk about its dead, but children still told ghost stories: about what if those people had done what they set out to do, which was to keep living on the same land where they were born—submerged. I thought in that moment that I had found proof, delivered us all from mourning.

But I've learned not to trust myself when I know what I wish. Look how many years I spent trying to excise my past like a tumor, believing that through blood and labor and terror-driven will I could escape what this place had made me. Or how, when it all collapsed, my mind dangled a series of fevered daydreams: Could it be that Ethan was only lost, that the ocean had spat him out whole and gasping onto some beach? Powder-blue sand, cluster of foxtail palms tossing softly the shade around. Like those people under the lake, he might have passed into a realm invisible to this one—could be there now.

Then the daydream would crumble, and I'd find the same hands in front of me, tan line from my dive watch and nails bitten down to the quick. It was only a wish, and I knew why I wished it: because, in the darkness and clean scrape of the seafloor, the glass cephalopods and blue luminescence haunting at the edge of sight, I was the one that lost him.

THE NIGHT I CAME HOME to Steels, my mother in her pastel nightgown spun around to fetch the whistling kettle off the stove and suddenly got so dizzy that she clutched at the oven handle, wrenching open its charred maw. I had to half carry her to the couch.

Just an hour earlier, on the ride from the bus station, Allie had filled me in: the kidney disease was getting worse, and our mother, Eugenia, refused to be put on the transplant list.

"They're pretty mild, but the symptoms are there—some days worse than others," she said. "I think she's having some dementia too."

Allie's eyes fixed on the road, like she was shy of me. It had been years since we'd seen each other. Her jawbone had grown sharp, her nose aquiline, the last childlike features melted away.

She dropped me off in the driveway. "Can't come in—I'm running late for the dinner shift." The restaurant where she waited tables was in the city, an hour's drive away.

As I opened the car door, she grabbed my wrist. We locked eyes then, and she smiled. "Stay a while this time."

She didn't know I had nowhere else to go.

THE DEMENTIA WASN'T NEWS. On our last call, my mother had asked three times if I was wearing my good coat, although summer on an oil rig on the Gulf of Mexico isn't exactly going to freeze your ass off. I didn't think much of it. She'd always had those moments when her mind went loose and wandered. She came back to herself in her own time.

But look at the place now. Heaps of magazines and boxes of collectible tea sets and folded paisley table runners and cages for birds when we'd never had birds. These towered against the walls three and four and five stacks deep, with hair and shit from the cat clotted at their feet.

My mother's dizzy spell left her exhausted—eyelids lilting, jaw clenched. I walked her upstairs to bed, then called Allie.

"I'm working, what's up?"

I told her what had happened.

"She had dialysis today. She gets lightheaded after," Allie said. "Let her rest."

I climbed back up the stairs, which were littered with feathers—maybe our mother did have a bird?—and piles of tabloids in chronological order, advancing as the stairs advanced. The collections had expanded threefold since I'd visited last.

When I walked into the bedroom Eugenia was sitting up, reading a magazine. Her eyes swept over my face, then returned to the wrinkled issue of *Time*.

"Otta Coates," she said. "When did you get in?"

"We talked downstairs, Mom."

She flipped the page. "Right, I remember." It sounded like a lie. But then, with one swift tug at the hook, she returned to herself: "I don't know why you took the bus. What are you here for, anyway?"

I CHECKED IN ON Eugenia a few times over the course of the night. She'd fallen asleep with the magazine on her chest and started to sweat, her forehead glossy beneath wild gray wires of hair. She was tossing in the face of I don't know what dream. I opened a window and the wind gnashed in carrying slices of rain, and still she sweated and kept sweating.

I rotated cool rags until she stilled. Then I crossed to the window and tried to mop up where droplets blotched the papers scattered across her dresser.

Beneath a stack of receipts, I found a leather-bound album, and flipped through it. It was a scrapbook of newspaper clippings, all from before the dam was built. On one article from 1978, I could see the headline and the first few paragraphs of the folded paper.

AMID RIFTS, COUNCIL STILL
REFUSES TO LEAVE VALLEY

> A group of some 400 people who have refused to evacuate Weber Valley has now splintered as a result of internal power disputes.
>
> The group, which calls itself the People's Council, has insisted on remaining in and around the

> town of Paintsville, even as construction wraps on a dam that will flood the area next year.
>
> The council was founded by a contingent of factory workers who seized control of the shuttered Weber Paint Co. more than a year ago. This group has spearheaded efforts to reinforce the factory and a number of buildings along Paintsville's Main Street in preparation for "underwater living." Other isolated homes and industrial structures have also been outfitted, including Paintsville Church, which stands on a hill at the valley's highest point.
>
> On Monday, Rev. Arnold Jewell of Paintsville Church told The Herald that he has broken ties with factory leadership due to "philosophical differences."
>
> "We are not guided by 'the people.' We will follow His word and His word alone in these final days," Rev. Jewell said.
>
> Community leaders have expressed mounting concerns that this mass delusion may in fact lead to

I shut the album. I'd heard the stories a hundred times growing up—though never from my mother.

I sat down beside her, watched the hinge of her jaw working at something she could never grind down.

The moon passed behind a cloud and I dozed, a crooked sleep that picked at my scabs and every hour tossed me awake. Haunted. Something, at last, my mother and I had in common.

WHEN I OPENED THE DOOR to the sunporch the next morning, a frothing black mold filled my lungs, and I coughed my way back into the kitchen.

I saw the problem fast enough: a corner of the roof had dry-rotted, and the ceiling drooped with damp. My mother had apparently covered the boxes she kept out there with a tarp but had made no attempt to fix the roof.

I was still sick in those first days home, damp in the lungs and hacking out something I'd caught down on the ocean floor. Breathing heliox at five hundred feet of depth had left the occasional tremors in my hands. When I was asleep I could still hear the dull shriek of metal through the comms as Ethan—weighed down by his dive gear and a million tons of water—wound the bolts into place, then tapped to test the solidity of the pipeline.

I took my mother's car and drove into Steels to find a contractor for the roof.

It was the first time I'd seen the town in years, and as I approached the single stoplight at the top of Main Street, my stomach churned. A wind tossed the light on its wire. I inched down the rust-dark corridor of storefronts, two redbrick stories beneath flaking cornices running down both sides of Main, huddled together against the brittle autumn. The plate-glass windows gaped through famished frames.

Nothing had changed since I'd left twelve years ago: a bank, a contractor's office, the diner where I waited tables in high school. It was as though the town had been sealed off completely from the outside world. Towering above it all was the eyeless edifice of Steels Evangelical Church, its oxidized steeple like a single raised finger of reproach.

I parked and went inside the contractor's office. The drowsy receptionist asked a few questions, then scribbled out an estimate that was far more than I could afford. My student loans were due, and it wasn't yet clear whether my last paycheck would be forwarded to me here.

I walked to the bank to see if I could set up a wire transfer. The teller, gulping through his tie knot, told me about a handyman living down on the lakeshore who would do it cheap.

"Jeffrey Clark," he said.

"Clark—the physics teacher?"

He nodded. He couldn't help with the wire.

I drove over a muddy creek and out of town. This road traced the boundary of a three-hundred-acre tract that my mother claimed had all been Coates farmland "for as far back as history goes." Eugenia liked to point out the landmarks: a clot of sugar maples where her grandmother, Ottilie—daughter of a French immigrant, after whom I was named—hung a tire swing; a span of field where her grandfather shot the buck whose head still hung in our house. Eugenia's father had sold almost all this land to developers.

I turned down the road to the lake, and a vine-gnarled forest swallowed the fields. The land around the lake was a state park, though it didn't get much traffic. The year after the valley flooded, the state health department detected dangerous levels of lead in the lake water and forbade anyone from swimming, boating, or eating the fish. The promise of a touristic boom of anglers and an influx of cash for Steels was dashed overnight.

Jeffrey Clark lived on a floating marina that had been built just before the bad news broke, in a bait shop that had never opened. I pulled into the empty parking lot. It was late September, and a swell of cicadas still quaked the surrounding woods.

As I walked down the gangway, whiskered bullheads swarmed the pylons, their keyhole mouths picking at floats of algae. Poisonous, maybe, but not poisoned.

I knocked, heard a grunt from inside the shop, and went in.

A counter with an old cash register ran along the back wall. There, a man wearing magnifier eyeglasses hunched over a battery pack with wires fraying out. A single shock of orange hair on the crown of his head cut through the gray. I'd seen him, years ago, shuffling through the halls of the high school with a leather folio. I never took his class; he was known for falling asleep in his chair.

"Shop's closed," he said, pushing the magnifiers up his nose.

"Going on thirty years, right?"

My joke didn't land. He scanned my face, the glasses dilating his pupils.

I searched the room for a change of subject and spotted a buoyancy compensator and crumpled wet suit in the corner.

"You scuba?" I asked, moving toward it by instinct until a twist in my gut stopped me short.

He shrugged.

"Turns out my asthma's too bad," he said. "Do you?"

"Yes."

He pulled off the magnifiers. His eyes gaped, and he blew out a puff of air.

"Well, how about that," he muttered.

I explained about my mother's roof. He was watching me closely, tugging at his beard.

Finally, he waved away the rest of my story: all the details of the sunporch's proportions, my hedging on the cost.

"I can start Monday, but only if I can bring a friend."

"A friend."

He nodded.

"She needs to learn how to dive," he said, "and she needs to learn fast."

WHEN I GOT HOME, Eugenia was out front, the wings of her straw hat flying up as, over and over, she thrust a hole digger into the ground.

"Do you feel well enough to be out here?" I asked.

She didn't answer.

"What are you trying to do?"

She wiped the sweat from her chin with the back of a gardening glove. "Rabbits."

"Can I help?"

"You don't know the first thing about it."

I heard the crunch of gravel at the foot of the drive. Allie parked and got out, but as she approached I gave a quick shake of the head. We left Eugenia to her mood and walked around the side of the house toward the woods.

When we were out of earshot, I burst out laughing. "What are you wearing?"

It was a frilly skirt with a laced tunic like a barmaid's uniform.

"Guess." She pirouetted, lace lifting around her.

"The Sound of Music."

"What else?" She did a waltz, then ducked beneath the low-hanging branch that marked a trailhead into the woods.

I followed. "Pretty sexy for community theater."

"You know I like to show them off." She spun around midgait to nudge up her boobs. When she'd had her top surgery, I was just starting grad school and didn't have the money to fly home. She told me later it had been the happiest day of her life—"more like in retrospect," she laughed, "because it hurt like a bitch." The bottom surgery was a few years later.

As she led me down the path now, I wondered if I would have recognized her in a dark bar. This visit was the first time I'd seen her since she fully transitioned. Her hair coiled down to her waist, and her long strides were assured—far from the hunched kid who used to follow me down this trail.

We passed beneath the alders whose pollen-yellow catkins Allie used to collect every spring on the way to the tilt—our name for the shelter of branches we'd leaned in an A-frame along the wandering arm of an oak.

We built it when I was eight, and Allie five. That year, the school bus dropped me off every afternoon at the foot of our driveway. It could reach our house only by passing through a new subdivision, constructed on the last parcel of land Eugenia's father had sold.

One day, as the bus pulled around our cul-de-sac, a boy from the subdivision pointed up the hill. "Your mama steal that car?"

I was confused. "No."

"My mama says she's a thief. So she must have stole that car."

Laughter rustled through the seats. I peeled my legs off the pleather and ran down the steps.

At the kitchen table, hot tears started rolling down my cheeks.

Allie—then called Alby, short for Albion, another family name—hugged my arm.

My mother set down two half sandwiches. "What's this now?"

As I explained, her lips pinched shut. She gazed out the window into a span of mown yard. When I was done, I gaped up at her, willing her arms to close down around me.

"Quit crying," she said. She crossed the kitchen and started banging around pots in the sink.

When she returned for our plates, we must have been staring.

"Get on outside and play. If I'm a thief, where you think I buried my treasure?"

That launched a concerted effort—one that would last for years—to dig up the hidden bounty. As springtime blushed awake, Allie and I wandered the woods kicking the underbrush and shining flashlights into the knotholes of trees. We made up stories about what had been stolen and from whom and how much. Come summer break, a diaphanous membrane sealed off our yard and the empty cul-de-sac. I passed through it only once, venturing down into the subdivision, which like a brain coral cemented the hillsides with tightly wound avenues of clones. Two boys from the bus passed on their bikes. I waved. Over my shoulder, their laughter trickled down the asphalt. That night, I told Allie we were going to build a clubhouse that no one else was allowed inside.

It took weeks to collect and assemble the long branches for the roof of the tilt. When it was finished, we stole a plastic rug from the sunporch to use as a stage and started putting on plays, acting out the discovery of the treasure. Allie always starred. She assembled leafy backdrops and patched costumes together from the clothes our mom bought at storage auctions. On that stage, with the twilight inking in, strands of fireflies laced out glittering tracks into the woods, whispering the route to us.

We traded off playing the part of our father, his canvas duffel weighed down with gold bars from his latest heist—treasure that our mom would later bury. The few times he'd visited, he never stayed the night. Eventually, though, there would be enough. He could stop being a thief and come home.

The autumn I turned ten, our dad brought me a keychain all the way from the Grand Canyon, with a picture on one side and a mirror on the other—"for doing your lipstick," he joked. Eugenia frowned and left us in the foyer with him crouched by his duffel, which I kicked, but which seemed soft like clothes. That was the last time he came.

Now, inside an overgrowth of clematis, Allie and I found the tilt. It was still intact, the branches woven in such a tight mesh that the ground beneath remained almost bare.

Allie leapt onto the plastic rug and took a bow. "My first stage."

I laughed. "A star is born in Steels."

"I told Mom this was out here."

"What'd she say?"

"Nothing, like usual." She plucked a clematis bloom and spun the four-petaled white burst in her fingers.

"I'm guessing she's the same way about the transplant list?"

"Of course. It was hard enough to convince her to start dialysis. You should try."

"If she won't listen to you, she definitely won't listen to me."

"You'd be surprised," Allie said. "She talks about you a lot."

I rolled my eyes. "She doesn't know anything about me."

Some of that was by design. The last thing I wanted now was to explain why I'd failed to become a marine biologist when that was the reason I left home in the first place. My interest in anything outside the farm—our four remaining acres, and the ghost of the rest—had always baffled our mother. Eugenia hadn't asked more than a dozen questions about my studies in the years since I'd left.

Allie shrugged, tucked the bloom behind her ear.

"Anyway, we'd need her birth certificate for the transplant list, and I can't find it. You're not leaving tomorrow or anything, are you?"

"No," I said. A famished void paced the margins of my vision: that image of Ethan—imagined, but impossible to shake—violet and swollen on the ocean floor. If I didn't keep my head down, it would swallow me whole.

"Okay, then, could you try and find it? I've been working doubles."

Dusk was crowding in, its little blues and stains.

"I can do that."

It was a purpose, and I was grateful for it. I would train all my focus on that glowing ember until it went to ash.

I STARTED THE SEARCH upstairs in Eugenia's office. Everywhere I looked—under papers, behind boxes, on shelves and side tables—I found mugs with moldy tea bags welded inside them. One, when I picked it up, emitted a fog of spores.

I dropped it on the table and took a step back, feeling in the swirling motes a sudden dislocation, like I was underwater and I'd just spit out a line of bubbles. They rose, spiraling around another column of breath—from whose mouth—

The blinds rattled against the glass, sending spears of light across the crates of books. I shook my head clear and waved my hand over the vent. It was off. But I could feel fresh air trickling from behind the nearest stack. Slowly, crate by crate, I began to carve a path.

A few rows deep, I pulled loose a framed poster leaning atop a bookshelf. Behind it was a window. It was cracked an inch, admitting slivers of breeze.

I'd forgotten about this window—even stopped noticing it in the façade of the house, the way the familiar always becomes invisible. I opened it and leaned out.

The front yard, years ago, had been overtaken by tall grasses creeping in from the woods. This too was so little changed that I had stopped seeing it. But now it jolted into focus. Someone was standing at the foot of the drive.

All I could make out was cropped hair, squared shoulders, galoshes. Still, across all that distance, it felt like they were staring back.

I shut the window and went downstairs.

When I walked outside, the figure was climbing the last stretch of hill. Checked blazer and patched pants, all oversized. They stopped at the foot of the stoop.

"Hello. I'm May." Tipped-up chin, mildly childish. "Jeffrey Clark the teacher sent me."

"Okay," I said. "Is he coming?"

"I think." That stare, still unbroken.

"Are you here to fix the roof?"

"Not me. I'm a mother."

A cold wind wrung the grasses along the front walk. She hugged her arms around herself and took one step closer.

"He said you could learn me to dive. My daughter is lost under the lake."

SOMEHOW, with Eugenia napping upstairs, I found myself walking inside her ghost—pacing across the kitchen, starting the teapot, fetching sugar and spoons and cups, serving at last a mug to the person at the table—this time, May, whom I had invited in at a loss for what else to do—and then standing at the counter, never sitting, never ever sitting down.

May's hair licked off in three directions, like she'd cut it herself. She appeared to be about my age, early thirties, but from some angles seemed much younger. When I set down her cup, I detected a scent of fresh and oil, like the outdoors.

I gripped the counter, sipped my tea, and said, "I don't recover bodies. You should go to the police."

"Bodies?" She squinted in the light dripping through the sunporch window.

"Your—your daughter."

"I can help her swim. She isn't heavy."

I searched her face for a twinge of what had entered my mother's, years ago—that spinning yarn she would watch just behind my head that meant half of her mind was elsewhere.

"I don't know what you mean," I said.

"Right." May shifted in her chair. "Mr. Clark said this would be confusing. I didn't know nothing of you either till I came to the Overlake. And I'm still learning, like with this."

She lifted her mug, tipped it so the water just reached her lips, and set it down again.

"Thank you, it's good," she said, and peered around herself. All at once, her eyes widened. She crouched to the floor. My mother's cat, a gray tabby, was frozen in the doorway, tip of her tail crooked.

"Hi hi hi," she whispered.

The tabby tiptoed toward her outstretched hand. She let May caress her once before exiting through the cat door.

May climbed back into her seat, gleaming.

"That's a cat?" She smelled her palms.

I didn't know if she was putting on an act or if she'd escaped from a locked room somewhere. But her mention of Clark gave me pause. The old man didn't strike me as a practical joker.

"A cat, yes. You were telling me—you're not from here, I guess."

"Right." She rubbed her palms on her thighs. "The thing you need to know is—my daughter and me. We're from the Chimneys and lived there our whole life. My daughter's name is Daphne. She left a week ago and I don't know to where. But she wouldn't have come here, to the Overlake, and so she must be Under—and I can't reach her on my own."

Nausea coiled my stomach. Everyone in town knew about the theft—and most of them knew, by my estimation, what Eugenia had done with the money. I'd learned the facts when I was twelve: She had given it all to the People's Council. They'd used it to fortify their houses, believing they could survive beneath the lake when the valley flooded. Every one of them drowned. Eugenia refused to talk about it, but for me, the blood on her hands colored everything that she did.

"This is ridiculous." I was shaking, and put down my tea. "Who sent you?"

She tilted her head. Birdlike, in her movements. "Jeffrey Clark sent me."

I flipped my phone open. No calls from him. May squinted at the device, as though trying to make out what it was.

"It's pathetic, really," I said. "We all know what my mother did. But at least she's not telling ghost stories about people living under the lake."

"Your mother?" May shook her head. "There *are* people living under the lake."

"Get out." That drowsing beast in my gut—it had been there as long as I could remember. But nothing stirred its gnarled limbs like being back in Steels, locked inside these low hills, where rumors spread like an infection, where no one could see past the closest horizon, much less imagine a world beyond.

I held open the sunporch door.

May stood, eyelashes matted.

"Daphne. She's my only daughter, my only only."

She walked out onto the porch, turned around.

"I'll be staying with Mr. Clark, learning myself to dive." She pushed through the screen door and down the steps. I could hear her faintly, just before it slammed:

"Please come."

As she plodded down the hill in her too-large galoshes, I watched for a grin back over her shoulder, some mischievous glint. There was none of this. Instead, halfway down, she paused beneath a cherry tree. She stood there, staring up. A wind passed through them both, and like two ships on the same swell, they listed.

She seemed lost inside that movement. I lost track of time, watching. My vision must have softened, curled back inside my mind. I hadn't slept well for weeks. When I blinked, she was gone.

May

For as long as I can remember the wires have delivered light out of the dark. Whenever the lake outside dims and flakes away into unknowing, whenever the sturgeon and the muskellunge tuck into their nests and the trout turn to nothing but thuds against the glass, there is a shiver of utter goneness and a caught single breath, shared between us all.

But then, surely and every, the lights flicker on. Bulb by bulb, they flare down the passageways that connect our cottages. The minnow troughs open back up their whiteless eyes and glint as diamonds—like those on the sculpture of the rising Him, that dimple His cheeks like tears. Every Sunday, beneath that sculpture, the reverend at his pulpit would burn his eyes along the pews. He could dig into any soul and find the rot in it, pull it out like a pin bone, and he loved it he relished the electric charge in it, you could see it from his curling lips.

After those sermons, the Reverend Jewell would collapse into his cottage and not be seen for days. It was understood how he needed rest in order to manage the stress of our tutelage, the guidance of us through salvation, which is the living mission of the Underlake, which I've been storied every day of my life—and which I stopped believing the day of my daughter's birth, to her own danger but also toward a different kind of salvation. My daughter is the only surviving child of her generation in the Chimneys. I have kept her alive by breaking every rule, and I don't regret one single crack of them.

It is the Jewells—the reverend and his family—that is encrusted with the telling of stories. Of the sinking Him and of the rising Him and of the arrival, one day most joyously, of the lake and the holy revelation that He raised the water for us. They tell us there was once a wicked world in the Overlake and there is not no more. They tell us how He entered the body of a minnow and now feeds us of His own skin whatever we catch. When I was little and alone down a passageway, I sometimes imagined I saw in a minnow trough the shape of the savior puzzle together in a formation of fry, only for it to crumble apart before my eyes. The passageways have a tricky light.

I believed it then: us the endowed only, tasked with rebuilding a virtuous world. To serve the mission, each family had an assigned fate: the minnow-blooming or the salt-packing or the wall-caulking or the allotment-setting. But me, I was here by accident. I wasn't born to any family but to a mother that no one talked about without shaking their heads, who didn't say—maybe didn't know—the father's name; but who also swapped her death for my life, which in my secret stomach I considered kind, but which left me without a last name and so without a fate—a noncontributor, with only the allotments others gave me as tithe.

The higher of the fates was the book-cleaning and the stockkeeping and the pronouncement-passing of whatever the reverend's family told them to pronounce. But the reverend always had the final word. Every Sunday he'd preach the stories of the First Books, pointing to the pictures in the stained-glass windows: His blood spilling from the crossed boughs of a tree, which is why trees are wicked; the parting of the sea, proof that even prophets could lack the true faith, which was proved only through submersion—which in all of history only we had done.

"We are washed clean," the reverend would say. "Will you stay clean?"

When the last steel beam was laid into the wall of Paintsville Church, the reverend gave the church its true name: the Shuttle, after how fools tried once to fly to the moon. We'd corrected that path to the righteous destination.

It was the Reverend Jewell who had wrote the Final Book about the sinking of the Overlake and the rising of the Underlake, an event that some in the Chimneys still remembered. He started writing it when they announced the dam and the lake's approach, which he revelated would bring the end of dark days. He finished the Book years later, on the very night that the lake's rise began.

The Rise happened on a series of seven days, like the beginning of the world. On the seventh, it reached the tops of our windows. That was the day I was born.

"What did they do to be wicked?" I asked one Sunday school, and the teacher gritted his teeth. But the next week, Mary Wallace asked the same question and he told her: "Grievous and bloody sins." When pressed, he added: "His chosen people were mixing with His unchosen people." And so the unchosen and any who'd mixed with them were left to the Overlake, where all of them over the next days were variously caught unawares by the rising waters and set to swimming while the gray waves gnashed and ripped off their little hats. And it drowned their cows and it drowned their pigs, and it dragged their airplanes out of the sky. And one by one they got tired and sunk to the bottom of the lake, where they fed the fish that now feed us, and that is why we call the lake the judge and justice, because it put the whole world back where it belonged: under our feet.

But here I must admit a thing. I have embellished. I've dreamed about their small legs climbing against the water. I've imagined many events I haven't seen and turned them into stories in my head. So that's what I'm coming back to now. That I have never told nothing that happened to me like it was a story, because stories are threads that spool from Jewells' mouths.

That was true and I believed it, until the day I sinned the greatest and went to the Overlake.

But I'm getting ahead of myself. Stories, I think, should be told in order, or they don't make the kind of sense that only one choice after another can make. I had trouble explaining to Otta what had led me here: all the million ways the Chimneys are different from her world of grass; the holy weight of water always haunting above our heads; the reasons my daughter left. It's hard to believe a story if you don't agree from the start what kind of world this is.

So what I want to do now is to be for my daughter a kind of body in words, a skin of minnows if minnows were letters, to tell from the beginning how it come exactly that she disappeared. Because if I can answer that, maybe it can help me bring her home.

ALL OF WHICH IS TO SAY, I'm going to tell about the night that I was born.

The snow churning down. Freezing water like the dead skin that scrapes off under your nails when you scratch. And portentous, a sign from Himself, was the snow that fell, because it fell in May, a month that was far too late for it. So I've been told.

I don't remember my birth and don't know if other people remember theirs. So I'll admit the gaps have been filled in by me.

The lake had been rising and was now halfway up the windows. Then at the door of the Shuttle there came an all-wet knocking. They called for the Reverend Jewell and when he heard the sound he declared, "We're here for anyone who deserves saving."

Which I bet he come to regret saying.

Someone called through the door that the knocker should come around the side of the Shuttle to a window box. All the window boxes got built in preparation for the lake's rise. Each one had an inner glass and an outer glass—plexiglass, it's called—that formed a huge container that could open and shut from the top. You'd dangle in the bait on a line, then pull a lever that shut it to the inside and opened it to the out, letting the lake pour in. You'd wait until a fish caught, then pull the lever again. When you opened the hatch on the inner glass, water would overflow from the top into a trough beneath, and then you could pull the fish out.

Now, seeing just the blur of a figure outside, the rising water up to their neck, someone pulled the lever to open the outside hatch. A woman, much pregnant, climbed down into the box with the lake slopping in around her. She was soaked so her dress clung to her legs and they could see the crests of her popped-out nipples. They flushed and brought over the wives.

Dark hair, a knotted riot down her shoulders. That's all I know. And maybe I don't even know that. I think, though, that she had green eyes and a fine fur down her arms and legs. I've seen photos of horses and how the muscles of their thighs carve up beneath their skin like they have nothing to hide. I think that she looked like that.

"Madge," they said, "Margaret." Their mouths hung open. Margaret used to sit in the back pews with her parents on Sundays, but she'd stopped coming a few years back.

"Help me," she said.

Those are the only words I know she ever spoke for a fact.

The wives led her out of the Shuttle and down a passageway to the cottage that once belonged to a family called Powell and so today is called Powell. It's the place I sleep now, with minnow-keepers and waste-collectors. They laid Margaret out on the floor and did their duty. They called for Peach Warren, the midwife, whose daughter is called Plum, whose baby daughters, each before they died, were called Blossom and Blossom and Blossom.

I remember, when I was small, seeing Peach many times stalking down the passageways, bent under the heft of her medicine bag. The passageways were lined with yellowing fluorescents—the best bulbs, for the many years they lasted—and these snaked out behind her, a holy protection, in their wobbling light. Whenever I saw her, I'd hide behind a minnow trough. I believed that on sight, she could melt me in my own disgrace. She'd also told it all to Plum, who was just a few years my elder and who taught both me and the other kids the word *bastard* and how it applied.

"SHAMELESS," Kella Partridge said later to Bethany Vaughan as they set a plate of trout's head in front of me. They'd been young women when my mother gave birth, and they were talking about the way she screamed.

Kella was bony and blonde and smelled like wax. She rendered me tithe every six months, same as Bethany; most others were on a tighter cycle. They were from high fates and good blood. Whenever I was there they would sit at the far end of the table, smoking their reverend's-stock cigarettes and chatting like I couldn't hear.

"Of course it was a blessed night"—Bethany leaned in at Kella and grinned—"but lakes! She just about ruined it for me." She bit her lips, a habit to keep them blushed.

Peach tended a long time to the birthing Margaret, but the baby wouldn't come. They had to burn down two candlesticks into the next morning, squirming eels against the walls. Many evenings in Powell cottage, I searched for the shadow of her shadow. I'd raise my hand in front of a lamp and play with its cast shape, pretend she was reaching out to me.

But there was a shadow of her there, clear enough. I just didn't like to look at it. The story goes that when I came through, the blood was pouring out around me like water from a window, and soaked all the way through the carpet, so that when they ripped it up it had stained even the wood beneath.

Sometimes when the Wallaces, who lived with me in Powell, got bitter about having to feed me, Erma Wallace would make me scrub at that stain.

THE BOOKS ALONG OUR SHELVES in Powell had pictures sometimes of men in robes, other times of buildings and beasts and jagged earth. One book was an encyclopedia of all the animals that had lived in the Overlake but were extinct now.

I loved those animals. When Mrs. Wallace was in a better mood, which in those days was Fridays when they got their blood-of-Him allotment, I'd ask her about the land animals. She'd seen almost all of them: horses and cows and sparrows and cats. One night, having also drunk Mr. Wallace's allotment, she told about her dog Toby, a yellow mutt who she had to leave outside the corner grocery. She'd held on to him hoping the rules would change, until the lake was rising already and it was too late. Her voice got quaky, and Mr. Wallace put her to bed.

One day it occurred to me that the grocery might still exist in the Underlake. I was only seven, and for me it was a revelation. I started to wonder, if someone was in the grocery looking out—sin to even think—what would we look like? No one in the Chimneys ever left—didn't swim, didn't climb the flues. None of this was allowed. I could glimpse the Chimneys from the outside through the windows, since the passageways spined out in all directions to link the different cottages. But the angles were hard. Usually, all you could see was the wink of windows through the silt and moss. I asked Mrs. Wallace where the grocery was and she pointed at a wall in Powell. We were the farthest cottage at this end of the Chimneys, separated from the others by a long passageway that placed us, for our low fates, far from the Shuttle. I pressed my face against a window, but it pointed in the wrong direction.

The first map I ever saw was in a brochure I found tucked inside a catalog. It was of a factory drawn like if you were swimming over it. I wanted to copy it. There was plenty of old books and magazines that us kids used for taking school notes. So in the back pages of an almanac, I drew Powell like from above: where the tables and chairs, where the shelves and knickknacks and bedrooms.

I was sitting at the table, focused on my sketch, and didn't hear Mrs. Wallace come in. She slapped me so hard I fell off the chair.

"Thief."

She tucked the brochure into her apron pocket.

After that, it was more interesting to me than ever. I would wait until the Wallaces left to tend minnows in the morning. That was a full day's work: feeding the fish, then scraping off the algae from inside the troughs, which lined every passageway. Peach Warren made vitamins with it. When they were gone, I'd sneak into their room and slip the brochure from under their mattress. It was called "A Worker-Owned Factory of the Future" and it had a picture of some people with their arms crossed. The brochure said they'd tried to stay in the Underlake also. I didn't recognize their faces, and I had met everyone there was to meet.

I showed the brochure once to Mary Wallace, who at that time still enjoyed small mischiefs like being my friend. She was a year younger, and slept on the bedroll next to mine in the living room. One day, while we were playing checkers, I whispered to her had she ever heard of the Factory of the Future. Mary leaned close, her dark eyes widened.

"Mom says that's where the lights come from." We peered at the bulb in the middle of the ceiling, one of the old fat-filament incandescents, which were lit three hours every night—dimmed to make them last.

"But where's the factory?" I asked. "Are there still people there?"

Mary sat up straight. "We are the righteous and only." It was the same phrase we encountered every day, in services or painted on walls or cross-stitched into aprons. I'd stitched it myself many times, undoing the threads in Mrs. Wallace's and remaking the design whenever she felt like "something fresh."

Mary got prim like that. She drifted closer to me and then away again. Mrs. Wallace raised us together as babies; I was an obligation tasked to her by the reverend's wife. But, as Mrs. Wallace liked to remind us, the two of us were in every way different. Mary had a fate. And aside from her friendship with me, she followed the rules better than anyone.

When I was eleven, Mrs. Wallace announced it was time we stopped consorting. But Mary didn't stop. For that I am ever grateful to her. At night, while her parents snored in their bedroom, we whispered between our pillows. Mary still slept on the floor beside me. Mrs. Wallace couldn't do much about that, there being a limit of beds.

When her parents were out, we did our homework at the table together. Mary helped me with literature—she liked the Final Book so frothingly much that she spoke sometimes like it—and I helped her with calculations.

"You're so smart for a girl," she told me a few times. She had the biggest round eyes of anyone alive, and a pink dot on each cheek. "Your fate should be calculating."

It was around that time that we invented a secret game between us. It was like a scavenger hunt. We would leave clues hidden around the Chimneys, each one leading to the next, and at the end of the hunt, there was some small beauty. It could be the full-color page ripped out of a magazine, or a braided-wire ring, or a new embroidery. I'd design one game, then she'd do the next. Sometimes I didn't even know a new hunt had started until, in a corner or under a chair, I spotted a scrap of yellow paper, or a strand of the colored thread I'd used reworking a tea towel. These were objects that only we could recognize. The thread might be tied around a wire or a pencil, and that clue would lead to the next.

The longest hunt ever created was made by Mary. It took me nine Sundays to solve, with thirteen clues along the chain, and at the end of it, hidden under a loose tile in a changing stall near the baths, was a drawing. It was on the torn-out page from the end of a chapter, where you could get blank space. It was done in careful pencil, with shadows carving the soft grooves of the skin where a dimple sunk in or the bone stuck out. It was a portrait of Jonas Vaughan.

Girls in the Chimneys weren't supposed to care about boys until we were fourteen and preparing for Rehearsal, with marriage to follow. This last part was not a guarantee for either of us. Mary had a lower fate, so she would be chosen later, and me—I could expect nothing. So with us not being allowed to talk about it yet, this was how she told me.

I would understand only later that in sharing the drawing she was also claiming him.

No. I'm lying about that. I understood it then. I've learned that lying always feels better than its opposite. That's how you know you're doing it.

After I found the portrait, we would whisper at night, not about our dreams or our secret books, but about Jonas—how he'd touched Mary's hand passing her a pencil, how he'd been in the allotment line in front of her, how she liked his longer hair better than his short. I'd pipe in with the kinds of questions I knew she wanted me to ask. It was enough to be a mirror to her. I couldn't wish for more.

WHEN I WAS TWELVE, Mr. Wallace started taking me around to tend minnows. He had a bad knee and needed me to help scrub out the algae.

Mr. Wallace was a lumbering, long gar with a hunchback from having to duck through doorways. He had so many memories sometimes they just spilled out his mouth. Before the Rise, he was a carpenter, which means building, so when the troughs had leaks he was good at fixing them, though he grumbled sometimes how he wasn't no blacksmith. Once I asked him what a blacksmith was, and his wispy eyebrows arched, surprised I'd heard him.

He waved me off. "Before the Rise, dead and gone." He kept his mouth shut the rest of that day. After that I stopped asking questions, and he was talking again soon enough.

I'd seen other parts of the Chimneys when I went on errands for Mrs. Wallace, who had headaches almost every week and would send me to fetch angelica from the Warrens. As I got older, more and more people complained of the same, and the angelica—a dried, ancient plant in airtight jars—was finally sealed off in the stockroom, alongside the replacement bulbs and the cigarettes and the blood-of-Him. The stockroom was attached to the reverend's cottage, and the Partridges' fate to guard.

Her headaches surged usually after visiting the chutes. Because on top of the minnow-tending, the Wallaces had the worst fate of all: removing the trash, and also, when it happened, the dead. They would load these on a cart and wheel them to a room on the far other end of the Chimneys. There, chutes sucked them down into the caves below, the first step for the dead on their journey to either the mantle or the core of the Earth.

Now, with Mr. Wallace, I saw passageways and cottages I hadn't even known about, and soon I decided to make a map of the whole Chimneys.

I'd peek inside the open doors of cottages as we passed by and make in my head the notes for my project. Carter cottage had a gold cross that glinted like teeth. Mann was blue-washed with a mounted dead paddlefish swimming through it.

One day, Mr. Wallace knocked on the half-open door of Mr. Teague, who had one son and a grandson my age. We crossed the threshold, and I leapt back in my shoes. A furred head with branching horns hung above the hearth.

Mr. Wallace sat right down in front of it. They started reminiscing on how Mr. Teague caught it: how he rose early dawn and disguised himself as the earth, how the hush of its hooves through the morning dark, how its thumping throat he felt before he saw it, how he aimed and felled the beast in one shot.

All the while, I stood behind Mr. Wallace's chair peeking up at the head. The eyes were smooth stones and reflected back the shape of the window. The wet lips were parted, like it had been slaughtered right on the verge of telling a secret. Telling what? And in what sound?

MR. TEAGUE'S SON, Robert Junior, came around twice a year to clean our chimney. It was only Teagues that was allowed to climb them, but I'd peeked up the shaft a few times. The rungs went all the way to the top. Up there, a tiny square of light poured down to us the only remaining good that came of the Overlake: air.

It was on that visit to their cottage that I noticed Robert Junior's son, Caleb, reading a book in the corner. Caleb was two years older than me and passed our classroom on the way to the sacristy, where boys had their last few years of schooling. Caleb was a middle fate but was friends with Jonas Vaughan, and so even if Mr. Wallace dared to visit Robert Senior, Caleb was far above someone I could even talk to.

Still, in the passageways, I'd watch for hints of stubble along his jaw, his tail-flick lashes. He never caught me doing it—but Jonas did. I locked eyes with him once and he seemed even to wink at me. I was sure I'd imagined it.

There were signs that gave me hope. Once, when I was alone in Powell, I heard a clatter from the chimney. It knocked all the way down and there fell right into the hearth a little round mirror with a keychain hanging off. I picked it up and turned it over in my palm. On the back, there was a drawing in brown printed onto it showing a yarn winding through a valley. At the top, in square announcing letters, it said THE GRAND CANYON.

I hid it right away inside my bedroll. But over the next months, I started carrying it with me, and the more I turned the cold metal disc in my pocket, the more I thought it meant something. Caleb was a chimney-cleaner, and out of our chimney had sprung treasure.

One day, while I was standing outside the door to the school, the boys went by and I glanced up. I heard a whispering and turned to see Jonas's sister, Leigh, leaning in to the ear of Lily Partridge. They were staring at me.

"What?" I knew better than to ask that.

"Lakes!"—Leigh Vaughan started to laugh—"you honestly think you could get my brother's attention, when he's going to marry her?" Leigh pointed at Lily, who plumped her lips. Lily had blonde locks halfway down her back. My hair was a middle brown and cropped short by Mrs. Wallace, who said she didn't like the stink of long hair.

They beckoned over a few others: pearl-toothed Asher, who liked poking girls with fish ribs too thin-as-hair to see; Noah, with putty lips and scrolls of dead skin peeling off his arms. Leigh told how I was looking at Jonas. I protested, but they talked like I wasn't there. Lily crossed her arms: "We should report this to Mr. Hudson."

Mr. Hudson, the teacher and a deacon, was thumping down the hall now on his beechwood cane. Before he could reach us, I slipped around the corner and ran down the passageway toward Powell.

But instead of disappearing into the twists of those poor-fate halls, I could hear this time their feet thudding after me. Over my shoulder I glimpsed Asher and Noah pursuing. They laughed, the echo knocking between the troughs. My gut smoked like paper. I'd once come around the corner to find Asher with a minnow flopping on the ground, watching it suffocate.

My advantage was, the closer we got to Powell, the more lost they'd get. The higher fates never came this far out. Around a few turns I could hear them losing ground. I slid through the front door of Powell and, with no one home, the only place I could think to hide was up the chimney.

I went four, five, six rungs up. When I heard their heavy panting and feet stomp into Powell, I held my breath. Then I noticed that the square of light at the chimney top was casting my shadow down into the hearth. So, quiet as I could, I climbed a few more rungs and over a narrow shelf of brick, until my shadow crawled out of sight.

I could hear the boys talking to each other, knocking tin dishes off the table, dragging out the chairs. Their voices grew louder and barking, any humor that there was now drained out. Their footsteps groaned the soft floorboard in front of the hearth, and I climbed higher, into the darkest part of the chimney.

Below me, I saw Asher's face dip into the firebox and squint up.

"Hey, bastard," he called.

Noah's face popped in. "Come out, come out." The chimney swallowed the sound.

Their heads disappeared. The voices that reached me now were hushed and overlapping and urgent. They knew, same as me, they weren't allowed up that chimney.

Asher leaned into the hearth and spat: "Come out or we come up, bitch." The lowest rung squealed in its mortar.

I scrambled up, up, along the darkest part of the flue, and when I was just shy of the square of light—decided before I knew I had. I shot up the last rungs and out the top.

Blinding.

I tumbled over the chimneyside and into the water.

I thrashed all my limbs. I tasted fish and sour, warm and live like skin, and it was the lake's skin and body and blood lashing me from all sides. The lake slipped up my cheeks and the crown of my head, and I leapt against it, caught a breath, and swallowed water as I sunk again.

Otta

You've seen it in movies when someone is drowning. They struggle against the water for a few agonizing moments until their limbs go limp. They black out, and sink away. It's almost peaceful.

But that's not always how it happens.

Blacking out is usually the result of hyperventilation. But an experienced diver knows how to control their breath and is unlikely to panic. So when a diver drowns—especially if they're in water that's very deep, or very cold—the cause of death will likely be a combination of oxygen deprivation and hypothermia. They might be conscious up until the precise moment of death, their eyes burning like bulbs into the churning dark.

The rescue crews will search for about eight hours—a generous approximation of possible survival time. The coast guard or a private SAR service contracted by the diver's employer will deploy a radar-equipped Jayhawk alongside a response boat using sonar and heat detection. In reality, neither vessel is equipped to retrieve a body at depth.

Consider, now, that deep-sea divers like me—like Ethan—are attached to the diving bell via an umbilical, a thick braid of tubes and wires that supplies them with air and comms. They don't have tanks. At best, they're equipped with a bail-out bottle that gives them five minutes of emergency air.

After just ten minutes, then, the search is no longer a search: it is a performance. The helicopter and boat make their sweeps, as though either could possibly scan enough ocean floor to locate one human body. As though the systems of that body could be—what?—so miraculously slowed by the frigidity of the water that the blood, crystallized in place, might still retain oxygen. Call it suspended animation: the eyes stamped and glassed, the fingers frozen around the handle of a core drill, the glove crusted in blue bioluminescence. Again, this is a performance, out of respect or—more likely—out of pure terror that most endeavors of hope are foolish. It's the embalming and last cake of makeup for a wake. It's an attempt to provide the same closure that a body would provide. It won't.

ETHAN AND I met in 2005 teaching scuba at a resort about thirty minutes' drive from campus. Another student in my doctoral cohort, Lindsay, was teaching there too—sun-streaked braid to her waist and the sinewy limbs that spring from a lifetime of tennis lessons, tissue paper, white tulips. My first day, I tried three times to talk to her, only to watch us wither into awkward silence. I knew it would play out like this. I was terrible at small talk. But I'd just started the PhD and was desperate to prove I belonged there.

When our last lesson wrapped and I was packing my gear, an instructor from pool two with pink hair and coconut-scented sunscreen popped his head out from behind my locker door.

"Daiquiris?"

We sidled up to the pool bar. I felt out of place in my clammy T-shirt, but Ethan ordered with the easy authority of a vacationer.

Within ten minutes, he had laid out his life story: born in Georgia, kicked out of the house, slept in bus stations then couches then hotels then apartments then seaside bungalows and vacation homes. He leaned close like he was letting me in on a secret.

"I don't actually have the rebreather cert." He slurped a clot of red ice through his straw. We were scheduled to teach a course the next week on rebreathers, devices that helped advanced divers swim deeper on recycled air.

He'd gotten the rest of his certifications in Cabo, he said, and took all the rebreather classes, but then he and his boyfriend broke up.

"Gerry didn't want to pay for the exam. Asshole had a Lamborghini." It was clear by now that he wasn't hitting on me, and I relaxed into my drink. He gnawed his straw, shaking his head. "Silver foxes, though. How about you—what's your weakness?"

I didn't know how to answer. I'd been hopping from town to town for years—for my bachelor's, my master's, some scattered naturalist jobs, and now for the PhD. Friends and entanglements turned over with every school year, and I'd kept most people at a safe distance. There had been one man—gold eyes, restless in his limbs, who drifted in and out of town for a few years while I was in Texas. Each time, he spent one night at my place before shredding me apart like wet paper. He couldn't keep a steady phone number, and I'd lost him.

"Nothing in particular," I said.

"That other instructor, maybe?" He grinned. "Lindsay?"

"Her?" The shame blushed down my neck: I'd been observed, flailing. "Oh no, she's just—" I couldn't say it: the person I wanted to be.

"You're mysterious." He sipped down the last of his drink, wink of green in his eye. "I like that."

Lindsay quit after two weeks. The hours were too demanding with her class schedule. Ethan and I stuck around. Every shift, he'd prod me for information as though I had something to tell. He trained his attention on me fully, captivated somehow, and I shared more than I meant to. I told him about the calls from my mother, how she hinted I should come home and then told me I didn't have to come home ever again as far as she was concerned. He picked over my scraps of memory from Steels, a long carpet of loneliness. One night at the bar, I started hiccup-sobbing into my beer, something about the diner where I used to work. Ethan walked me home and put me to bed. He returned the next morning with a styrofoam container of steaming waffles. I'll never forget that. Then, one day, he showed up at my door with three suitcases and a cockatiel and never left. When his ex tracked him down a few weeks later and took the bird back, that was the only time I ever saw him cry.

Living with Ethan revealed in him an undercurrent of introversion and meticulousness. Each time we dove a reef, the first thing he'd do when we got home was draw the animals and plants he'd seen from memory, shading them to life in colored pencil. It was how he memorized names and the subtle morphologies that distinguished species, and the catalog he'd built up in his mind was impressive. Whenever I urged him to go to college, he only laughed and said, "I have commitment issues." I'll admit it now: part of me was glad he didn't go. There were two types of people who succeeded in leveraging their PhD into one of the scarce jobs in marine biology: the trust-fund kids who could work for free in perpetuity, and the ones who were truly brilliant.

I was neither.

Ethan was brilliant.

Now, back at my mother's house, those nights when I managed to get a few hours of sleep, I'd sit straight up out of dreaming and start scraping at the afterimage in a panic, panic. Blood thrummed in my ears. I tried to carve his incandescent shape out of the dark: flash of canine, crooked smile. Until the rushing release of a pipe in the wall, I wasn't sure I was alive. I liked that. The both of us together gone.

Otta

Two days after May's visit, a massive thunderstorm lurched across the state. On its heels came a spate of flash tornadoes that flattened a few houses and even picked up a horse, dragging it across two fields before dropping it into the boughs of a walnut tree, dead. Under all that weight, the branches held. The scene would attract dozens of news crews and hundreds of visitors, all of them waiting for the trunk to crack.

The next morning, I found a quarter of the sunporch roof ripped away. Dull flusters of mold were already creeping across the cardboard heaps. I drove down to see Clark. I had a headache, and a stewing outrage.

Spits of fog crawled over the lake's surface like begging dogs. A low breeze, trapped between the hills, chased its own tail. This used to be called Weber Valley and was now Weber Lake, named after the family that had owned everything from the drugstore to the newspaper to the paint factory—the reason that Paintsville was called Paintsville—all of which were now underwater.

I thumped my fist on the bait shop door. Clark opened it half-bent and holding his hip.

"You didn't come fix the roof, and now the storms knocked it in," I said. Looking at him now, the accusation felt sodden, dumb.

"Wasn't in great shape in the first place, was it?" He grinned, revealing a missing bicuspid. "Tripped down a few steps at the school. Doctor says I didn't break nothing."

"That's good."

He wiped his brow with a handkerchief.

"Hear it didn't go so good with May," he said.

"I don't know why you sent her. This town never forgets a freaking thing." I censored myself last-minute, remembering he was a teacher.

"No it does not." He dug through a toolbox just inside the door and pulled out an Allen wrench. "Help me with something?"

I could hardly say no. "All right."

He grabbed a walking stick—"Just temporary," he said—and stepped outside. As we crossed the gangplank from the marina, boils of bullhead rose to the surface and followed him with gaping mouths. He beamed over his shoulder. "My babies."

We walked to the south end of the parking lot, where a metal sign stuck out of the dirt:

WARNING: TOXIC

NO SWIMMING

NO FISHING

NO BOATING

We picked up a trail that hugged the edge of the lake.

"I know the lead in the water's no good for us," Clark said, lurching up the rocky slope at a surprising clip, "but with the fish, it's like there's more than ever. Just turned some of the trout tails black, is all."

Clumps of pin oak and sourwood shaded our path. I'd walked this trail, years ago, with Allie.

Clark paused to take a puff off his inhaler. The fog was receding, and in the distance, I could just make out where the western branch of the lake reached into a sleeve of hills too brambled and steep for trails. The lake was split into three arms: one to the south, where the dam was; one to the west; and one to the east, where the marina sat.

Clark pointed to a coiled stillness in the water's surface about two hundred yards out from the marina and its single dock.

"A hill, if you'll believe it. Used to be a church there. If you were driving from Steels, you'd follow the road right through where that dock is now, past the church, and on down another mile until you hit Paintsville." He traced the road with his finger as he spoke, landing where the lake's three arms met. "And if you kept going west from there, you'd reach the factory at the foot of the slope. Deepest part of the lake now."

Clark thumped his stick on the ground. "But this used to be Coates land, right?"

"So my mother says."

I'd thought Eugenia was the only one who remembered. But it was true that just before the dam was built, the Webers had bought as much acreage as they could in and around Steels. Hence the slow selling-off, parcel by parcel, of Coates farmland to the Webers, until Eugenia's father came down with Alzheimer's and she took possession of what little remained.

There were several years during my childhood when we'd accompany our mother to city council meetings every month. Eugenia would deliver packets of documentation, or strongly worded letters, or monologues at the podium. She insisted that the sale of certain plots hadn't been legal, pointing to the fine print and to the mental state of her father, who died soon after I was born. I'd sit in the back row passing Allie a succession of picture books.

One evening, the night before my twelfth birthday, the council started a closed session. We waited in the lobby of city hall along with Lena Davis, maiden name Weber, and the church committee, there to request a permit for the annual Steels Evangelical fundraiser.

The committee gathered in front of the RC machine. It was an unfortunate choice. For ten minutes, my mother paced back and forth, waiting for them to move. Rail-thin as she was, upright and stiff as a mantis, she had a hefty sugar tooth, and she wanted the grape soda she bought out of that machine every time we came.

Eugenia had always been both tensely aware of what others thought avoiding any direct encounter, though she knew every family in Steels—and unaware of the impression she projected: the uncombed hair, the oversized clothes on her frame, shirts with logos hilariously ill-suited to her interests: Carhartt, People's Bank 5K Run '88, Trix Are for Kids.

Finally, she took me and Allie by the hand and marched across the lobby. "Excuse me," she said, and shoved through the circle of women to reach the machine.

"Honestly," said a committee member, shaking her head. Mrs. Davis watched our mother dig the coins out of her pocket.

"Coming to the Fall Fundraiser, Eugenia?" she said. The mascara weighed down her eyes like the overextended arms of a live oak.

Our mother reviewed the machine's lit buttons as though she'd forgotten what she wanted. "When is it?"

"First week of October."

"I don't know."

I squeezed Allie's hand, willing our mother to move.

"Might be a good way to give back. Or at least start to."

Eugenia dropped a quarter on the floor and crouched to retrieve it. Then she pinched her lips, stood, and stepped right up to Mrs. Davis. "I don't owe you nothing, Lena."

Mrs. Davis took one staggering step back, then settled into her easy hammock of a smile.

"Repentance is the first step toward salvation," she said.

"And you think I need salvation?" Eugenia crossed her arms, jutting her jaw. It was a stance I recognized: no argument could penetrate it.

"Well, I'd say so." Mrs. Davis was in her stride now. She popped the clasp on her handbag and pulled out a change purse. "As I recall, you thought my family's land should belong to you, same story as today, and you were going to use stolen church funds to buy it back."

Mrs. Davis slotted two quarters, one after another, into the machine. She pressed a button and a root beer tumbled down.

"And when my grandpa wouldn't sell it to you, you turned around and gave the money to those factory workers—what, just to spite us? Helping those misguided people stay in Paintsville—and then all of them dying like that. My own uncle was one of them—but you know that. Really, Eugenia. It's just a shame we couldn't prove it was you."

Mrs. Davis retrieved the root beer, taking care with the flap not to damage her French tips. She held out the can.

I could see the muscles working in my mother's jaw. Lena Davis had managed to puncture her defenses. She perched her hands on the talon-sharp bones of her hips.

"Sure it was to spite you," Eugenia sneered. "It was about time someone did."

She retook our hands and dragged us toward the lobby door.

"Those poor children," Mrs. Davis intoned. The committee murmured. Her victory was cemented.

Eugenia tugged us down the stairs of city hall, planted me and Allie in the back seat of the car, and sped into the night-clotted hills that had shuttled us through every sojourn homeward—our protectors, and the source of all our pain.

THE LAKE TRAIL continued along a ridge that rose some twenty feet above the water.

Clark stopped short and poked at the ground with his stick.

"Arrowhead." He peeked at me. "Not always Coates land, was it?"

In the shadow of the drop-off to our right, a beach appeared. I recognized the web of tree roots that Allie and I had climbed down, twenty years ago now.

After that night at city hall, everything clicked: Eugenia's secretiveness, her bitter interactions with everyone in town and their iciness toward Allie and me by extension. Our mother was a thief—and worse, her vindictiveness had contributed to the deaths of more than two hundred people.

No wonder my father left. He couldn't bear the sight of her—and he was never coming back.

Through the years that followed—the screaming matches with Eugenia, the nights I slept in the woods, the mascara and pints of vodka I shoplifted from the Food Lion—Allie stayed close. She was soft-spoken, huddled into flannels and extra-large hoodies, but with a smile that could disarm anyone.

In my freshman year, the whole school—elementary, middle, and high, all of which were in the same building—took a field trip to the lake. By that time, I was barely speaking to my mother. The buses unloaded at the marina, and Allie found me in the crowd. The teachers explained how the dam worked: how the sluice gates opened and shut to keep the water level steady, usually when it was raining. Then they set us loose with plastic bags to pick up trash. In the context of a lake visit, my classmates' snide remarks—"Don't drown us, okay, Coates?"—had started on the bus, so the first chance I got, I led Allie down a trail away from the marina.

We rounded a curve and the beach opened up beneath us like a fistful of coins. Smooth stones glistened as though lit from within. And there, on the lake's lapping edge, was a rowboat.

I began to climb down the web of roots that laced the escarpment's bare edge. Allie hung back.

"We'll get in trouble," she said. She was growing out her hair, and it fell across her eyes.

"Don't be a baby."

Careless for the safety of others, even then.

The stones crunched beneath my feet as I surveyed the boat's chipped blue hull. On the bottom boards lay two wooden oars. We each grabbed a rusted oarlock and together shoved the boat into the shallows. I helped Allie over the gunwale and leapt in after.

The oars were heavier than I'd expected, and we took one each. For a while we went around in circles. Then, with a jolt, I noticed we were much farther out into the lake than I'd intended. The water was a bitter green, and dead quiet. The teachers had warned us that the lake would make us sick if we even touched it—yet here we were. Allie looked so small rowing at her oar, mouth set and stern at the task.

All at once, the boat lurched. Out in the full depth of the lake, something scraped so hard along the prow that we tipped to one side. I reached to grab my flying oar and fell in.

For a moment, I believed I'd fallen asleep. I was suspended in a slow stir of water, and it held me there, weightless.

I didn't want for air. I didn't struggle. The particulate churned around me as though the lake was powered by some internal engine, and squinting to see through it, I thought I glimpsed ahead, near the prow, a tower of bricks winding up through the silt.

Then I felt a tug at my collar and Allie hauled me toward the surface. I scrambled over the side of the boat.

We collapsed into the hull. Allie was half wailing my name, but she seemed far away. Light brimmed my vision, ice-cold and hushed, and I felt bright and torn open. Thrill dripped down my cheeks.

I regained my breath. The boat shrank back around me, along with it Allie's sobs. I squeezed her hand until she settled down.

I sat up. We'd floated some distance off from whatever we had hit, but I could see it: a squared-off brick protrusion standing just a few inches above the surface of the lake.

"What is it?" Allie said. I grabbed the remaining oar and tried to row us there, but we were going in circles again, working against a current that tugged us back toward the beach.

"Hold the oar," I said.

I balanced myself in the boat's rounded belly and stood.

"It looks hollow."

There was a pebble in the bottom of the boat. I picked it up and tossed it, but it missed the hole and the lake swallowed it without a sound.

I searched my pockets. All I had was my house key, attached to it the mirrored keychain our dad had given me. I turned it over in my hand, its drawing in sepia like an old movie, symbol of a grand adventure and a promise of return. It didn't mean any of that now. I spiraled off my key.

Weighing the keychain in my hand, I eyed my target. I waited for the boat to steady, then launched it into the air.

We heard it clank against the brick, then rattle down, falling as though into a well. I shrieked with triumph. The boat rocked beneath me, and I sat down.

We gave up on rowing with the one oar and watched the obstacle shrink into the distance until the current delivered us back onto the beach.

Now, seeing that beach again, I felt the icy water drool down my skin, watched Allie's finger press and leave a white print in the meat of my arm. "Are you poisoned?" There was no boat in sight.

Clark and I followed the trail another quarter mile as it descended along the lakeshore, emerging at last onto a bluff three feet above the water. On a grassy outcropping nearby hummed a huge machine—a metal cabinet six feet across. Two steel pipes, each a foot in diameter, emerged from the cabinet and traveled along the stone bluff. They bent at a right angle, drove down into the water, and disappeared. A PVC pipe emerged from the water but ended midair, capped at the top.

Clark gave one of the steel pipes a shove. It was attached to the bluff with metal straps, and one of the bolts had rusted loose.

"All right," he said, "I'm not so good getting down on my knees right now." He produced the Allen wrench. I knelt and loosened the bolt.

"What is all this?" I said. I dropped the old bolt into Clark's hand and exchanged it for a new one. His eyelashes glinted, orange hairs mixed with white.

"It's hard to explain," he said. "But there's more going on here than May knows."

Rust crusted the hole in the brace. I gouged it out, then slid the new bolt through.

"May's daughter is down there," he said. "And if you don't believe her, you should just swim down yourself and see."

"You want me to dive into heavily leaded water, just to see?"

For a moment, light managed to slice through the surface of the lake. A sash of silver bass changed direction, then sank out of sight.

"All I know is she needs help now that I can't give her," Clark said. "Show her how to dive, and I'll fix your roof for free. Is that enough?"

HOW DID I KNOW this in dreams? Beams of light carving the water, shoals of tuna with their fresh-bruise meat, sharks carving maps and letters into the current—I knew it by the time I was six years old, though I wouldn't see the ocean until I was eighteen.

After I fell into the lake, the sea of my one recurring dream emptied out completely. Only one thing was left inside: a fish—big, dumb, slow, like a bison—moving away from me. Her chest-wide hull rippled with green, and her swaying tail sent back currents that lifted and plunged me in her wake. I kicked as hard as I could, scooped the water with my arms and shoved it behind me. I was never strong enough to reach her.

But one night I came so close, I felt her tail brush my lips. I stopped swimming. All at once, I was afraid to know where she was going—because maybe she wasn't going anywhere.

MY LETTER OF TERMINATION arrived the next day. It was stapled to my paycheck—a bellman's rate, docked for damaged equipment.

The sunporch roof was groaning in the slightest breeze. I couldn't afford to fix it, least of all now that I'd found Eugenia's birth certificate under a collectible 1992 Barbie Porsche Carrera and convinced her (after a two-hour argument) to join the transplant list. We needed to save up for whatever that would cost.

Eugenia and I drove to a hospital in the city to sign her up. On the ride home, she scanned through every radio station, then shouted over the newscast what she'd read in the *Farmer's Almanac:* that this year's harvest would be bountiful, but that winter would bring heavy snows. "If I live to see it."

I turned down the volume. "I don't know why you have to talk that way."

"I don't know why you got to force me into these treatments." She let out a whimper. "I don't do no one no good."

I knew better than to engage.

At home, Eugenia kept picking at the scab, vying for pity, pacing between the kitchen and living room with her half-empty teacup. The tea had always been a strange habit; no one within five hundred miles drank tea. I think she did it out of pure defiance.

"Go to bed," I said at last, and she slunk up the stairs like I'd hit her. Allie indulged this kind of behavior. I wondered how much she knew about our mother's past.

I washed the teacup and went digging through the built-in cabinet in the foyer. I found the cut-glass decanter in its usual spot, still stocked with vodka. When I was sixteen, I'd started taking covert sips—little flames to get me through the nighttime. That had sustained me during the last year of high school.

I poured a vodka neat. It ripped through me, a lit match.

Back at the bait shop, Clark had insisted that lead levels in the lake were low enough that short-term exposure would have no adverse effect. As it turned out, he had some authority on the subject: the state EPA paid him a meager sum to live on that marina and take regular measurements.

"Look at me." He'd held out his hand, steady as a shelf. "No symptoms of lead exposure. Good brain, good kidneys, no headaches, no joint pain. And I been living here for thirty years."

I sprawled on the couch with my drink on my chest. I was not my mother; I could take responsibility for what I'd done. Whatever harm the lead might bring me, I'd inflicted worse. So even if Clark was wrong, it would feel good to get my due.

I FOUND MAY at the end of the dock, trying to suck air through a mouthpiece with the tank valve shut. She was wearing a wet suit, leaning over an ancient, wrinkled instruction manual. When she saw me she tried to hide the hose in her lap.

"Hello," she said.

I sat down, dangling my legs over the dock's edge, and pulled the tank toward me.

"You have to turn on the air to get anything through the regulator." I showed her how to rotate the knob—slow until it was fully open, then a quarter turn back.

May put the mouthpiece to her lips again and inhaled. "Thank you, yes."

She looked away. The short crop of her hair nudged the breeze.

"Look," I said, "I'll help you."

May's hands shot up and clasped beneath her chin. "Otta, thank you, I—"

She stammered a few half words. It was clear from looking at her now: she really believed the story she had told me.

"It's just"—I broached it gently—"why don't you think your daughter could be here? On land?"

May shook her head. "I tried to bring her. She never wanted to come."

"Do you know why she left?"

A flush crossed her face, drip of paint on wet paper. "She went looking for good water."

"You mean water without lead in it?"

She squinted. "Lead—I don't know. Clean water, good for drinking."

"All right," I said. "So if she's under the lake—where, exactly?"

"I don't know. She went deeper, I think. Because Mr. Clark told me the good water is in a cave underneath the lake."

"You mean the aquifer?" I asked. The county's more secluded houses still pumped their water from it: a massive reservoir of permeable rock, four counties wide and flooded with groundwater. For all the caves that punctuated the area, the aquifer lay even deeper in the earth. My mother's house used to draw well water from it, brown and sour in recent years, until she finally agreed to tap into the pipes of city water that the subdivision had laid.

"Yes. I think. That's what Mr. Clark told me. Caves of air, and beneath those, caves of water."

"How would she get there?"

"She must have swam out into the lake. But she doesn't have a scuba suit."

"So how could she be—" I couldn't peel the words from my tongue.

"She's alive," May said. She raised her chin. "I know she is. She's my daughter."

She exhaled, expelling a shiver from her lungs.

"Maybe she made it to those air caves. I just— I can't think where to start." She shook her head, shook and shook it, fist knotted against her ribs.

How had this narrative formed in May's mind? Had her daughter left a note on the kitchen table, spots of wet on the page? Or while they camped on the shoreline, maybe Daphne stripped down to her swimsuit and dove, swam out as far as she could, and disappeared from sight.

A throb of swallowed air wormed down my throat. I hadn't been in the water since Ethan—two months ago now. Was it two? The marked units of time dilated around me.

I dragged in a breath, picked up the BCD butterflied behind her. "This is a buoyancy vest."

I explained how to strap her tank to the vest and put it on; how to inflate and deflate it so you could stay balanced at a steady depth. I expected the same boredom to wash over May's face that I'd seen in the resort tourists. Instead, she blinked with open-mouthed enthrall. She asked how to plan a dive, why you had to limit your time at pressure, how long to decompress.

"You and I are never going to stay under long enough that we'd need to do real decompression stops," I said. That was a decision I'd already made.

"But what if Daphne's very deep? How can we bring her back up?"

The knot of air expanded in my chest; my ears were ringing. The light quivered and was suddenly hard to hold on to. Were we really planning for the rescue from depth of a living human being? It appeared in my mind as a complete scene, a diorama within a cube of pale light: Ethan on the seafloor, his legs crossed, subsisting in hibernation on a pea of air so compressed that he could live on it for a hundred days. Or was it ninety days—eighty? Was there still time? Had I given up on him sooner than I should have, realized the truth too late, by only seconds—

LIGHT BLUED IN. May's face hovered above me, and I sucked in a fist of air.

I sat up. The wood grain of the dock was stable, sane. I moved to stand, but May placed a hand on my shoulder.

"Sit a minute," she said. "This happens to Mrs. Wallace. Standing fast doesn't do her good."

I blinked, trying to clear the dark edges from my vision. "I just haven't been sleeping."

She studied me, wringing out a washcloth. Where had it come from? "Not sleeping, yes. That can make it happen."

I shivered at the cloth's cold touch.

Something about the claustrophobia of her wet suit, how it squeezed her skin, how after I strapped her into the BCD it had swollen itself shut—my airway had started to narrow, a straw that couldn't feed me.

"I want to ask," she said, dabbing my forehead. "Maybe it isn't my business. But what is Ethan?"

I'd spoken? I couldn't grasp how long I'd been out.

"There's a garden with a name like that."

She let the silence swell up between us.

"Ethan is a person's name," I said.

"I thought it might be," she said, nodding. "And he left, like Daphne?"

"Why would you think that?"

But I knew. I felt the salt drying in runnels down my face.

"Ethan didn't leave." I said it clipped, final. I stumbled to my feet.

A breeze licked across the water, drying my cheeks and bringing me back to earth. May took my arm. My legs were trembling, so I let her.

We started toward the bait shop.

"I can't think why Daphne left," May said. Her brow was knotted, pained. "I gave her everything she needed."

Fluttering down, on frail wings: an image of Ethan, socks half off his feet, rubbing the sleep from his eyes. I made him scrambled eggs every morning. I was good at them. My gratitude toward him, the urge to wake that crooked smile: what was I grateful for, exactly? Maybe for every day he hadn't left.

"In the end," I said, "people only care about themselves."

May stopped short. "I don't believe that. Not family."

"Family especially." I started to chuckle, then at the look on her face fell silent.

We reached a picnic table on the floating pier that housed the bait shop and sat. May twisted her hands in her lap.

"Maybe—because of Ethan—you can't help." Behind that kindness, her face was like a bag emptied out.

The lake's spineless gray expanse swallowed gallons of light and returned nothing. This was not that water. It was tideless, stagnant, its elephantine hide barely stirring in its sleep. I stuffed down the last flurries of my heart.

"I can do it," I said. I needed something to occupy my mind.

"Really?" She gasped a great lot of air into her chest. "If you're sure."

"I'm sure."

Her gaze traced mine out into the flooded valley, lingered, then returned altered, like the lake had whispered to her something.

"Mr. Clark said he's fixing your roof to thank you for helping me. So I guess you'll say that's you caring only for yourself." She squinted. "But I don't think so."

She twisted up her mouth with the easy defiance of a teenager.

"You want to save her." She bolted from her seat, like she'd surprised herself. "Ha!" And she sauntered off toward the boathouse.

She was wrong. Until that night, around 2 a.m., when I tossed out of a yawning nightmare and realized she was right.

May

Up and out—gallop of endless water. Then, when I dragged myself to the surface, endless sky—as I'd heard it called—sky that He'd forsaken, though He used to keep heaven there.

I churned my legs and arms and gasped through my thrashing heart, and then maybe it was instinct that all at once, I just settled. I took a deep breath, tilted onto my back, and floated. The sky was a flat un-lake blue, and I imagined it cut smooth across the top with scissors.

The air shifted across my face. It tasted sweet. But it was so dry that I started coughing, and tipped up again, grabbing the chimney edge that nudged just above the surface of the water.

I listened. I peeked over the lip down into the flue. Nothing.

The boys weren't climbing after me. They didn't dare. I grinned to myself. Then I felt a pang in my stomach like the grin was wicked, then I liked that it was wicked, and liked the pang when it came again.

I let go of the chimney and kicked away from it and back, paddling my arms one over the other, taking myself farther away with each lap. I copied as best I could the fishes I'd watched every day of my life through the windows.

I was good at it—right away I was. I got maybe too prideful. The next time I swam out from the chimney my belly cramped—just balled up like paper. I churned to keep my head above water. I gasped at air, but water rushed into my open mouth, and I knew the lake would take me now, gulp me down into all that I deserved—

Then a rip at my scalp. I was pulled up by my hair. Two hands heaved me from the armpits up and over a hard edge. There, on a dais floating in the middle of the lake, was a man with bass-belly hair.

I couldn't catch on what I was seeing or what it was the man said to me now. He had a strange way of talking. He smacked me on the back and I spit up water.

"You hear me?"

I nodded.

"How the hell you get out here? Anyone else? A boat sunk?"

I shook my head.

"You swam?"

Nodded.

"You know swimming's not allowed."

I blinked lake from my eyes.

"Don't feed me excuses. We got signs posted everywhere."

He rubbed at his chin and sat down at a wheel. I recognized now from the encyclopedia that this was a boat. The man turned a key beside the wheel and shoved a lever. A roar surged from behind us that like to knocked me over the railing, except for he grabbed me by the sleeve.

Water foamed from our sides and we rushed toward the edge of the lake, a lip where it collided with a dark tangle of hair. I felt on the verge of sick until he pulled back the lever and the boat slowed.

We crept up to a wooden walkway on the water. He turned the key and the roar cut. He climbed out, tied us down, then helped me out.

But when he tried to lure me away from the lake's edge I wouldn't go. So he told me to wait and walked down the gangplank to where it expanded into a floating platform. At its middle was a house made of steel and whitewash. He disappeared inside and came out with a towel under his arm. He returned to where I stood dripping, draped it around my shoulders, then put a glass of water in my hand.

None of it made sense. Everything living on the surface of the Earth had been in His wrath sliced down. I didn't know if this man had bubbled up somehow from the Chimneys, or if he was an Overlaker left alive—sin to even think. And I wondered should I drink from the glass he gave me.

He could see my hesitations.

"I'm Jeffrey Clark," he said. "What's your name?"

"May."

"All right, May. Well, I'm a teacher at the high school. I also look after the lake to make sure no one gets hurt," he said, "like from swimming."

His eyes were soft like mud. I couldn't remember the last time someone looked me in the eye.

So I took a sip—then another, and another. I drank and kept drinking till the glass was gone. I felt even more thirsty after, and he went and fetched another glass, then the third time fetched a whole jug, and didn't ask questions and didn't ration me to it.

It was magnificent. I don't never use that word. It was like when you've bathed with soap and you lick the own skin of your arm and it's sour and soft. It was better than the wafers, better than the blood-of-Him wine.

When it was over, I had drunk half the jug itself and my belly swole out in front of me. The cold water made me tremble. I pulled the towel close around.

By now the man was watching me funny. "Where you from?"

I shrugged. I'd never been asked the question.

When he kept on waiting for an answer, I tried a recitation. "The Underlake where all the righteous and only."

He stared at me, then squeezed his eyes shut and open. "Goddamn."

The curse put me on guard. But the lake kept calm and lapping at our feet.

"And you, where from?" I said.

"I'm from here." Like I should know what *here* was. Surrounding us on all sides was a dark lace of what must be trees, clambering up the slopes, and inside them—what tongues and fur and canines sniffing and swallowing the wet earth, lungs and all manner of organs sewn tight into beastly shapes?

"Goddamn," he said again, slapped his knee. "You took long enough."

We sat on the dock together for hours. At first, I was sure he was a demon come to lure me down into the mantle of the Earth. But never did he pull out his spear or teach me strange tongues or roll around in the dust. He said he'd been waiting these many years to hear from us, the people of the Underlake, to see if we survived the Rise. The flood, he called it.

"How's Henry?" he asked. "Still kicking?"

"There's no Henry."

"Henry Weber? You never met him?"

"No." This I was sure about. "I met everyone there is."

He tugged at his beard. The next time he talked came slow, like he was working through a calculation. "How'd you get up here? You couldn't have swum."

"I swum a little. You saw me." I was defensive even; I felt it living already inside my limbs.

"But from that deep—"

"From the deep I climbed."

I described the chimney and its rungs like I was talking to a child. Told him how you shouldn't climb them, but that I did and that I wasn't afraid to do it, which I surprised myself to say. The ice-bones terror of running from those boys, the iron rungs numbing my knuckles—somehow it all seemed far away. Unreal, the way horses felt unreal when I read about horses.

When I was done he rubbed his beard a bunch. He paced the dock, shaded his eyes out at the lake. The sun was blearing the tops of the trees.

He said it was getting dark and I looked up at the sky unblueing and it was.

HE HAD TO EXPLAIN all about his boat—*pontoon,* he called it—before I would get back in. Back out on the lake, we found the chimney where I'd come up.

The sky was becoming of crushed velvet, the way it rots and scrapes away from itself—but here, scrapes of clouds, white slow-shifting sheaves that glowed while the blue flaked off around them. The clouds were new, and I couldn't fathom their purpose.

Rung by rung, I slipped down the chimney, pausing just above the firebox. Not a sound. I sprinted down the last rungs and ducked through the hearth. No one was home.

I'd left the Underlake like a sinner and returned a sinner. But as I waited now in the bulblight, no punishment came.

And it came not the next day or the day after.

For weeks, I shivered to go around corners for what might be waiting—the floor to open, the mantle to swallow me down. I expected the reverend to know it from my face that Sunday in the Shuttle. But he only ignored me like always. No one saw in me the crimes that I'd done.

I even started to relish my secret. I liked the taste of wickedness, how licked and sweet, and nothing anyone could do.

Soon it made me bolder. If I could go to the Overlake once, why couldn't I again? I felt it tugging. At every hearth I could see its trembling wick of air, smell its leaves and clouds.

Curiosity drew me: wondering how sharp the grass and how the trees smelled, about Mr. Clark the teacher, and whether there was anybody else still living. It was all of these things, sure. But what made me go back up the chimney again—and again, and again—was thirst. A powerful one.

MONTH AFTER MONTH, I returned. I sat with the teacher on the dock, and learned myself to swim, and come to expect the dry clothes that he kept for me. Even come winter—he told me, winter—I loved the shock of plunging into the lake, how it shot up bright shards. I was awake—felt like this was where awake was.

Mr. Clark insisted to come and fetch me in his pontoon. We decided I would flash the Canyon mirror when I reached the chimneytop; it caught the sunlight and he could see it from shore. Every thirty days I went, because those were the days that the Wallaces, after a full shift at their fates, had to wait in the allotment lines.

Mr. Clark let me untangle ropes or feed the fish that pleated by the gangway or mop the floating deck around the bait shop. I thrilled to have what felt like a fate, except that I could choose which task to do and even to not do it.

When I got tired of the work, I'd nudge at the edges of the world. I went first to where the concrete parking lot ended and stepped into the grass. It sunk beneath my feet, and I knelt and laced my fingers through. A blue bird with risen crest dropped right down in front of me, leapt, and picked a bead up in its mouth. I held my breath for so quivering long. I'd never seen a miracle before.

Soon I ventured farther, to where trunks of trees scrawled up the air and mustered into dark, moiling leaves. I felt the texture of them, a skin as dry as shingles, but they stood unmoving and didn't mind. So I touched them, one after another, each a new version, each more fragrant, delicate. They pulsed with a kind of life I never saw before but now couldn't stop seeing it, how it boiled and stitched and sang inside everything around.

A FEW MONTHS AFTER my first visit to the Overlake, I turned fourteen. The girls in my class—nine in all—graduated, hosted their Rehearsal, and were most of them picked for courting. I hadn't been invited. The answer now was clear: I was never going to be married.

Caleb had attended his first Rehearsal, but I learned later that he didn't choose anyone. I locked this, blue-bright bird, inside my stomach, but left no air for it to breathe.

Mary's Rehearsal was coming the next year. That was when she stopped talking to me about it. She pitied me, I think.

But the anticipation of it swallowed all the air around her. Every night, Mary and her mother plaited hair and embroidered clothes and crafted fishhooks. Mrs. Wallace maybe took it even more serious than most mothers, who had usually at least six children, where Mary was her only one—what Mrs. Wallace called a "late-in-life baby."

Meanwhile, if I hadn't shared about Caleb, I knew for sure I couldn't tell Mary about the most blasphemous thing I'd ever done. As passionate as she was about the Final Book, me going to the Overlake would be unforgivable.

So it was that silence piled up between us. More and more nights, I turned on my side and went to sleep without saying a word. I could feel her receiving that like a relief.

EVERY YEAR, the Day of Risen Lake marked the seventh and final day of the lake's rise, when it lipped over the tops of our windows. On this anniversary, the Reverend Jewell would deliver his longest sermon of the year, where he would tell the story of how we got here: How one day, a snake appeared to him and pronounced the return of the garden. How He built a wall around us, then the snake churned a river into milky froth and made the lake to rise.

All the Overlake's sinners sunk into the mantle to be damned forever. Us, the righteous and only, white and delightsome, were left to replenish the population here in the Under, second only to heaven, which was deeper still, in the core of the Earth.

There were others who had wanted to live in the Underlake, who built electric and tubes and pipes, "and we can thank them for our glorious light," the reverend said, pointing at the yellowed fluorescent tubes along the wall. But they had failed to hear His word, and so had drowned with the rest.

After was a feast. The Partridges unlocked the stockroom, bringing out some reverend's-stock vinegars for pickling. This was now the only time of year when people would get their blood-of-Him allotment, which made Mrs. Wallace jolly leading up to it for weeks.

This particular day and me swollen with my secrets, I sat in the back pew in a mull of light that the cathedral window cast down. It was my fourteenth birthday. It was always my birthday on Days of Risen Lake. My presence was offensive because of this, so every celebration I kept my eyes low, only daring to look as high as the choir's feet.

But today, as I listened to the sermon, it occurred to me that there had been countless wisdoms shared by the Reverend Jewell, truths that only he knew, but now there was something I knew that he didn't. And this made me raise my eyes to the choir's knees.

Nothing happened. No jolt of flame from the bulbs. I swallowed into my chest and looked up at the choir full-on.

I'd always imagined a row of core-bright faces, porcelain plates with an oval mouth hole stamped into each. What I saw instead was the same boys I went to school with: sweaty, pimpled, one with close-set eyes, another with the bad haircut his mother gave.

Jonas was the exception. He glowed—gazed at the top of the cathedral window like a stained-glass seraph. I peeked behind me. Not even a fish stirred the glass.

When I turned back, he was looking straight at me. He saw that

I saw and kept on. A smile sparked his lips, and he raised his eyes again.

That was it. I had blasphemed, but he had also blasphemed. I didn't know if one canceled out the other. I waited there in my seat the whole rest of service for punishment, and again none came.

For days, I walked on tiptoes. But over time, I grew more certain that no judgment would slice me down. And I began to wonder, only to myself, about the wrath of Him the Lakebringer and His rightful justice, and who got to tell the stories and what else they didn't know.

WHEN OTTA FAINTED, I saw a crack pass across her skin, beaming through it a new-colored light. This friend, Ethan—she wouldn't say where he'd gone. But in the way she had no words to tell it—and in the gap he'd left behind—it felt all at once like seeing myself mirrored. Like we shared that shell of protection racked open by the only person whose abandonment we had let matter.

Maybe I imagined this, dressed her up in my own suffering. But it sent an electric charge through my limbs. I was all at once too bold: "You want to save her." Then I barked out my nerves and fled, peculiar to myself.

That evening, on my cot in the boathouse, I watched the particles of ice along the ceiling catch the moonlight and shiver to life, bloom and splinter and spread. My blankets were warm and the heater burned its fiery laces, and that night I slept deeper than I had in weeks.

THE FIRST TWO DAYS of training, Otta wouldn't let me even touch the water. She showed me the gauges on the tank and how to hook up the tubes. She showed me her watch, called a dive computer, and how she used it to track bottom time, which was how long you stayed at the deepest part of your dive. The danger, she said, started below twenty feet. After that, the pressure of the water above you started squeezing the air in your lungs, and it could be dangerous to come up too quick.

I'd heard something like this before. When Daphne was seven, she came home from a day down at the chutes with Mrs. Wallace. Most of the other children by that time were sick, but not Daphne. So people took an extra joy in her, including Mrs. Wallace.

Daphne grabbed my wrist and started leaping up and down between us like a jump rope.

"Mrs. Wallace says the chute goes down into the earth," she huffed, "like a passageway. And the air tries to suck us down, but we can't go or we couldn't come back up. We'd be trapped under heavy air."

I was confused. Mrs. Wallace shrugged. "She wanted to go down the chute with the trash." She beamed down at my girl.

Now, with Otta explaining, this idea of being trapped locked into cold clarity. Otta called it *the bends,* said it could kill us. Which meant it could kill Daphne.

On the third morning of training, Otta got there late with sunglasses over her eyes.

"Today?" I asked.

She dropped her gear on the dock's edge. A wind tossed little fits and chops across the water.

She took a long sip from her mug.

"Why not?"

Otta

There is nothing closer to bliss. The water wraps around you, sustains you. It pays attention.

Ethan had a favorite joke: "Let's get narced," he'd say, then put in his mouthpiece and fall back over the gunwale. We took all the precautions, but the rule of thumb was that every thirty-three feet you descended was equivalent to drinking one martini. *L'ivresse des profondeurs,* Cousteau called it. The rapture of the deep.

Scuba divers usually won't admit it, but free divers will: that the narcosis—that buzz of release—is one of the reasons we're here. You slip out of your life, discard your skin. Suddenly, nothing matters but what's in front of you. Everyone you ever knew, everything you've done wrong, is scrubbed clear. It's freedom.

I followed the fish from my recurring dream out of Steels, out of state—as far away as I could get. I trailed it through undergrad and grad school and focused every fellowship application on getting to the West Pacific to study the bumphead parrotfish, its closest approximation. I got good grades; I graduated with honors; I chose the library over friendships. And eventually, I made the bumphead parrotfish the topic of my dissertation.

But coming from a backwater town was an anchor I had to swim against. I couldn't get into the better colleges, which paved the way to the best internships, the right publications. I swam, I churned, I came up for air only rarely. And when I did, the exhaustion manifested like a rip in a space suit, dragging me into the void.

I'd wake up groggy a few days later, escaping the bed of someone who had looked, for a moment, like relief. I was exhausted by my own presence, by the same nagging flashbacks: heaps of dead leaves beneath autumn's gray heavy; school bus windows swimming with eyes; those last years at home when I couldn't look at myself in the mirror. My own ghost dragged along behind me wherever I went.

I thought I understood the dream. But no matter how hard I kicked, the person I was supposed to become kept its distance: like the fish, just out of reach.

By the third year of the PhD, my best moments were spent with Ethan. We'd dive reefs, wrecks, stands of shoal grass tucked with turtles and scallops. One day, I spotted a shift inside a dark depression of reef. Tentacle by tentacle, an octopus emerged. Ripples of color passed over its skin, green to purple to white, the way light trickles down the water. The octopus glided along the reef, transforming into anything it passed: staghorn corals, anemones, sea fans. Everything but what it was.

I started driving us to farther-flung reefs where we could see octopuses. Ethan complained about the early mornings; he was working late shifts at the bar on our street. So after dives, we'd set up camp beneath the palms and nap before driving home.

"Shouldn't you be studying?" he said one day, out of nowhere. I looked up from my magazine. He was lying in his hammock. I wasn't sure how long he'd been awake.

"I'm relaxing," I said. "It's been a shitty week."

My advisor had insisted again that I needed more fieldwork. Two days later, I was turned down for a research fellowship at the Great Barrier Reef.

"I don't get why you don't just study a different animal," Ethan said. His curls—bright green, the latest dye job—poked through the mesh. "Something that lives around here. You like octopuses."

"Too late to change," I said, and turned a page. "Everyone else is already way ahead of me."

"Who is? Lindsay?" He pressed a sad-clown grimace into the weave of the hammock.

After Lindsay quit the resort, I'd managed to spark a meager friendship with her. We studied together, traded notes, and even shared a bike lock outside the biology department for half a semester after she lost hers. A month ago, she'd invited me to a party. Her townhome was furnished with Moroccan rugs and Mexican ceramics, overrun by assistant professors and turtlenecked "friends from New York." I didn't belong there. I hadn't spoken to her since.

"You're as good as any of them," Ethan said. He thought Lindsay was a snob. It was one of the things that had endeared him to me: somehow, he liked me better.

I shut the magazine and started loading our beach bag. He didn't know what he was talking about.

"Let's go."

We walked down the beach in silence. A bloom of jellyfish pocked the sand, spent bulbs.

"Okay, look," he said. "Remember I told you why I left New Orleans? That I hated it? Well, that was bullshit. I loved it—I wanted to stay. But there was a guy. We lived together for a year."

"You never told me that."

Ethan actively avoided serious relationships. He also didn't like rehashing his past, except in reference to how far he'd come. *Lingering isn't a good look,* he'd said once.

"Great sex, breakfast in bed, candlelit dinners." His eyes trained on the water line. "For a year, I didn't dive, didn't go running, didn't draw. I kickboxed because he kickboxed, drank Negronis because he drank Negronis. His friends became my friends. That's how he liked it. But I like myself."

We veered around a clump of flea-swarmed seaweed. Blue crabs fled into the foam.

"I get it," I said. "I like being alone too."

"You like being alone because you don't have to talk."

I felt the cold prickle of having been observed without realizing it. He knew me sometimes better than I knew myself. "Okay."

"I mean, I only know your full name because you were drunk when you told me."

"No one needs to know about Ottilie." I tried to laugh.

"She sounds like a badass."

I was taken aback. I didn't remember telling him about my great-grandmother. Ottilie was the last one to run the farm as a successful business, and Eugenia talked about her endlessly. I shuddered to imagine the same sentimental stories coming out of my mouth. "Why are we talking about this?"

"Because." He was studying me with the kind of seriousness usually reserved for his drawings. "Look, I love you. But it's like you're waiting for someone else's approval."

"I *am* waiting." I was raising my voice; I couldn't help it. "There's only one scenario where I don't turn out to be a complete failure. I need to pass exams and defend my dissertation and get fellowships and get hired, and all of that is about other people judging me. That's the fucking point."

We forged the rest of the distance to the car in silence, a saccharine afternoon sun drawing the clouds around it like a cloak.

I started the car and rolled down the windows.

"Let's just enjoy the rest of the day, okay?"

Ethan turned the radio up. It was blasting a song we both hated and secretly loved.

"I can do that," he said.

WE FLOATED, we held on to each other, we dove beneath the taller waves. Ethan moved through the world letting little of it cling to him.

I wanted to be like this.

But autumn curdled in, then winter, and now the wind carried the scent of waters farther out to sea: the swarm of tin tarpon, the scamp grouper scouring the hard-bottom reefs of the Edges, where a few months back, blacktip sharks had been observed schooling in the hundreds, strange behavior and inexplicable to the point that, in my classes, the questions had settled into an uncomfortable silence.

My recurring dream warped and taunted. Sometimes I waited for the fish and she never came. A few times, swimming after her frothing green form, I reached out to touch her fin and it became the rice-paper skin of my mother's hand. She blinked at me and turned away.

Ethan and I worked the resort job until the ocean got too cold for tourists. I picked up shifts at the bar with him for extra cash. After close, we'd fill our water bottles from the keg and walk down the road beneath the orange cast of streetlamps, sand shifting along the curbs. Once we reached the beach, we'd drop onto the sand, and the night expanded into a great wide hiss of air.

I don't remember the date, I only remember that Ethan raised his first beer for a toast: "Rot in peace." His dad was five years dead that day. We joked like always, laughed ourselves to tears, danced to the songs left on the jukebox. But Ethan had a charge running through him that wouldn't wind down, and when we got to the beach he sang up at the sky, then stripped down to his swim trunks. I dove in after him.

The water was cold, and once we swam past the break point, the bioluminescent bacteria started to swarm. The sparks spiraled down in cyclones beneath our kicking feet. We dove with our eyes wide open. We swam back and forth, watching them bloom around our arms.

The chain of lights along the beach grew faint. I felt the muscles in my thighs start to seize.

"Let's go in," I said, and started swimming for shore. I swore I could hear him kicking behind me. I reached the shallows, put my feet down, and looked over my shoulder.

He wasn't there.

All I saw was ocean—broad, brown, sending row upon row of foam toward shore, devouring each back into itself.

I called his name. The wind swallowed up the sound. My heart against my sternum felt swollen and strange. I swam back out to where I thought we'd been.

I treaded water. I called and called and no response. I dove, but the bioluminescence had vanished, and the water was tea-black and thick with itself. The sea in every direction opened up like a mouth—hungry, hungry, with teeth.

ETHAN BURST THROUGH THE SURFACE, spouting water from his mouth. I swam to him, slung his arm over my shoulder, and started toward shore.

My left thigh was cramping. But I managed to kick, dragging us forward and finally submitting us to the waves, which carried us until our knees hit sand. I pulled us both to our feet and staggered just beyond the surf.

We fell onto the beach. I could hear him cough out water. Then he started to giggle. He was still drunk.

"Dove too deep," he said.

No rebreather certification: the fact returned to me in a flash. I hadn't protested, hadn't insisted he finish the cert before he taught a class about it.

The next morning, from my bed, I watched a slant of light carve its way toward the far wall. The desk was piled with index cards and books—heaps of labor, for what. In the half-open closet hung a tattered T-shirt from a high school field trip to the aquarium. My walls were bare aside from a tacked-up bill from one of Allie's plays. I hadn't flown back to see it. *When are you going to actually start making a living,* my mother had asked on the phone, *so you can come home?* All these artifacts—familiar, mean—I could blur away for months if I tried. But now the full picture shifted into focus, painful in its detail: myself, in all my failures—inescapable as the blood in my veins.

Otta

I had felt for weeks a mounting suspicion of my own mind. After fainting in front of May, I was suspicious of my body too.

I avoided the water training as long as I could. But I could see the panic urging into May's eyes. Every moment of delay presented a greater threat to Daphne. Or that's what May believed.

So on the third morning, with a headache and a night of bad sleep under my belt, I waded in. The water was clouded with pea-green algae. I signaled to check if May was ready. She signaled back.

When we dove headfirst into the lake, that sound—a broad static. It stretched out like a piece of chewing gum, hard to knock against and dull as cartilage.

We swam out twenty yards and hovered. I tried to tamp down my heart. I hadn't dived since Ethan.

May bobbed beside me, awaiting direction. I led us back toward the shallows, and we put down our feet. The slime of seaweed stroked my ankles. I took out my mouthpiece.

"Catch your breath," I told her. I could barely catch my own. My head thudded as I tried to rip the image from my mind.

May shuffled forward and wrapped her arms around me. I was startled, but her chest rose and fell—even, slow. I matched it.

At last she pulled away and studied me. Her eyes grew wide. "Didn't leave, but—?"

I nodded.

The understanding washed across her face.

Somehow, it was a relief to see it there. She was the first person I'd told, and I hadn't had to speak the words. I could never speak them.

Suddenly, there were tears in her eyes. Between the trails of lake water on her cheeks, one streaked down.

I hadn't cried. It was a sealed valve, with what incomprehensible flood behind it. I turned away.

I fixed my eyes on the flat line of water slicing between the hills. No matter how colossal—cliff, island, mountain—some greater force can always cut it down.

I could control this.

"Go again."

We waded back in. We swam out beneath the stargrass that carpeted the water around the marina. It cast down speckles of light. This time, I could pace my heart, keep my breathing steady.

We did four more dives that day, each one farther from shore, each deeper. The lake water was heavy with particulate, scales, plant matter. It was nothing like the sea. I uncoupled it in my mind, link by link, from any other diving I'd done. And as I watched the fish dart and shift, the green coils of sourceless current, I was even able to forget my own mind. Everything outside this moment—erased. For a while, at least.

THAT AFTERNOON, after May and I peeled off our wet suits, we climbed into the car and headed for Steels. I needed a Bloody Mary, but I had another motive.

The last few afternoons, Clark had come by to start work on the roof—mostly taking measurements, since his hip wasn't healed. After he left, I'd slip out of the house and drive into town. I didn't know how to describe her, or even how to phrase it—I'd just ask at the checkouts, the gas station counter, the sandwich shop, had they seen someone named Daphne. A stranger, I said.

The idea of saving her—something about it had lodged inside my chest. It could make me, for a while, useful. But I knew we wouldn't find Daphne diving. Either she'd run away or—I cringed to think—May was lost inside her grief. May had stuck to her story, and Clark, whenever I could corner him, insisted she was telling the truth. It was clear that it was all too tender to broach directly. But I figured if I found Daphne for her, I could stop all of this from going too far.

My visits to town yielded nothing. The cashiers only shook their heads, eyes like sockets. I wondered if they knew who I was. In Steels, I wore my mother's shame, her famed half lunacy, like a sign around my neck.

I wanted to try one more time, but with May by my side. If we were in town together, maybe she would notice a clue, or even catch sight of Daphne. So I took May to one of the busiest spots in Steels.

When I cut the ignition in front of Bud's Diner, May was biting a white ring into her upper lip.

"You all right?"

"I don't . . ." She blinked at the plate-glass windows, where an old man smacked the heel of a ketchup bottle and a server—ruffled apron, paper hat—scrubbed down the lunch counter. It occurred to me that part of May's delusion may have been fueled by a crippling anxiety. I remembered those years in middle school when Allie had to throw up before I could coax her down to the bus stop. "It's a lot of people," May said.

Instinctively, like when I held back Allie's hair, I put my hand on the nape of May's neck.

"I've got you," I said.

She nodded, unbit her lip. We walked into the diner together, a bell chirping our arrival, the door hissing shut behind us. An old dread sent a puff of smoke from between my ribs. I'd worked here for three years, starting at fifteen.

We sat in the booth farthest from the door. The paper-hatted server, a woman in her sixties with a twitchy mouth, dropped two menus on the table.

"Drinks? Coffee?"

May blinked at me.

"A Coke for her," I said, "and a Bloody Mary."

I studied the menu, and when I looked up, all the color had drained from May's face. My heart skipped.

"What's wrong?" I thought she might faint.

"Grievous and bloody sins," she whispered, digging her nails into her arm.

The server slopped two drinks down on the table. "Ready to order?"

"We need a minute."

May gaped at my cup.

"May—it's tomato juice." I rattled the ice and choked back a laugh. "It's vegetables. See?"

I sipped it and offered her the straw.

"It's—" Relief pooled across her face. She released her arm—chain of white prints—and then she was grinning broadly. Both of us burst out laughing. Soon the old man was frowning from three booths down and the server glowered up from her magazine.

"I just—" May stammered, a tear streaking her cheek. She caught it with a napkin and hiccupped. "I have—had a friend named Mary. Which makes it worse," she squealed, dabbing her eyes.

Finally, May exhaled and took a sip of Coke. Her eyes widened; she coughed, touched her throat, and took another sip.

The bell tinkled and a woman strode across the threshold. I watched her approach the counter and click her pink nails along the Formica. Amber Hastings. I wiped my eyes clear.

"Is my order ready?" Amber asked.

The server glanced up from her magazine and disappeared into the kitchen.

Amber strolled along the counter and settled on the stool closest to us. She scanned us from beneath her penciled brows.

May was halfway through her Coke already.

"Wow," she said, her pupils dilated. "Have you had one of these?"

"Sweetie, don't tell me you haven't had a Coke," Amber said.

"First time!" May said. The sugar seemed to have gone to her head, and she turned to Amber. "It itches," she said, pointing to her throat.

Amber's nails laced over her knee. "You must be new here."

May nodded.

"Where you from?"

May opened her mouth. She looked at me.

"The city," I said. Amber's eyes flicked over my face. She recognized me.

"City girl."

"Sure," said May.

"Tell me more."

"What do you mean?"

"I mean, what's it like? I've lived here all my life, so I don't really know. Is it dangerous?"

I could see May's mind folding and slicing and stitching Amber's words back together. What she said next inched out like a receipt from a printer.

"It's not dangerous," May said, "if you have a lot of friends, like me. They invite me into their houses—which I have one. Sometimes I make meals for them. Yes. A lot. They sit at my table. That's what it's like, to live in the city."

She grinned triumphantly, tottering side to side from the rush and sugar.

"Wow," Amber said. "That sounds amazing."

"Oh, it is."

May had missed the sarcasm.

The server reappeared, dropped Amber's to-go bag on the counter, and switched out May's Coke with a fresh one, which May set upon immediately.

"How about you?" Amber asked me, threading her index finger through the bag handles. "Was your life that glamorous, wherever you ran off to?"

Words failed me. I felt the walls of myself collapse like brown paper, and I was sixteen, had always been sixteen, hadn't progressed a single squirming inch.

"Guess you weren't cut out for it," she said, then glided across the diner and out the door. Chirp, hiss.

My heart pounded, and I buried my nose in the menu. But May was buzzing in her seat.

"Did you see that?" she beamed. "She really liked me. And she doesn't even know who I am."

She cackled into her straw. She should have seemed off her rocker, but I recognized this particular kind of giddiness. It was the euphoric release of anonymity—how, when no one knows you, your old self flakes off like a bad dream. I'd tasted that freedom only rarely, in all the years I'd been chasing it.

Maybe I was jealous.

"Amber Hastings doesn't like anyone," I said.

Right away I regretted it, but May looked more perplexed than disappointed. "You know her?"

"Yes."

"How?"

I stirred the celery in my drink. I'd gotten myself into this. "I used to wait tables here. Amber and her friends would come in after school."

"And you'd sit with them."

"No. I was working." I finished the Bloody Mary. Somehow, I felt more comfortable with May than I should have. "They'd sit at the tables dropping pennies into their water glasses until they overflowed. A game. They called it Drown Town. And when they left, I had to clean it up."

Mop up your mama's mess, Amber would sneer on her way out the door. Chirp, hiss.

May considered for a moment; nodded.

"I see," she said. "I know some people like that."

"What did they make fun of you for?"

She bit into her lip again and couldn't look at me for a moment. When she did, her eyes were half-wild; pleading. "Don't tell, okay?"

"Okay." My chest crumpled: the raw, sweet sight of her.

"I don't—" She lowered her voice so that it was almost inaudible. "I don't have a father."

Her pulse thumped in the crook of her throat.

"Hey," I said. I reached across the table, squeezed her hand. "Me neither."

Her brow furrowed, and I could see her searching my face for the deception. "Really?"

"Yeah." I laughed, an expulsion of nerves.

She jabbed her straw down in the ice, swirled it around.

"I never met no one else like that, besides me and Daphne," she muttered at last, in full astonishment.

"Mine left a long time ago. It happens."

I'd like to say I never looked back after throwing that keychain down the chimney. But somewhere in my mother's house was a blue leather journal with my letters to him. Nowhere to send them, of course. *Come and visit soon. xo. Mom said no one taught Alby how to be a man. You're mad at her but I am too. xo. Come and get us. I got an A+ in Biology. Are you happy? Come and get us. I promise I'll be good.*

"I didn't know that—that it happens," May said.

"It's okay." I jogged her arm. "Now decide what you want to eat already."

May spent the next five minutes staring at the first page of the menu. In the end, I ordered us two burgers.

We ate for a while in silence, May chewing overlong at every bite. At three, when school let out, kids flooded the sidewalks. As May watched them pass, I studied her face. No flash of recognition; no sign that she saw Daphne among them. Soon, the street was empty again.

"Drown Town," May said. She pulled the pickle off her burger, licked it, and set it aside. "I don't know that game."

"You wouldn't. They made it up—a joke on my mom. She stole some money and gave it to people living in the valley—where the lake is now. Everyone hated her for that. They hated me and my sister too."

I'd spoken this aloud rarely—maybe never. I shrugged it off like rain.

"Why did she steal it?"

"To try and buy our farm back. It's a long story. The real reason is that she's selfish. She never wanted the farm for us—she wanted it because she can't let anything go. I mean, she was pregnant with me when she did it. Didn't care how being the town thief would affect her kids."

"Hm." May winced, shook out some salt on her side plate. She tipped her sparrow head at me. "That doesn't make much sense."

"What?"

"I mean. Ever since I got pregnant, everything I done was in service to Daphne. She must have cared a little. Every step she took, *weighed* with you."

"You don't know my mother."

"Maybe." She drew a spiral into the salt, her ear on her shoulder. "But I know how it is to be a woman without a husband, because . . . I am also one." She paused, scanned me for a reaction. She began again, almost breathless. "And the things they said about me—selfish, immoral—those are the things you're saying now."

It took me aback—wall of water cresting a seawall. I'd never seen it. But she wasn't wrong.

We packed up our doggie bags and stepped outside. A whorl of leaves barreled down Main, slamming the door behind us. Across the street, a Gadsden flag with its coiled rattlesnake fluttered on a pole outside the contractor's office.

"Don't tread on me," May read aloud. "Ha!"

As we climbed into the car she was still chuckling to herself. "Who'd hurt a snake?" she said. "He speaks the truth."

MAY PROVED TO BE a confident swimmer. And outside the water, she was diligent. I'd find her at the picnic table every free moment she got, leaning over her notebook, mapping out dive plans, doing all the calculations under her breath.

On the evening of the second day of water training, we dragged our tanks up the boat ramp and collapsed at the table. I couldn't delay any longer.

"All right," I said. "What's the plan for our first dive?"

May expelled a sigh of relief, tucked a smile into the corners of her mouth.

She opened her notebook to a plan outlining two quick bounce dives reaching forty-five feet of depth, forty minutes of bottom time each.

"Good work," I said. "But where do you want to start?"

This was the moment when it should have crumbled—the delusion of underwater pockets of air, of a daughter run away for some noble purpose, rather than the crushing truth.

"I think . . . Let me think on it," May said. "Can I tell you in the morning?"

"Sure."

A strand of breeze passed between us, and her round cheeks flushed. She seemed so young sometimes. So long as I could keep her safe, maybe I was doing her a kindness, ferrying her through this loss to the other side. Once we swam down and found nothing, she'd be forced to face reality.

"If we see your daughter," I said, "how will I recognize her?"

She thought for a moment, turned to a blank page, and started to draw: wave after wave of long hair, then the outline of a body, tilted at an angle—swimming.

May set down her pencil. "This is how I been dreaming her since she left. Do you think that means something?"

The question turned my stomach. "She's strong, and she's young. That's to her advantage."

May nodded. "Sixteen."

She pulled the picture toward her.

"I think it means she's moving fast," she said, "and we'll have to move fast too."

THE NEXT MORNING, May was waiting outside in her wet suit, her eyes burning like pennies through the dawn haze.

I changed in the boathouse and sat down beside her on the edge of the dock. Her flippers twitched up and down, slapping the water.

"Stick to the plan," I said.

"I will."

We pulled on our masks and slipped off the dock.

We blew the air out of our lungs and began to swim. Morning light, scrubbed and fresh, tilted down in pale sheets.

We descended. As we'd agreed, May pulled a few feet ahead to lead the way. She kept level with me so I could control our depth. She swam fluently, tilted forward like the figurehead on the prow of a ship.

Visibility through the thick reams of silt was no more than twenty feet, but May started to urge ahead faster. She stopped kicking her feet, instead using her hips to whip her legs from side to side like a fish.

I tried to slow our pace, lagged as a signal for her to do the same. But she didn't ease up. We were already at thirty-five feet and still angling deeper. My heart fluttered a warning. She was pulling ahead farther than agreed—five feet, six, too far for me to tap her ankle. A single panicked thought clicked on like a bulb: what was I doing, taking someone diving who was not well, who in her delusion or grief really believed—

May pulled up short—tipped her torso above her feet and hovered. Ahead, a huge form carved up through the silt.

It was a church. Cotton algae matted the red brick, flagging off its paint-stripped cornices. A steeple rose above our heads. It extended past where it should have tapered, converting into a shaft like a chimney that reached the water's surface.

Grasses crawled up the lower wall. They seethed with fish, cadres of minuscule darters. Tangles of fishing line nodded in the current.

May and I drifted closer. The wall extended to our right, reached a corner, and dropped away. Just beyond this was the wavering shape of another structure: shipping containers laid end to end and traveling off into the silt, like a corridor.

I signaled to May. She was okay. She pointed left and started to swim; I followed.

We rounded the corner of the building and encountered a broad façade with morning light spilling down its face. A cathedral window yawned at its center, flanked by two lancets of stained glass. As we moved closer, I saw that a layer of plexiglass had been installed over them from the outside.

Through the cathedral window, I glimpsed a shift, a movement in shades. At first I dismissed it as one of those flickers in the corner of your vision that disappear as soon as you look. But then I saw it again: a shadow—shadows—a procession, moving with an organic and inexplicable gravity. I squinted; I rubbed my mask. But they didn't dissipate. Instead, they started to cluster, school, all in the same direction, not fish but—we were dropping lower in the water—body after body, humans, passing along a pew, turning toward an altar, women with hair rivering down their backs and men shaved close, waxy cheeks shining, raising up their arms—drowned, and come back to life.

II

May

Otta thought, in the search for Daphne, that she was cradling my madness. I knew that. I had to prove to her first the livingness of us. To show her the Chimneys and make her understand.

She climbed out of the lake that day coughing water, words slipping from her mouth like minnows out a fist. She paced on the dock talking back and forth, half to herself, half in questions.

The wet dripped down her. A chill of wind sliced the valley, hoisting spins of brown leaves.

"We need to warm up," I said.

It was early still, and the shop was locked with Mr. Clark gone at his fate, so Otta drove us to her house. She fetched me some dry clothes and went upstairs to change. When I came out of the bathroom, smells coiled through the house and I followed them.

In the kitchen was an old woman. She stooped over a clutch of hot plates, warming a slice of butter in a pan. I'd seen Mr. Clark put this on his toast.

"Who are you?" I asked.

The lady jumped in her skin. She looked me up and down, trying not to seem surprised in her face.

"I should be asking the same thing. You're in my house."

"You're Otta's mother." Since I first heard of her, I'd been trying to picture her face—if she might talk in the accent of Otta, if she chewed also the insides of her cheeks and had hard eyes. The hardness, yes—but in the rest of her, I couldn't see Otta at all. "Eugenia, right? I'm May."

"Never heard of you."

She cracked two shells on a bowl and they spilled out, sun-bright and glossy. Then with a fork she sliced it all to liquid and bits.

"You want an egg?"

I nodded, sat down at the table.

She tipped her mixture into the pan. It wheezed and smoked. It was only a minute before she poured it onto two plates and sat down across from me.

I took a bite. The richness almost made me spit it out, but I chewed and chewed, and swallowed it down.

"So how do you know my daughter?"

"She's teaching me diving."

She narrowed her eyes. I took another bite. I was hungry and the eggs I was starting to like very much. "So it's you she's been going out with."

"Yes."

She glared at her fork. "I guess you know how wrong that is. Disrespectful. But, just like my daughter, you're choosing to do it anyways."

I nodded. I wasn't sure what the answer she wanted.

"You come up here with Otta from the university?"

"No."

"Where you from, then?"

I said what Mr. Clark had said: "Here."

"Who's your parents?"

This one I wasn't ready for; I sputtered. "Margaret."

"Family name?"

I froze. Then for some reason blurted out the secret name I'd given my daughter, in the lack of us having one: "Clark."

Her face seemed unbelieving. "Clark. Really. What's your daddy's name?"

I shook my head down at my plate. The eggs tilted in my stomach.

"Okay, all right." She patted my hand. When I looked up, her face was softer, skin loose and pink in the pits of her cheeks. "Men—who needs 'em?"

And then I remembered: Otta, also fatherless. A baffling thing. When she told me in the diner, I could see all at once a little glass and fragile, the risen bumps on her arms. And now here was Eugenia—husbandless, like me. That there could be more of us in the world changed the world itself.

Otta's mother gulped down her last slippery egg.

"Margaret," she said. "I only ever known one. We went to Paintsville Church together. She passed in the flood. Was that her?"

"I—" All these questions tumbled my mind to mud.

"Good woman. Had to overcome a lot. You should appreciate that."

The blue tubes of her eyes spiraled me down. My mother had always been a flat thing—a shadow in the corner of my vision, frozen inside her final wailing image. But what if Eugenia had witnessed her moving in full flesh, through a lifelong life? I couldn't fathom it. I had a million questions. I did. And I couldn't put words to not even one.

Eugenia scratched at her scalp.

"See, Margaret wasn't spoiled," she said. "She stuck around and took care of her mom. That woman wasn't right in the head. Meanwhile, Otta up and leaves the minute she turns eighteen. After I put a roof over her head, gave her everything she needed."

These last words thumped like a stone. I'd said them out of my own mouth. The woman sitting across from me was starting to look so much like myself, it made me dizzy—down to the daughter that abandoned her.

Otta had told me her mother didn't care. She did; I could see it in the drawn corners of her mouth. But Otta didn't feel it. Like even after food, and shelter, she'd wanted something more.

"Well—at least—you must be proud of her," I stuttered. "With her diving. I never met someone who knew so much."

Eugenia waved it away. "She's not living in the real world."

We heard Otta coming down the stairs. Her mother poked at my shoulder and whispered, "Maybe you can snap her out of it."

She passed Otta in the kitchen doorway. Neither said a word.

OTTA SAT ACROSS FROM ME. Her eyes sheened like dishes, but she was calmer now.

"I'm sorry I didn't believe you," she said. "If you could, tell it all to me one more time."

Her fingers wove together, bone-thin with the nails bitten down. *They hated me,* she'd said in the diner, then shrugged. But the effect was opposite of what she wanted—not the slick shell of a mussel shut. Instead, I saw the soft meat glinting—saw it because I knew it. A bruise fused forever to the body.

I explained it all again. I told about the Chimneys and the reverend and the people there. How Daphne disappeared overnight and the note she left. What I couldn't say, sour in the pit of my throat, was how I was the one that told her—trying to explain how much bigger the world was, trying to make her care—what Mr. Clark had told me. That just like there was a lake above, there was a lake below, an aquifer inside a great sponge of rock, and that the water there was still fresh and good. Good water was what Daphne was after. It was my fault she left.

Otta took my hand. There was a sob rising in me. Mary only heard me cry once, in the pit of night, for no reason. She'd rolled over and wrapped her arm around my chest. We never talked about it after. I was ashamed. But in my most hopeful heart, I imagined that Mary's face in the dark looked kindly, no pool of pity but like I'd opened up a faucet for us both. Like the way Otta looked at me now.

ONE THING I'VE LEARNED is to keep everything a secret unless there's a reason to tell it. I broke that rule when I told Otta I was a bastard. That felt dangerous, like with broken glass beneath my feet, choosing to step.

There are secrets I want to say now. I want to learn how to tell them in the telling. Because I wonder if there's a way you can know the future by understanding better what has already happened.

To start, look again at the mighty windows of the Shuttle, their colors gnashing into the nave. As Otta and I floated, I felt like the eyes of the lake itself.

Even through the twisting light, I caught sight of him: dust-brown hair clipped three inches to his head, the curls oiled and tamed. I'd known whenever he was close every day for seventeen years—not from sight but before sight, like reflex.

Time slips: the present seeps into the past, the past into the present. It's hard to hold them into separate threads, like time is not a line but a braid.

Let me say first that Mary didn't abandon me. I kept secrets from her and so built a distance between us. She tried still to ask me about my day and my books, how my map was coming and what did I eat at tithe. But we were born to different fates, and I withdrew as a way to help her do what she couldn't do herself. I saw it as a mercy to her. I don't know now if it was.

So it come to pass in my fourteenth year, with Mary's preparations for Rehearsal swelling the walls of Powell, that I started spending more time in the lime kiln, a round room with a hollow pillar of brick in the middle of it. Inside that pillar was an open hearth that led up to the first chimney—the inspiration for the rest of them, so says the Final Book. Before the flood, the kiln had been used like an oven to make quicklime for plastering our walls with, the Book says. Now it funneled air and light down.

The kiln was the only place I could be really alone. I'd sit on the floor, lean against the pillar, and do my calculations in the purple glow cast down through the chimney. I lost track of time, urged into my work, forgetting all the reasons it was foolish of me, impudent even—Mrs. Wallace's favorite word—to think that my maps and calculations were anything more than vanities.

I wouldn't dare shut the door for fear of looking like I was claiming this holy place for myself. So whenever people walked by, I hunched over my workbook. It was a quiet passageway because it led to the sacristy, which only certain boys and men had the keys for.

Over a few weeks' time, I come to be aware that one figure passed by more often, and walking slower than the others. So one day, when I heard footsteps, I watched through the door, and Jonas appeared.

Curls fell over his forehead and when he turned to look, a light caught his eyes, like how a spark lifts off a flame and wanders. He paused, let a smile cross his mouth (pink, flash of teeth), and walked on.

It was how he'd looked at me from the choir on that Day of Risen Lake. Ever since, I'd lingered on the curve of his lips, their corners dimpling into his cheeks; wondered, if I touched them, would they feel like my lips. I'd never felt any lips but mine.

After that day, I postured my body different when I heard him coming. I straightened my back, arched out my chest. I borrowed Mary's embroidered tops, and stretched the neck so my collarbones showed.

I felt sick in my stomach. I didn't know why I was doing it. All I knew was he was the only person who'd ever looked at me like that, and I didn't want it to stop.

One day, instead of glancing into the kiln and moving on, Jonas leaned in the doorway. He was wearing his sacristy robe, and the lines of his body showed under the draping.

"What are you doing in here?" he said.

"Homework."

He laughed. A short burst. "Come on."

In truth, it was lately hard to get the teacher to give me assignments. I should have finished school last year with all the other girls my age, but with nothing else to occupy my time, I was repeating the year.

"That's what I'm doing," I said, deadening my features against him.

He held my eyes for a moment, then—against all expectation—flopped down beside me on the floor. He twisted his head to see my workbook, a stack of numbers all up and down the margins of a seed catalog.

"Not the Final Book?"

"You think all girls care about is literature."

"Yes." He smiled my defiance back.

"Well, I guess you know I'm different."

"I do."

"So." I didn't know what to say. "What do you need, then?"

"Need?" That laugh again. "Just being friendly."

"Okay."

"Is that strange?"

"Yes."

"Maybe I like being strange." He sounded sincere. And as he stared at me, it even seemed that he lost his words for a minute.

"So, why calculations?" he asked. "I'm shitty at them."

I cringed at the curse but couldn't help grinning.

"Well, I'm trying to figure out the full dimensions of the Chimneys. The length and width and volume. It's for a map I'm making."

"Why?"

I shrugged. "No one's ever made one."

"Because we all know where everything is." He was teasing.

"Well, you know, before the lake, they made maps of towns and countries and even the whole Earth, although they thought they knew where everything was." I was telling him what I'd read in a book, one I'd hidden to keep it from being repurposed. There was danger in sharing this. We weren't supposed to read unapproved texts, which he'd especially know since his family were book-cleaners, who'd tear out pages or even remove whole books from the shelves. "I think making the map helped them find things they didn't know were there."

"How would it do that?"

"Maybe made them ask questions they wouldn't have asked—shouldn't have asked."

I tacked on the last bit without thinking. A warm surprise edged across his face.

"And what have you asked?"

"I don't know."

"Come on."

I retreated. I explained to him more about my map and the ways I calculated its dimensions. While we talked, the world outside this room melted into distance. He looked me straight in my eyes, and I realized how much I wanted to really trust someone—something like what I'd had with Mary, that we'd lost.

"But I haven't seen everywhere," I said. "Not every room of every cottage. So it's hard to map those. And some of the sacred—the—"

"The Jewells' house." He leaned in. A wicked twinkling. "The sacristy." He jangled the keys in his pocket.

I felt his breath on my neck.

Then he stood. "I'm going there now. You distracted me."

The smile still hung on his lips.

"You coming?"

We both laughed in our angled ways.

He left.

But he came back.

AGAIN AND AGAIN, for weeks on weeks, he came. The kiln chimney's mouth spat out bursts of wind, tossing the pages of my texts, kicking up spirals of dust and the dry shreds of leaves. Jonas sat beside me, turned the pages of my book. Our palms brushed, then our shoulders, then our shoulders touched for long moments, then his palm rested on my knee, and lakes, it sent the slick of a new-caught fish down my spine, and he let it, he knew and he let it.

We found every day new things to talk about, which every day stunned me, and some of them forbidden: how he didn't want to do his fate, didn't want to start courtship; how he wondered sometimes did the Overlake still have living animals, fur and scales pasted all over them, writhing in the dirt. All this nudged me closer to trusting him, because any of these secrets repeated would be a shame on his family. So when he asked about me, I told—and said things that even caught myself off guard. That I dreamed sometimes of my mother's face leaning close, speaking a language I couldn't untangle. That I sometimes got my calculations wrong so as not to alarm the teacher. That I'd dreamed of the Overlake too—just dreamed it.

Because that, I still kept to myself: that I'd been to the Overlake half a dozen times; that these visits had shifted something in my mind; that they were the only reason I was brave enough to talk to him now.

He acted like what I said was worth hearing. He asked did I like my fish sautéed or boiled, did I sleep on my stomach at night, where did I think the toilets went when they roared open and snapped again shut—when he asked this one, twinkled and poked me in the stomach. Did I read any books he didn't know about; did I touch my thighs in the dark; and once, he asked did I like not having a fate. "Does it feel free?"

That question halted me.

"What do you mean?"

"Having no responsibilities, no one expecting anything of you." He was lying back on his elbows. He'd nudged the door to the kiln almost shut with his toe. "That sounds perfect."

A bitter fist turned in my gut.

"Perfect? Being uncourtable, untouchable, and the bastard that your own mother, Jonas Vaughan, grudges to feed: that sounds perfect to you?"

I hated the hot lake in my eyes. I turned my face to the ceiling where the chimney arched into the room.

"But you're not." He sat up and put his hands on the sides of my face. "You're not untouchable." His breath, I could feel it on my lips—then I could feel his lips—and they surprised me, they were nothing like I imagined. They opened to his mouth, hotter and darker, with his tongue flicking through the breach, and then they traveled along my cheek and down my neck and ran down my arms, my chest, my waist. He pushed the door all the way shut, and I didn't know what it was but everything he asked I gave, and feeling across his miles of skin, the incalculable galaxy of him, I believed that of all the worlds I knew about, below and above, this was the one I belonged inside, now and for the rest of my life.

THOSE AFTERNOONS I met Jonas in the kiln were the closest to sacred I'd ever felt. More than anything I'd experienced listening to the reverend or reading the Final Book or sitting in a pew. So I'll leave the most private moments where sacred things lie: in the dark.

He spoke so openly as I lay with my head on his chest, or his head on my stomach, that I believed there were no two people in the world who knew each other better. He told me about the dream that had haunted after him ever since he was small: a mantle worm burrowing itself up, up, up, inch by inch, toward his bed. He started and stopped a few times to say what some boys did in the sacristy. He told me how his father pinned his mother against the wall, punched her on the chest, the shoulders, the stomach, so it wouldn't show on her face. I'd seen Mr. Wallace hit Mrs. Wallace, but the hiding of it seemed worse. He said that when he had a wife he didn't want to be like that. I saw his eyes grayed against a pain I couldn't see the bottom of, and I thought he was the gentlest man I knew.

When I have a wife. I thrilled at those words, felt a surge of something I hadn't dared. But over time, I dared it. For many months, we met in the kiln at dinnertimes—Jonas claiming to be sick, and no one missing me at tithe. He'd shut the door so swift that the air shushed from the room, then pressed my face between his hands, or dipped me to the floor like I was the softest animal. If he broke my gaze, it was to watch how my skin moved over my ribs, or how the hairs on my stomach rose to his fingertips. Many months may sound short, but it was an entire lived life and I came out the other side different, brightened and sharp like a flesh left in vinegar. All that time, not least because he was important and high-fated, I was growing prouder—like with every hour we spent, he belonged to me more, in a way he would not be able to deny.

Jonas gave me shimmers of hope that this was true. He started venturing farther from the Shuttle and the cottages nearby, which belonged to the higher fates. I glimpsed him once along the passageway to Powell, crouched beside a minnow trough. He was playing Upside-Down, a game for little kids where you turned over a drinking glass and pushed it down into the water, trying not to bust the air bubble inside. He didn't say a word as I passed, but he sparked beneath his brow.

When others were around, it was different—like when he walked by a group of us who were gathered at the schoolhouse door. Those times, he ignored me in a way that came almost too easy.

Mary crumpled every time his eyes chanced on her. It was painful to watch her wheedle and hope, knowing that his glances meant nothing. Or hoping they did—which was worse.

All the wickedness I'd come to relish—when I visited the Overlake, whenever his hand brushed mine—all of it turned to a sick pit of stomach when I remembered how Mary adored him. She knew so little about him, but I wondered many times if her love was better than mine—even because of that ignorance, its starch and tin shine; because each of them was fated, where I shouldn't have even survived the Rise.

One night, I heard her roll onto her side.

"May."

I wanted to pretend I was asleep, but my breathing wasn't right. "Yes?"

"Guess what happened today?"

"What?"

"Jonas said he was excited to see me at Rehearsal. *Me.*"

That pit in my stomach moaned. I tried to think of something to say and could not. I remembered him lying in the mauve light that rippled down through the hearth, arms behind his head.

"Mary," I said, "that's great news."

She pressed her face into the pillow and let out a squeal. "I know. It's good, right? It means he'll be considering. I think it must mean that."

"I think it must."

She rolled onto her back.

That night I dreamed every fish in the lake locked together to form a net and started pressing their sides against the walls and windows of the Shuttle. The plexiglass groaned and bent. The murals painted on the brick—bass and muskellunge and grasses spiraling outward from His pulsing violet palm-shaped heart—cracked under the weight of them. The fish were not meek before Him but wrathing, wrathing, and what had enraged them I didn't know, I didn't know what we'd done.

I ASKED JONAS ABOUT IT LATER, standing with my back against the kiln chimney. A specter had slipped into the room and was slithering low along the floor.

He laughed. "She's obsessed with me. Thought I'd give her something to live for."

I felt a twinge of anger for Mary—and relief. "So you weren't serious."

"No. Come on." He paced around the chimney with his hand trailing the wall.

"You haven't asked me if I'm going to Rehearsal," I said.

He came around the other side, glanced at me, and started his second lap of the room. "Well, I mean . . ."

"What?"

"It feels pretty written in stone."

"And that doesn't bother you?"

"I don't make the rules."

"Don't you?"

He tossed his chin up for one laughing burst. It was a peculiarity I loved, except that now it seemed in spite of me. "My mom likes to make us out as more important than we are."

Jonas started his third lap. His mind was elsewhere. When we were in the kiln, we'd always sealed the rest of the world out—but here it was, eeling around our feet. Glinting through now was a part of him I didn't know: the outside- and Vaughan-him, the courting and white-toothed, the twinkle that could gain any favor, from anyone, that could melt them like Mary—like me.

"You shouldn't play with her," I told him. "She cares about you."

He shrugged. Lap four. "She doesn't know me."

"Well, I do."

He didn't answer.

Then, against all my instincts, I blurted it out.

"Have you considered me?"

It sounded painful, meek.

He passed in front of me. His fingers traced the grooves in the stucco, up and down and over, a jigsaw where accidental images loomed in certain slants of light. I'd studied these shapes more than my books in the time that we'd spent here.

"Considered you for what?" he said.

I blocked his path.

"Okay, okay," he said. "I'll talk to my parents."

"When?"

"I've got to find the right time."

He turned for the door. I reached for his hand, but it slicked free before I could grasp it.

"I've got to go, it's been busy."

He left.

WHEN I WAS SMALL, the air and the water around us swarmed and tumbled with the holy-holy. The Lakebringer reigned and was all-knowing—and knew me, my crumpled-paper self.

As I grew older, I felt His presence less and less. Once *bastard* stained every tongue; after visiting the Overlake and witnessing the lake contained; after Jonas wrung and drained me and kept what he took.

Then I dove the lake with Otta and saw the Chimneys laid out before me. I can't describe it. Maybe it's like seeing all your skin turned inside out.

It had been mulling for years at the back of my mind, but now gasped into focus: that the Chimneys and even the lake were two organs inside a much larger body. And that body, a land that yawned out in all directions, had its own ends and designs no one could know.

It wasn't until diving with Otta, until seeing the whole Chimneys from the outside, that I remembered that feeling: the holy-holy, the all-surrounding. And when it returned to me, what it had to do with Him was nothing.

OTTA CUT THE ENGINE, morning light swilling in the foam. On the table in the middle of the pontoon, she laid out a chart of depths beside a map of the prelake town.

"Most of the structures are along Main Street." She pointed at the spot where the lake's three arms met—where our boat was floating now. "We can start there with bounce dives."

Otta and me had talked it all out—our plan for finding Daphne. Mrs. Wallace had told us a few times how she'd left her dog at the corner grocery, down the hill into town. One night she'd said—in a hushed voice slurred with blood-of-Him—that the grocery was sealed off from water before the flood. In the end, the people there had panicked and tried to flee, and drowned with the rest of the world. The Final Book confirmed this. But after Mrs. Wallace went to bed, Daphne had turned on her bedroll to me and said, "Could there still be air inside?" I said I guessed there might.

That was a year ago. Daphne must have been mapping it out even then: the path she would take to find good water. The grocery might be a first step deeper toward the caves.

According to the prelake map, the grocery sat on Main Street. The road was flanked on each side one or two cottages deep, and then continued west past a few scattered houses until it reached a structure ten times the size of any cottage. It was labeled *Weber Paint Co.*

Otta saw me studying this part of the map and shook her head.

"West of town, depth drops another fifty feet," she said. "We'd need another gas mixture, or even rebreathers to get enough bottom time. We can't dive that end of the lake."

We pulled up our wet suits. Otta was somber, crooked in her mouth, the exhilaration gone from seeing the Chimneys the day before. We would go deeper this dive than we'd ever done. Every foot of depth meant less bottom time, she said, and less room for error.

We strapped on our BCD vests—and then it hit me: a kind of dizzy, like unlinking from the earth. I held tight to the railing as we moved toward the stern. The Final Book taught that every living soul outside the Chimneys had died during the Rise. But that had already proven wrong. Now I wondered if whole other worlds, other Jewells and Vaughans and Wallaces, could be down under the lake, stirring. And if they'd seen Daphne—what had happened next? I felt the ballast of her body below me like a guide. Was she safe and herself and whole? I hadn't dared to ask. And couldn't. I wiped it from my mind. We sat on the stern and slipped into the water.

BUBBLES FILLED MY EARS and clouded my vision and the silt tossed in sheaves. We descended.

I glimpsed beneath us a hard glint of roof, metal and rippling and—strangest of all—with no chimney. Otta kicked forward and down and I followed.

Otta raised the hose above her head, released some air from her BCD, and sunk along the side of the house. I copied after, pushing the air from my lungs. I liked the mechanics of it all, the small tweaks and negotiations and then settling in on what was true. It was like numbers.

The wall was furred with pondweed. The cottage had two window boxes for catching fish, but they were so grimed with algae that there was no seeing inside. We circled the house, but found no door—just the shape of one bricked over. A steel pipe traveled along the lake bed and then entered the house above that bricked-in door. Near the wall, the pipe was bent, almost to the point of pinching shut.

On the far side of the house, we found a gaping mouth in the lake floor, a wooden hatch flung open around it, and a staircase into the earth. Otta flicked on her dive light.

In the flooded cellar, spare lengths of rope and bottles marked for milk hung suspended. A staircase climbed to an opening in the ceiling, a square of even darker dark. *Daphne*. We went up and through.

LAKE SLICKED OFF OUR SIDES. We discovered ourselves inside a box of air. We'd passed through a seam of water, which now lay shining in the floor like a fingernail. It quivered in balance with the room without shoving in to fill it up. The whole cottage was like a game of Upside-Down: air trapped and squeezed inside an upturned glass.

Otta pulled her respirator out of her mouth, inhaled, and nodded. She barely glanced at the pool, but I couldn't look away—not until she touched my shoulder, said, "Save your air," and pulled my mouthpiece out herself.

In the dive light's beam, the wallpaper was stamped with small roses. Black mold blotted out the pictures in their frames.

Otta lifted the flashlight above her head, and her hand struck something that sent a rattling wave across the room. The whole ceiling became an undulating skin, and I thought the lake was slicing through with vengeance. I yelped and dropped to my knees.

The stirring calmed; the water didn't swallow us. I started to see what the quaking really was: thousands of fish bones hanging from the ceiling, each on its own hair-thin thread. They were so dense that every inch of air contained one. Ribs, vertebrae, the spines from fin rays hung at various depths so that the bones, when they finally stilled, made a formation like the rolling of hills.

I climbed to my feet and shuffled in my flippers toward a cluster of jaws opened to the earth with their pinprick teeth.

Then I tripped. I fell forward, and landed on a softness.

"You okay?" Otta shone the light down.

I froze. I was face-to-face with a human being.

Scale-gray skin. Eyelids shut, but so thin I could see the pupils through them. Their body was cool beneath my palms. But I could feel, barely, a rising and falling: breath.

Otta pulled me to my feet. We saw now that there were bodies laid across the whole floor.

Otta locked her elbow in mine and we tried to calm our thumping hearts, like we'd practiced for diving. But it was hard to catch my breath, like there wasn't as much air as there should be.

"What is this?" she rasped.

A wave passed along the bodies. Above, the fish bones whispered it back. They were all breathing—the whole room, in the same single pulse—but deep asleep.

There were about fifteen people, all adults, with belly-white hair not the shade of aging but like the color had drained out. They lay side by side, pressed so close together that I couldn't see the floor between them.

Otta covered her nose with her arm. "That smell."

I hadn't noticed. But when I inhaled again I recognized it. It was the scent of fish and their flesh and cleaned bones, mixed with the warm sour of sweat. It was how the Chimneys smelled.

"Hello?" My voice came out louder than I meant. The fish bones quaked.

No one stirred.

"We don't have much time," said Otta. She sucked once on her mouthpiece. "Air seems thin. You feel all right?"

I nodded.

And so we circled this mat of people, searching for Daphne. Each face seemed almost a print of the next, except for small differences: that nose with a bump, these brows pinched. The knobs in their wrists gouged up like new fingers trying to be born. Some had collars stitched shut around their necks where the buttons had been lost. One had refinished the end of their sleeve by knitting the thread from the shirt back onto itself. It was the same cable pattern in miniature that Mrs. Wallace had taught to Mary and me.

Daphne would have been easy to find. She was sixteen with dark churning locks.

She wasn't there.

The relief curdled through me.

"It's like they're in hibernation," Otta said. She passed her light along a side table. The bulbs had been unscrewed from their lamps and collected in a tin. She sucked more air through her mouthpiece and I did the same. "I mean, I've heard of it—early humans, people living in extreme cold . . ."

"That pinched pipe . . . ," I said, but couldn't complete the thought. It was all slipping from realness—everything around.

"Right," Otta said. "If it's an air pipe, that might explain it."

She checked her watch. We only had forty minutes of bottom time and they were half gone. We sat and dangled our legs into that enchanted pupil of water in the floor. Otta noticed how I awed at it.

"It's a moon pool," she said. "They have them on research vessels and drilling rigs. So long as the air and water are at the same pressure, it maintains stasis."

The lake's pitch-cold shock was a relief. I started to swim. My muscles tensed and thawed. The whole drowsy scene began to slip away like dreaming does. We left the cellar behind and with each kick shed a piece of that house. It's hard for me now even to recall any more particulars. For instance, I don't remember—though I know, though I touched it—how their skin felt.

–79 ft.

Through the glass, the bass teem.

Inside the grocery, the shelves are arranged in neat aisles. The residents wake each morning to the sunlight fluttering through the plate-glass windows along the front of the store. The eelgrass has been cut away from the cracked road out front to keep the light on shining.

They sleep along the aisles. At dawn, they roll up their mats and stock them on the lowest shelves. They don ensembles of brown paper, folded and woven with pointed shoulders, pleated Elizabethan ruffs, swallow-tailed collars, and braided sandals for their feet.

Thus adorned, the younger ones go visiting. They glide down the centers of the aisles. The families living in each aisle greet the visitors as they pass. Behind them, cans of soup or boxes of cereal or jars of sauce array the shelves, almost all of them empty, but reconstructed to their former glory, re-placed on the shelf as archive.

The visitors admire the authentic maintenance of the aisle and the craftsmanship of its product. Some individuals are renowned for this skill, and are elected over and over to the Council of Preservation. This is the governing body, because preservation is the foundation of life, because memory slips when one's surroundings don't reinforce it, and because without memory there is no way for people to relate to each other.

After the visiting ends, the harvesters get back to their harvesting, choosing of the cans that remain which ones to open. The fishers drop through the moon pool and swim out with air swollen in their lungs to net catfish with plastic bags. The farmers plunge along Main Street clipping strands of pondweed and eelgrass from the crops they maintain in old flower beds. The cooks gut and scale and debone each fish, tucking in two kernels of creamed corn or a cube of Spam. Then they wrap the fish in eelgrass and place them in the walk-in to smoke. The preservers reseal cans with isinglass glue, touching back any tatters of paper to recomplete the label, dabbing with the tiniest paintbrushes where fading has occurred, and laying these out to dry along the shelves where they were originally stocked.

At the front of the store is a throne crafted of aluminum cans, the only artifacts that haven't retained their original form. Years back, the Council of Preservation declared that a sufficient number of these cans had been preserved. All color was stripped from the rest. The aluminum was hammered and bent into a core structure. This was covered with embellishments in the shapes of angels with small wings, or more recently—because the throne has been crafted over decades—angels with fins, angels with smoke rolling out of their chests, angels with legs like eels and eyes like bulbs.

The king of the Council of Preservation sits all day on his throne. He is asked to approve any newly sealed cans; plastic bags tented with reconstructed bread (eelgrass draped over a form and dried); peanut butter jars filled with lake bed silt; cardboard boxes for rotini repacked with laces of paint shaved off the walls; cracker boxes stocked with crackers made of boxes; Heinz bottles filled over the course of many accidents with a dark liquid; sacks that once contained rice, but now, sewn inside them, collections of dead skin, clipped nails, shed hair—the unique scent of each individual amalgamated over a lifetime and then sealed forever after their death. Inside these sacks is the answer to a question they've all been asking since they can remember—and they're closer to answering it than ever, any day now they'll wake up and know.

May

In my fifteenth year, I volunteered to help prepare the Shuttle for Rehearsal.

Me and some older women dragged all the pews against one wall. We popped the fluorescent bulbs from their fixtures along the Shuttle walls, wrapped them in blankets, and stowed them behind the altar. We set up two long tables to face each other.

But as the women filed out, I hid behind the pulpit. We had moved it into the shadows at the back of the dais, where two steel beams drove into the air, all the way up the chimney-steeple.

The moondrip was high and white through the cathedral window and cast its shape along the floor. Two stained-glass lancet windows flanked it, dripping a colored pattern across one of the long tables, where we'd set out the butchering sheets. The colors blotted out the faint smears of fishblood. On the other table, cast in white light, we'd laid out tablecloths crispy with age and lace napkins and the Jewells' lent silver.

Eight boys, all sixteen or older, filed in first in their best clothes. And there was Jonas—the robes I'd run my hand along, that he'd shown me how to unzip and lift above his head. He took a seat alongside the other boys at the table cast in white.

The Shuttle door opened again and nine girls entered. They wore dresses embroidered for this day. Mary's heart-sharp jaw was bowed like the rest, and all the girls' hair was pleated, but Mary's was the most fine—practiced and refined with her mother for months—and the moon like milk down her nape. Despite her being low-born, I thought there was no one more beautiful.

The girls took their places along the butchering table and, while the boys observed, each tugged the end of a line from her pocket and threaded the eye of her fishhook. We'd all been trained from seven years old how to fish, it being the role of each family's women. The lower fates made their own wire hooks, but for higher-ups, the luthier crafted them from bone.

Behind the girls was a long row of troughs with a window box above them, used for baptisms. Now each fetched a live minnow from the troughs. I knew Mary sometimes hesitated, but this time she pierced it in one swipe. Droplets and small blood leaked onto the butchering sheet.

The girls lined up along the window box and dropped their hooks into the water. Together, two dragged down the lever, a bronze contraption that triggered a groaning nest of wheels and cogs. The inside lid sealed, then the outside lid of the box opened. Lake water flooded in.

They waited.

The hooks flagged in the water.

The girls took each other's hands and, stepping pointedly, began to draw a wide circle around the tables.

The boys fidgeted in their seats. Some glanced over their shoulders, but outside of the bright lancets that the windows cast, all you could see were the flickers of hems.

The girls circled three times and stopped in front of the window. None had caught a fish.

The boys started to whisper among themselves.

Asher, with a shimmer of teeth, took up his fork and knife in his fists and slammed them into the table. Jonas spit out a laugh and did the same. Soon enough they had all joined in, thumping to a beat, and then started to chant—*Eat—Eat—Eat*—and the chants changed as each boy called out the next—*Yes—Yes—Meat—Meat*— The rhythm built on itself, spiraled up, twanged in the steel beams. Even the lures quaked.

Then the first hook caught. It was a rainbow trout with a pink flush down its side: good to eat, hard to catch. It whipped against its line but only dug itself deeper onto the barb, until a small oily pool expanded from its mouth and it fell still. The hook belonged to Lily Partridge.

The boys, who had been rapt watching it, let out a cheer and banged their silverware on the table, walloped down their plates, roared and punched each other's shoulders and wrung at the tablecloth.

Other fish ventured in to pick at the trout. They soon got hooked themselves: two bass, a sunfish, a chain pickerel, a pumpkinseed. With every one that caught, a roar rose up.

Mary stood there shifting in her mother's velvet shoes. The moondrip had stretched the full length of the tables now. Finally, I saw a whip at her hook. When it settled, it revealed itself to be a small warmouth—good but gamy.

The slant of moon touched the lowest step of the dais where I was hiding. A few girls shoved the lever up. The outer lid on the box shut, then they pulled the release. Water spilled over the top of the window box into the troughs.

Each girl pulled out her line, untied it, and brought her fish back to the butchering table. With the electricity humming along its three nightly hours, some plugged hot plates into an extension cord hidden beneath the draping. A few opened vials of their family's prized vinegar. While the girls prepared their meals—and although some displayed special tricks with the knife, or a hand so deft that the head and guts were swept instantly out of sight—the boys leaned back in their chairs and chatted among themselves.

Then the moon hit the top step of the dais, and Jonas and two other high-fate boys stood.

The girls hurried their meals onto the plates in front of them and froze in place.

The face I saw on Jonas as he approached the table sent an eel through me. It was like that time, in the middle of the night, when I'd tried to call the ghost of my mother. I sensed a shade draw near—then realized it was not human but something primal, thrumming and blind like the dark water that hung beyond the lit, like the mantle of the Earth that moaned up at us from the toilets and dragged everything toward it. The core was heaven but the mantle was hell, and this presence, scuttling low across the floor, stinking of waste and drownedness, murmured a message I was too terrified to hear. Jonas's eyes hooded into shadow, the sharp shelf of his cheeks, his mouth turned down like the concrete Him on the altar in all His judgment—he was not anyone I knew.

Jonas and the two boys walked along the butchering, inspecting each plate, leaning to smell them, looking up and down the girls in their statued grace. Jonas paused at the girls he was supposed to pause at, and the lower fates mostly drifted by—but slow, I think for the spectacle.

Mary at the far end of the table bit into her cheeks. But she kept her hands folded and her eyes straight ahead and when Jonas reached her, I saw him hesitate. Everyone in the room was poised on the edge of the knife that was Jonas's choice. He observed her, then continued on his way.

The three boys assembled before the butchering. A small, single curl escaped from Jonas's oiled-back hair.

I hadn't thought he would do it—didn't realize how hopelessly I'd believed.

Jonas pointed.

He pointed at Lily Partridge and it was done.

The rest unraveled fast enough. The next boys made their selections, and the others filed in order of rank along the plates and took their pick. Lily placed her plate in front of Jonas's seat, stood there to watch him eat it, and Jonas as much as everyone else nodded and hawed and finally, when he was full, began to speak to her. The courtships would go on for another year, but we all knew what was coming.

I found myself floating above the floor, darkness dripping from the edges of my vision. I had to go in search of my body, which I found at last through the icy sting of the steel beam against my spine. I dragged the air into my lungs by force.

I managed to climb to my knees. I peeked again around the side of the pulpit. The broad stalk of it cast me in shadow, but I was pinned in on all sides. Moon poured down the altar in gallons and the glittering jewels of His cheeks cast wild specks of light up the walls. On the dark end of the dining table, a few candles had been lit, and I could see Mary, chin on her chest, leaning over with a fork and knife to pick bones out of the warmouth for Caleb Teague.

−91 ft.

Through the glass, the bass teem.

The muskellunge with their blushed fins weave between the columns of a veranda encircling the Weber family's antebellum home.

Henry Weber in his generosity donated his own family's mansion to the forty-odd people of Paintsville whose apartments and houses couldn't be battened down against the flood. When Henry moved to the factory, he took with him two sofas, one painting, and a four-poster bed. He left behind more riches than anyone there had ever seen: pots and pans of bright copper, a lockbox of jewelry beneath the floorboards, damask armchairs, and a library of leather-bound volumes.

Henry had run his own family out of the place. His father left in such disgust that he hadn't even bothered to pack, and took only what the help could wedge into two Cadillacs.

Henry had then undertaken the painstaking task of tracking down the descendants of those slaves who had worked on the plantation in its prewar years. But the one family he could locate turned down his offer to move in and left town with the rest of the preflood exodus. Those in the mansion who claimed to know Henry personally whispered in their late-night stories how they had never seen him in such a rage, that he had split a clipboard over his knee and burned some papers in a barrel out back. But the stories always ended with Henry's revelation of who the rightful inheritors of the mansion really were. He opened his doors to the common people of Paintsville, whose skills were not needed elsewhere but who wanted to stay because they believed in his vision.

Those living in the pharmacy were assigned to distribute messages and medicine to Underlake houses via pneumatic tubes, since it was too far to swim between most of them. Those in the factory would build the batteries that provided the electricity every night. But when the flood came and the people in the mansion still had no tasks assigned to them, Henry promised he would send instructions by tube. After several years of polite bulletins on newsprint, the messages stopped arriving altogether.

In their secret hearts, many were relieved not to have been assigned an occupation, and took it all as a gift from Henry, recompense for their years of labor. As one resident eloquently put it, injustice anywhere is a threat to justice everywhere. So every moment they lived below the lake was an act of resistance against the state, which had stripped away the land that had been rightfully theirs since their forefathers carved it from a savage frontier.

Their occupations, in the end, they chose for themselves. Many men became adept spear fishers and could swim out the moon pool, snag a quillback, and be back in less than three minutes. The old folks scraped algae off the windows, which they ate for the vitamins. A troupe of women started scavenging mud from the lake floor and sculpting dishes and cups, with mediocre results. Their creations shifted over the years toward greater abstraction, and now their mealy, emotional sculptures were on display throughout the mansion, perforated with catfish whiskers and small stones.

Others took to the kitchen and refined a technique of wrapping fish with pondweed, then smoking them beneath the range hood. Sometimes smoke enveloped the kitchen, and they would stagger out with pools for pupils, babbling about the shapes they had seen in the haze. People started to ask them for oracular visions, and soon they were oversmoking the fires on purpose. Their scent of smolder and scales came to be linked with great wisdom.

A group of ladies, nine in total, had been children when the valley flooded. When they reached their late teens, one got pregnant. She insisted it was an immaculate child, come to her in the pitch of night through a bolt of dark lightning and sour pain. The child was stillborn, and all the young ladies were thrust into a collective despair. They gathered each night and wailed until they fell asleep—all except the not-mother, whose eyes were ever after emptied out, like they were printed on her face.

No one knows if the pact was spoken, but none of them married. Some were even said to collaborate with the kitchen to generate concoctions that would seal their hymens and even—if some questionable encounter occurred—wipe away any whisper of a fetus. They attained an air of untouchability akin to vestal virgins.

One year, a deacon and his wife announced that they were putting on a play. At first, they cycled through as many of the classics from the library's archives as they could. But eventually, the collective obsession landed not so much on any particular play, but on a concept: Queen Mab, fairy monarch of mischief who travels in a carriage with spider-leg spokes and disturbs people's dreams. The productions featuring her character were the most requested, and the role of Mab coveted, until most people could recite the lines freely:

> This is the hag, when maids lie on their backs,
> That presses them and learns them first to bear,
> Making them women of good carriage.

The communal fixation on Mab seemed driven, most of all, by her capriciousness: that she could deliver terrors in the dark simply because she wanted to. Everyone was at her mercy. They had all heard the deep-night yelps and small weeping, here and there a shift or shutting of doors. When they spoke of it, if they spoke of it, with the sun up, they called it the fairy queen passing through, doling out her whims, and whoever was her target must lie and bear it, then roll back into sleep again.

May

The steel air pipe sticking out the side of that first cottage (fish bones, dreamers) traveled along the lake floor, anchored with metal posts, and branched off in all directions. Over nearly a week, we followed it to another cottage, then a tool store, then a grocery. We could never stay underwater more than forty minutes, and we could bounce dive twice a day only because we had two tanks each.

That first stop, for a long time, was the worst. Every other cottage we visited, if it had people inside, they were awake. They lived by breathing air from the pipes, which arrived at the same pressure as the water around them. This kept the moon pools from surging into the rooms. Otta explained to me all this.

At one house, we emerged through the floor to find an ancient couple seated before an unlit hearth. Their silver hair hung all the way down the backs of their rockers. When they saw us, the woman peeped and then passed out in her seat.

They were startled, but not surprised at the fact of us. Even though none of the cottages were connected by passageways, and most were too far to swim between without scuba gear, they seemed to know that other people were alive in the Underlake—not like us in the Chimneys. That kind of existence, so alone, made each cottage peculiar to itself, stretched and drawn and obsessed with singular things.

"What news?" the old man asked, rocking and patting the hand of the woman, who now was huffing through some dream. The ruts of the rockers had dug halfway through the floorboards. He said the newspaper used to come through tubes and asked could it start to come again—the medicine also. He thought we were from the factory and we couldn't convince him otherwise.

"We are looking for my daughter," I said. But the more I described her, the more he squinted like he didn't understand.

He wasn't the last like that. Most of the people we visited were welcoming enough after the shock of us passed, but distracted by their own minds, eyes shifting up into their skulls, forgetting the ends of their sentences. Some seemed to pinch little secrets to their chests—questions they wanted to ask, needs. A small family with gum-grinning parents (old) and three children (also old) hosted us at their table with hot water and bass. But when we went to leave, one of the children (a man) gripped my arm. "Save us," he whispered. It was hard to pry loose his hand.

What could we do? It wasn't just that we had to find Daphne—that every day we didn't find her I felt my certainty flaking off of itself. Ever since she was born, I would tug at a little thread knotted to my navel a dozen times a day, checking—*Are you all right?* She always was. Anyway, I knew she'd taken food with her, a little water. But she'd been gone almost three weeks now.

The other problem was that, as Otta reminded me, these people couldn't just swim to the surface. They'd been living at pressure a long time. Swimming up fast, without tanks or wet suits, could kill them.

I noticed it more with each visit: gaping eyes from a corner, ropes straining in someone's neck. The desperation. But we were desperate too. We would have to come back.

WITH EACH VISIT, the number of people in the world multiplied, and the number of ways they had of living. Every cottage had different angles to their speech, habits and decorations and rituals as holy to them as ours in the Chimneys were to us. They had their own scents, ways of touching each other's arms or avoiding touch; to each their reverends and kings.

But the cottages had one thing in common: a sound in the walls, hushed shifts and groans—the lake testing weak points, tugging at the foundations to see would they hold, and beneath that, all the secrets the lake muttered to itself that had nothing to do with us.

I'd never known it was a sound until I went to the Overlake for the first time and it was gone. In the years that followed, I began to hear it in the reverend's sermons, how it wove its music into the way he spoke—him and everyone else. I saw how we stepped to the pace of it, shifted our bodies toward the walls when it quivered through the floor. And after returning to the Overlake and hearing again the lilting voice of Mr. Clark, of Otta, of her mother, and finally meeting these others living under the lake, I heard its song at last out of my own mouth.

I WAITED FOR HIM in the kiln for weeks like a fool. I was sour in my lungs, and food made me sick. But I carried my workbook down the sacristy passageway, humming in my chest, sat against the kiln chimney with the door wide, and tried to calculate.

The numbers made little sense. I'd stopped loving them, stopped loving my map. The world had hollowed itself out, jagged and scraped like I pictured the cave below us where we sent our dead. I started to feel its presence in the soles of my feet: its mute stonework, the quivering glass eye of what Mr. Clark called the aquifer—shadow to the lake and, in its holy distance, just as uncaring.

MARY LEFT EVERY AFTERNOON for her courtship with Caleb. She came home sooty from standing at the feets of chimneys. Every night, she cried under her pillow. I wanted to comfort her, to pull her to my chest like she had done for me. But I couldn't tell her the truth: how there was no one in the world that could understand better what had shredded her apart. Every time I opened my mouth to speak, I felt a thread flagging in the back of my throat. If she said his name, I wouldn't be able to keep it sewn. So instead, I hummed to drown her out. Night after night, I hummed myself to sleep.

I knew why I was being punished. According to the Final Book, it was because of what I did with Jonas. But the time we spent together had never felt wrong to me. It felt like the Overlake: another world that this one had no standing in.

No. I was being punished for what I took from Mary.

For what I tried to take.

TWO WEEKS AFTER REHEARSAL, I came around a corner and saw him walking in my direction. He was with a group of men, having the kind of discussion—lively, bloated—that seemed important because of who they were.

I kept on my way. Jonas may have glanced at me as they passed. I wasn't sure. I ran to the kiln and shut the door and my face cracked open and I almost wailed. But I pinned it in, set to humming and pacing and humming.

Still he didn't come.

I was sick to my stomach for a month. I felt weak from it, battened up in Powell and slept much. But one allotment day, I woke suddenly desperate for a different kind of air. At the top of the chimney, I flashed my mirror for Mr. Clark. Sure enough, he came to fetch me. He drove us to shore, and in the bait shop gave me a glass of water, which I drank and drank like I'd never drank it.

Mr. Clark never asked me personal questions. But this time, after watching me drink with a quizzed look on his face, he finally asked, "Something going on with you?"

I shook my head.

But when I got to my feet I was trembling, and Mr. Clark laid me down on a cot in the corner.

He covered me with a blanket. The sickness swept away, and I slept.

When I woke, blue light softened through the window. Mr. Clark raced me to the chimney so I could be back before allotments ended. But this time, he insisted I take some water with me. He'd sealed it inside a sack—*waterskin,* he called it—covered in the fur of I-shivered-to-think what animal.

As we bobbed beside the chimney, he tied a rope around the nozzle and showed me how to tie the same knot again.

"I can't take it," I insisted, knowing even as I said it how thirsty I was.

"Hang it from the top rung," he said. "No one will find it there."

So I climbed into the chimney and did what he told. I tied the knot, and even when I knocked the waterskin going down, it thudded mute against the brick.

I lived off that water for three weeks, and when it was getting low went back to find that it was filled again. Every week after that—for months, for what would become years—he came and filled it for me. It felt like a debt that every day stacked higher. But I drank the water ravenous, and the faster I drank it the faster he filled it.

I learned when my belly was out past my breasts what must have happened. One Sunday, Kella Partridge blocked my way into the Shuttle.

"Look at you," she said. "Just like your mother."

I didn't know what she meant. Bethany Vaughan—Jonas's mom—walked up behind her, fingers laced on her chest.

"This is a place of mercy," Bethany said. "But we can't let whores into the sanctuary."

Then I understood.

Later, when it all sank in, my reaction was not what anyone

would have thought, including me. Because the next Sunday, and the next and next, I felt freer than I had ever felt.

The whole Chimneys during those services emptied out. I wandered with my belly bulging out ahead. I peeked into doorways and stepped over thresholds and trailed my fingers along other people's walls. In Powell, I snuck into the Wallaces' room and laid on their bed. I flipped through the magazines under their mattress.

My wickedness. It ran through my veins, a fate passed down from my mother. Now I didn't try to stop it. It was as much mine as this baby in my stomach, this baby which was a piece of Jonas that he could not take back.

I expected them to ask but no one ever did. Who the father was. And after the whole world found out I was with child, I expected him to come. He didn't.

I passed him in a passageway once, and he looked. I know he looked. I'd fantasized he might fall to his knees, press his ear to my belly, stroke my hip, my neck, my cheek. But he didn't even slow his pace.

I CONSIDERED, many times, leaving for the Overlake. Mr. Clark said there was a town beyond the trees. But even if it did exist, what could I want with another town? It would be just one more place where I was an intruder without a name or fate.

And maybe I stayed because I believed in my stupid heart that he might change his mind. If not now that I was pregnant, when the baby came out and had eyes like his, lips like his. Or when she took her first step, said her first word. She would be irresistible to him, his own body folded and remade into living flesh.

So before she was born, I waited. After she was born, I waited. I never admitted to myself what I was doing. I can admit it now.

I WANTED HIM worse than thirst. For a long time, I did.

But the moment she was born, I stopped needing him.

When my water broke and the pain mounted, Mrs. Wallace at first tried to manage the situation. After a few hours, I was groaning through my gritted teeth. The blood started to spill out, right at the spot in the middle of the floor that my mother had stained with herself. The Wallaces had to beg Plum Warren the midwife to come. When she arrived and saw the situation, she started mumbling and laying down towels, felt my belly, and shoved her fingers up in me without asking or explaining why.

Mrs. Wallace asked what was happening and Plum kept saying *breach* and *breech*. Finally, she looked me in the face.

"I'm going to try to turn the baby."

The next minutes were agonizing beyond what I knew was possible. I stopped trying to hold back the screams and let them hurtle down the passageways. I had a vision of them surging into corners, under the feets of tables and between the pages of books and spilling into the sacristy cups. The screaming coiled around people's arms and braided through their fingers and crawled down their throats, and somewhere, behind a door behind a door behind a door, it stirred the fine hairs along Jonas's nape, planted something in him that he would have to keep.

Plum shook her head and spoke to Mrs. Wallace. Then surged forth a convulsion like I hadn't yet felt. What came next was a blur of pain and mission, a tunnel with no beginning and no end where my only reason for being alive was to learn the rhythms and respond to them, to train my muscles to their pace, to buoy her—I knew now it was a *her*—along her journey from under to over, from water to air, the sky to crack open and pour down in sheets, a bounty, bounty, and how much love there could be—she would show us all.

WHEN THEY LAID HER against my chest, she was blue but wailing the pink back into her cheeks. Her legs had been swaddled together with a strip of cloth. One was broken. She calmed into sobs, and I felt how her skin was my skin, and nothing I had ever feared did I fear now, and no one could ever make me feel shame again.

A BABY WAS ALWAYS AN EVENT in the Chimneys, but it had seemed until this moment that mine would be the exception. The change came when word got round of her little broken leg, and how the midwife saved her. Everyone wanted to see her, cradle her, touch her cheeks.

Daphne, I called her, after a sculpture I'd seen in a book called *Renaissance:* a woman escaping.

I didn't want to let her go. But it was useful to be loved, and this was her chance. I placed her into their arms, visitor after visitor, and she gazed up at each one like they'd saved her themselves. Rocking her at our kitchen table, the women had to speak to me again. They asked how she was nursing, offered to lend me their hand-me-down onesies. They asked could I bring her to the Shuttle with me on Sundays.

When she started walking we noticed a limp, which the ladies and even the men overtended to, and liked to hold her hand down the passageways. Most of the children weren't as healthy as she was: pale and prone to stomach ailments, spending weeks in their beds. One baby, belonging to Lily Partridge's sister Beulah, had died. After that, the squeals and proddings that greeted any child shrouded a sickly dread. Mr. Partridge, Beulah's father, stalked in and out of the reverend's offices. He and his wife didn't come to service once for three weeks in a row, until at last Lily was moved to a better cottage, one of the Jewells' personal ownerships.

Lily by that time was pregnant.

Her and Jonas.

ALL THIS TIME, the waterskin kept filling up dutiful and every week. I couldn't stand to leave Daphne alone down there, so instead of visiting the Overlake, I started leaving notes pinned to the rope to tell Mr. Clark what was happening: that I had a child, that her name was Daphne, that she was doing good and healthy. I let him believe I had a husband but didn't mention it direct.

This went on for years.

I started going to Sunday service again. I knew she would need to fit in there. I relished walking through the great arched door, feeling the naked skin of my legs swishing beneath my dress, my breasts that they all knew had been touched. Jonas sat in the front row and never once looked at me or the child, though everyone looked at the child.

She shone. The gold off the altar sparkled her irises. Whenever her gaze landed on anyone, they gripped the sides of their seats, hankering to drop to their knees and scoop her into their hold.

The only other person who wasn't charmed by her was Mary.

Her heart was folded, maybe, around other things. Jonas and Lily were the first to marry after the Rehearsal. Others had played out the one-year courtship that was convention. Mary, I think, saw this slowness as proof of her modesty—or that's what she put on. Each time she left Powell that year, if I caught her eye, I saw it waver. I could feel her suffering, but I left her alone in it. That was one more crime I committed against her.

She finally married Caleb and moved into his cottage. Six months later, she'd come home only twice, and flinched every time she saw Daphne. Mrs. Wallace told me she was trying to get pregnant herself, without success.

Caleb came by more often, wanting to provide the Wallaces with a top-notch chimney service. He would stay to chat and flatter Mrs. Wallace on her embroideries (mostly done by me). I hadn't noticed before how, beyond his handsomeness, he was kind. Caleb was better-stationed and could have picked a higher fate than Mary, but he was sincere about her. When I saw how he looked at her during the wedding and, even when her eyes were cast down, never looked at anything else, it occurred to me that Jonas's face may not have held as much love as I'd thought.

Every time I knew Caleb was coming to clean the chimney, I'd bring down the waterskin and tuck it into the bottom of the basket where Daphne slept. As I rocked her in my lap or Caleb cooed at her, there that water was, just a blanket's depth away from his fingertips.

I COME TO LEARN years later that Mary suffered many miscarriages. She wasn't alone. Where people used to have seven or eight children, the number of births had been dropping for years. The year after Daphne was born was the start of a long shadow. The reverend had grown hunched and gray-skinned from a progressing ailment, but once he was behind the pulpit, he would straighten up and quiver like a candle flame. His voice hammered between the walls. He spoke about the sickness eeling through the Chimneys, that whispered into cradles and crawled into toddlers' beds.

"What have you done?" he demanded. His eyes sliced through us, each word a hook through a different lip. "What have you done today that you should not have done?"

Wave after wave of illness washed through the children. We believed for years that they passed it to each other—and then, when isolation didn't help, forgot that belief. Next, people rumored that the sickness was choosing children for the sins of the parents, or the sins of their ancestors, or the sins of even their thinking. The reverend spoke more and more about purity of thought. People crowded the door of Plum Warren, her being trained also in medicines and tinctures. They traded their vinegar and vitamin allotments for remedies—dried herbs, powdered lichens, chalky ancient pills—not only for their children but for themselves, that could purify their minds or turn them off completely.

Then Plum Warren's third daughter, Blossom, died at the age of three. She had lived the shortest of all Plum's children. After that, people lost faith in her treatments. They started conducting rituals that the Jewells at first didn't support but then, when people kept doing them, had to. They delivered babies into troughs of lake, into troughs of live fry and lake, into troughs of fresh-caught fish and lake. Mothers wrapped their newborns in woven water milfoil, or ground algae to a paste and painted their lips with it. When the child wouldn't eat, they fed them a broth of scales. When the child vomited, they submerged them in lake water. Some children were born deaf, and people believed they could hear messages sent up from the core. There were others who had spells that made their limbs jerk or their bodies stiffen, and if they survived these, people concluded they had visited the mantle and brought bad omens back. Most refused to be in a room with them.

The problem with all of these theories—why none of them could hold for long—was me. Daphne was the healthiest child by far, even with her limp. And yet I had committed a cardinal sin. Just the survival of Daphne crumbled every explanation.

It's a deepest secret I don't like to admit. But sometimes I felt a wicked pride about keeping my beautiful girl alive when no one else could. Everyone fed off her presence—fed, I say, because year after year they seemed more hungry for it. And somehow, young as she was, she understood what people needed from her, and was generous beyond what any child should be.

The older she grew, the more she drew her strength from Him. She started crossing her chest and belly to punctuate her sentences. She dipped her thumb in the troughs as we passed and pressed it to the walls, to the tables, to other people's foreheads—reverending.

When she was nine, I found her in a passageway, crouched over a dead minnow. Every morning we found a few of these: ones that had flopped out the tank overnight and suffocated. But this one, she was giving rites. She sprinkled lake on its face, she milk-churned the air around it. On the floor, she'd drawn in water the snake that came to the Reverend Jewell—that returns to us in death to lead us coreward.

I wrenched her to her feet. Terror soaked my chest, and the fluorescents hummed loud in their ballasts. I don't remember what I said—a panicked scold, veiled and in half-truths. What I do remember is how she stared at me. Calm, like it washed over her and couldn't touch.

When I was done, she took my hand.

"Mama, it's all right."

It was the way she comforted everyone. But I was not everyone—I was her mother. Sometimes I felt like I was drinking her love through a straw. It was never enough.

I didn't scold her that way again. We were so close, like she was still attached to my body. I didn't want to see the seam.

HOW COULD I BELIEVE that she would not live inside this world? That she would not swallow what she was fed? There was no reason for her to reject what had not rejected her. I had even engineered her acceptance; I fed on it myself like someone starving.

But she was in other ways independent in her thinking. The children with jerking spells, she visited when no one else would. She played games with the deaf ones, though they were supposed to be listening for divine missives. In both cases, she begged and begged me to take her until I gave in. Nothing bad ever happened. In this way, she settled the worst waves of hysteria. Those final years, the last children—we were gentler with them.

When I tossed awake in the dark, tears mulling in my throat, she tucked her chin into the crook of my neck. In the passageways, any barb directed my way, she clung to my arm until the attacker blushed and turned away. She was my protection.

Around her twelfth year, the reverend started to notice us. He burned his pale eyes through us from the dais, watched me into the sanctuary with gritted teeth. Whatever story he told, I complicated it. I was the knot in a clean line that could not be teased out.

I tried to relish in it. But in his presence, I could not. When he looked at us, it wasn't scornful or prideful or even disgust. It was a blue-burning hatred that I knew someday would be a danger to us both.

−109 ft.

Through the glass, the bass teem, blurred by a sheet of plastic sealed across the window.

Before the flood, the pharmacy and the bank were in adjacent storefronts on Main Street, and in a stroke of genius, the wall between them was knocked down to gain access to the bank's pneumatic tubes. Weber had had a sudden influx of cash (he never said from where) and this funded the expansion of the tube system, the installation of air pipes between houses, and the reinforcement of older buildings with steel I-beams. It also ensured an ample stockpile of drugs.

The pharmacist was personally selected by Henry Weber to care for the people of the Underlake. Requests would be sent to the pharmacy by tube. (The church had parted ways with the People's Council, and their reverend turned down tube hookup for fear of "staining.")

The pharmacy, by virtue of its tube system, would also be the central trafficker of messages between every "refuge," as Weber had termed them, calling the people of the Underlake "refugees of a world obsessed with change." The postmaster moved in, and seized upon the safety deposit boxes as an efficient infrastructure for message organization. A few neighbors signed on too, with the promise of supporting pharmacy and post operations.

For several years, this refuge of about thirty people succeeded in its mission. The pharmacist made diagnoses based on described symptoms and sent along the appropriate drugs, and the postmaster distributed letters and newspaper bulletins. The fishers from the grocery store down Main Street swam by, waving through the window boxes, though they couldn't visit, since the pharmacy had opted against a moon pool and wouldn't open the windows to them for reasons of security.

When the tube service stopped, it wasn't because they were running short on medicine. Rather, it was because everyone in the pharmacy had become suddenly very ill. The sickness started in the children, then swept through the adults. It was characterized by severe stomach cramps, headaches, and hallucinatory visions of psychedelic tunnels, or of trees climbing out of the ground and pulling their roots along like skirts. Some grew overly jolly. Others felt an ineffable dread. One man, who had been in the navy, theorized that the water pressure at this depth was causing neurological problems. But the pharmacist couldn't identify the illness and so could only treat the symptoms.

The sickness dampened the mood of the whole enterprise. But it wasn't the only culprit. The children gave voice to it first: how the light filtering down through the water was a meager broth; how they missed the crunch of grass beneath their feet; how they were forgetting the way horses smelled and all the shapes there were of clouds.

One day, a boy of twelve snuck out a window box. He had told his friends he was going to the surface. He didn't get far: the boy's shirt got caught on a chain-link fence along the back of the property, and he remained suspended there, in view of the window, for a long time. In the hysteria that ensued, the pharmacist decided that the medicine should be administered to everyone at regular intervals.

All this upheaval made it difficult for the pharmacy to fulfill its duties. For a while, the postmaster was so ill that everyone thought he was going to die. His wife and children, sick themselves and despondent, tried to keep up with the messages coming in but couldn't figure out his filing system, and many were lost or sent to the wrong refuge.

Requests for medicine continued to come in, but the pharmacist chose to delay some shipments. Fishers from the grocery even came looking for the medicine themselves, thumping their fists on the windows, to no response. Meanwhile, the pharmacist started to grind down pills so that they could be meted out with greater fastidiousness, and this was when the first plastic went up behind the counter—so that if someone sneezed, or if the circulation system started pulling up air through the vents, the powder could be recovered, nothing gone to waste.

He was now spending most of his day at the mortar. So each family set up their own sealed space in which to grind their prescriptions.

The daily distribution of the medicine and the installation of plastic sheeting, an ever-expanding project of refinement and ingenuity—all of this gave people a sense of purpose again. They felt, instead of pain, a slow churning along their veins, the lake *yes*-ing through them. It was a community like never before, and a blessing to be in it, and if life was suffering without the medicine, then the medicine was the meaning and the pulsing heart of life.

The polyethylene sheeting—originally for sealing off shipments from water—now lines all the walls of the pharmacy to within an inch of every corner. The powder is distributed in envelopes folded from the notes that stopped coming in years ago. At that time, the pharmacist and the postmaster agreed that the other refuges would need to be on their own, for resources were scarce, and the medicine should stay where the medicine is properly understood and revered for the blessings that it brings.

May

Whose story am I living inside of? Am I the dream that folds away into its drawer? Sometimes I turn and believe she will be right over my shoulder, believe that believing will make it so, and am surprised to not find her there.

As a child, I thought sometimes I wasn't real. For weeks, I could go without anyone saying to me a word. I even wondered was I invisible, a ghost haunting someone else's story.

Then the story became Daphne's. She was like the character in a book, and I the words that told it. Everything I did was in service of her joy.

Sometimes, in my weakest heart, I was selfish. I liked most those moments of me brushing Daphne's hair, or playing Upside-Down together at the minnow troughs. I liked the quiet of mornings, with everyone off at their fates. I'd slip up the chimney to fetch the water-skin, and pour her a glass of the only water I let her drink.

"Our secret," she would repeat back to me.

Then we'd leave to tend minnows. Mr. Wallace was dead, and them being without sons, Mrs. Wallace had let me take on half the troughs, though it wasn't my fate. I liked watching the minnows flood to my palm, prickle and warm it with their mouths, like they were glad of me—like they had missed me. While I scrubbed off the algae, water would spiral around my hand, and I'd even enter a kind of trance. I liked it—the complete untethering from here.

By her teenage years, Daphne was so close with many of the women that they'd show up at our door crying when they were upset, or flushed when they were angry. She would clutch their hands, sitting together on the leather trunk in the corner of Powell, which was filled with gifts of candles and mussel buttons and yarn, the most valuable items people could spare, just because they liked to make her smile.

There was much they needed solace about. Almost everyone in the Chimneys was in mourning. By the year that would have been Daphne's Rehearsal, there wasn't anyone to invite.

When the reverend set his sights on her at last—announced from the pulpit one Sunday with quivering wrists that he had discovered the cure, that the cure was a purge, that the purged was a false idol, that the false idol was the product of sin, and when his eyes wouldn't break from her face—the very next day his illness progressed to the point that he couldn't leave his rooms, and the day after that he died.

The night of that sermon, I told her everything: about the Overlake, about Mr. Clark, about how it was him that filled the waterskin, about the caves and aquifer below. I gave into her possession the mirrored keychain. I said that if she was in danger, she could climb the chimney and give the signal, and Mr. Clark would come and fetch her—keep her safe.

She turned it over in her hand. "The Grand Canyon?"

With everything I'd told her, that was the only question she asked.

She didn't scold me for the sins I'd committed. But I could feel something inside her take a step back. And when I suggested for us to leave that night, to go to Mr. Clark, she said we should wait.

"One more week."

Nothing happened to us the next day, or the day after. The reverend's eldest son, Jabez, became the new Reverend Jewell. He had always been a cautious disciple. When I was in school, the teacher sometimes brought him in as a guest lecturer, but he almost refused to speak. He'd draw out genealogies on the board, erasing and redrawing unstraight lines, and then repeat each name many times, I guess to memorize them to us.

Meanwhile, the sentiment grew throughout the Chimneys—and no one spoke it, no one spoke it—that for all the elder Reverend Jewell had got right, he had made one small miscalculation with regards to Daphne. The new Reverend Jewell seemed to catch the scent of this. Moving forward, it was as if that last sermon never happened. The first talk the new reverend gave, and many after, repaired any doubts. He said over and over how we were all of us lambs of the same flock, guided by *our shepherd*—as he called the elder reverend, until everyone come to call him that, though we knew not much about lambs or why they needed guiding.

Daphne proved to be little curious about the Overlake. But she asked about the water. Asked did Mr. Clark make it—no. Asked had the other children drank it—no. Asked could we share it—no; asked this many times—no, there wasn't enough to share.

Two weeks after the elder reverend's passage to the core, I was anxious not so much of what Jabez would do, but of the way Daphne's eyes no longer met mine; how she spent more time huddled on the trunk, writing her journal between the lines of *Little Women*.

I'd never touched that journal in all the years she'd kept it. This, even though I was jealous to it, wondered what she could tell it that she couldn't tell me. But now the dread itched down my veins. I wasn't sleeping, couldn't stand still without a spasm shooting down my legs. So one day, left alone in Powell, I slipped the book out from under Daphne's bedroll.

The writing was tiny enough to fit between the print. I flipped to the later pages.

> . . . and he is holy who does not wish for more then he has, who knows that what he is been endowed through the Rise is what was fated for a reason.
>
> But. He fated our babies to be born skinny and shrunk . . . why? To live their whole lives sick and pained and to lose them so young. Donald . . . we invented all those signs together. Even though he was deaf, I think he would of been my match in the Rehearsal if he'd of made it.
>
> I am being tested in this gulping lonely that I should make something good of it and not let it swallow me down.
>
> All the girls in this *Little Women* . . . I stop to read it sometimes . . . married, married, married. (Not poor Beth.) Their love is sickly, they can't control it, it drains from them like their insides might collapse . . . but then it turns around and gives them so much strength. That surprised me. I look around for a love like that here . . . no one has it. Donald's parents don't look at eachother anymore. Mrs. Wallace wept for Mr. Wallace and now she does her knitting in peace. My mom loves me . . . but like it hurts her. More like needing.
>
> Is the love in this book real? A sin of the unchosen? It doesn't sound like sin.
>
> I am being tested. Is aloneness my purpose? I wonder when He will show me what it is.

I looked up. Daphne stood in the doorway. The journal slipped from my hands and thudded on the floor. When she picked it up, her cheeks were all-over flushed.

"Can we talk about it?" She was, as always, gentle.

My throat—raw as cut glass. That she could feel lonely, when here I was. I blamed Him. He had sunk all His teeth in her.

I shook my head.

"But, Mom, there are things I . . ."

I fled. I left Powell behind in its coils of dust. I erased the scene, erased what I'd read. She'd return soon enough to herself. She was my body, I was hers. It would put itself back.

I HAD ALWAYS KEPT a part of myself aside—my gleeful wrongness, my foolish hopes. It stayed locked in a cave inside my belly that I'd stocked over many years with shelves of unapproved books, pictures of long-gone animals, and drawings—hidden even deeper—of how I hoped he might look at me again.

Maybe I believed she should stuff it down. That we were all supposed to lock away what was ugly. Now that she's gone, every word she wrote is precious, and it doesn't matter what they say, only that they were hers.

I wonder why she abandoned me and it makes me lose my breath. But I abandoned her first. I let her down because I couldn't find the words. I'm trying to find them now.

THERE WAS SOMETHING ELSE locked inside that cave.

One of those drawings was us together: Jonas, me, Daphne, sitting in the front pew with our arms around each other.

Then there's what really happened.

The first time was wordless. As we approached each other down an empty passageway, Jonas blocked my path. He pushed me into a doorway and kissed me. I felt down the belt of his pants; he felt down mine; then I ripped myself away, and before I could say a word, he was gone.

The second time, I was scrubbing at a trough. I didn't hear him approach. Then a hand settled on my hip.

I stood and spun around. He had filled out in his proportions, broader in his shoulders from the work they did to move the glistening Him in and out of the Shuttle, to climb the walls each month and scrub them down. He slicked his hair back for Sundays but on other days would let the curls spright out.

He pressed me against the wall. He rubbed his hand down the middle of my thighs like he used to do, like not more than an hour had passed from that time to this.

It swole around me. His hot breath, his lips grazing my neck. I melted into its control.

"Come to the kiln," he said.

The recollection of that place, where I'd waited so many months alone, made me pause. I planted my palm on his chest and pressed away.

"And what happens after that?"

A wash of impatience crossed his face.

"You'll claim us?"

Now he dropped his hands into his pockets, paced away and back.

"You know you want to," he said.

"That doesn't matter."

"Of course it does." He placed his hand on my cheek. He searched my face, but whatever he wanted to find—it had little to do with me, I think. "The best times of our lives—they were when we did whatever we wanted. Right? When we were free?"

I wiped his hand away. My own muscles resisted the gesture—but I did it. "You don't know the best times of my life. You don't know Daphne."

He shook his head, started down the passageway.

"You'll regret it." He peered over his shoulder.

But he couldn't hold my gaze and so went on around the corner.

Later I would walk a few times along the passageway to the sacristy, and the kiln door, which was never shut, was shut. He never tried with me again.

Why do I tell this now? It's a story about a thing *not* happening. But I wasn't proud of saying no to him. Instead, I wondered what could have happened. I wondered if he might have remembered that he cared for me; if he would have started visiting Daphne—because if he had, he'd have come to adore her. He was childless. He and Lily, like everyone else, had suffered several losses. And so the only moments I could find alone, climbing the ladder for the waterskin, I clung to the cold iron and let the sobs seize me, my body spasming and silent against the rungs. I told myself it was because I'd failed her. I sobbed because that was a lie. I sobbed because I wanted just a few more moments with his body against mine—to make me important, grand, real. I had shaved myself down to a point, to be one thing only: the mother Daphne needed. Soon I might be so thin I'd disappear completely.

THEN I CAME HOME to Powell one night after cleaning the troughs and Daphne had left a note on the table—simple, like she'd be back in an hour: *Gone for water. I love you.*

The candles in her leather trunk, gone. The trout jerky we'd been drying in Mrs. Wallace's mirror box, also gone.

I rushed from cottage to cottage searching. She was nowhere to be found.

The worry mounted through the Chimneys. It passed from mouth to mouth until a low rumble rattled the walls, until there were gatherings at the junctions.

One person had seen her outside the Warrens', another crouched beside a minnow trough, another helping remold candles from old wax. This was five hours ago, last night, two days past.

They started to turn it onto me—Plum Warren, then the rest: *What did you do? What did you say? You're her mother, you're supposed to protect her, we knew you couldn't—*

I'd taken their affection for her onto my own heart. I'd stood in the corner of her light and thought it shone on me. It was always, only hers.

I didn't tell them what the note said. I couldn't reveal what I'd come to realize about our water. That it made us sick. That giving her good Overlake water was how I made sure she was healthy.

Maybe keeping this secret was the worst thing I ever did. But you turn a deaf ear on the truth, and what comes next—you reap.

That's what I've been taught.

−123 ft.

Through the glass, the bass teem.

Ornamental moulding frames every door in the Victorian, the baseboards and windows ice-creamy with it. Every inch is sanded and polished, so you'd never know that the exterior walls were at one time gutted and reinforced with steel beams and scrap metal, then restored down to the photographs hanging on their original nails.

When the lake rose, the house's three occupants were considered old maids. They lived off a stockpile of canned and jarred foods that would take them, as they told everyone around, to "the end."

One living room wall had been reinforced using sections of an iron fence that once encircled the yard—a sentimental gesture. The wall was therefore magnetic, and proved useful in storing an array of scissors, nuts, bolts, and sewing needles.

In the corner, an eight-track tape starts to play every night when the electricity comes on. Over time, the magnets have warped each recording further and further away from itself. The tape player is on a wheeled cart, which the old maids rotated countless times in an attempt to place it in an orientation relative to the wall that might restore the original quality of the tapes. This only succeeded in tangling them more.

Over many years, the lyrics from the recordings—mostly sentimental ballads from the nineteenth century—started shuffling to form new sentences. These told the future but especially the past, reinterpreting the memories of the old maids so that they became in fact truer than what the women had originally recalled. Later, the words twisted into other words, some of them recognizable, others that had to be interpreted. Meanwhile, the music wilted and reflowered. The ladies would stand and sway to it, discovering within their bodies new shapes that they had never imagined possible.

The dance laced over the shreds and shrubs of music and the music laced over the words and the words wove a fabric that shuddered and stretched. The long-gone men who slept with them but would not stay were pasted over with wallpaper. The alcoholic mother was corked like a note into a bottle and tossed out to sea. And the best girlfriend who ran one night out into the yard, the wine gone to her head, was now carried away by a migration of monarchs. Reaching out behind her, her trailing arm desired to cross that breach—and oh, how the old maid too desired it, said it out loud, said and said it and was not ashamed:

Darling, stay.

Otta

Morphology, health indicators, feeding habits: I approached our encounters with the people of the Underlake as I'd been trained. I observed how the peculiarities of each microhabitat might influence social interactions, how group size and demographics may have molded their reactions to our arrival. Any conclusions, truth be told, were entirely anecdotal, a distraction to stave off the dreamlike quality of it all, my quivering knees at every stop, and some uncomfortable parallels: the dead who were not dead; the saved who were not saved.

We visited a dozen houses in less than a week, several of them occupied. Some Underlakers froze at the sight of us, one fainted, and a few didn't believe we were real. We were the only visitors any of them had ever had.

I could feel, with each stop, a mounting menace. We had one or two run-ins with people asking to swim out with us. One man, pits of dark between his few teeth, would not stop tugging at May's arm until we promised we'd come back for him. Others, I saw it in their eyes: a thumping hunger, more than they could manage in words. We couldn't help, not now. I wasn't sure yet how to help, and the search for Daphne came first. But each encounter felt like one more crush of paper in my stomach: more to carry.

I learned to move in and out of these visits quickly. We'd explain how we had gotten there, learn a bit about them, promise to return when we could, then ask if they'd seen Daphne. The answer was always no.

We could never stay long, anyway. The deeper we dove, the shorter our bottom time. I never let us hit our no-decompression limit. If we did, we'd have to make stops on the way up. We'd also be at greater risk of the bends.

More than one person asked if Henry Weber had sent us from the factory. I was surprised to hear that name. The Webers had sold much of the valley's land to the state expressly to make way for the lake and dam. Henry's father, Charles Weber Jr., had resisted every effort of the Anti-Dam movement and, after that had failed to stop the dam's construction, had tried many times to crush the organization that rose up in its stead, the People's Council. The last person I'd expect to join either of these efforts was a Weber.

I started to ask more about Henry and the factory, but each house had its own version of the story.

At the mansion, an old woman told us that Henry was "one of our great men." She said that he'd composed an epic poem about the tribulations of the faction and that the newsmen were busy binding it into books.

At the grocery store, their leader declared from his aluminum throne that the factory was filled with socialists and had fallen to pieces as a result. All the while he was talking, he stroked a taxidermied dog at his side. May couldn't stop gaping at it. As we turned to leave, she whispered: "I think that's Mrs. Wallace's yellow mutt."

Only once, in the hardware store, did we meet someone who actually seemed to have visited the factory after the flood. We were invited to sit in a circle of plastic chairs, enclosed by curtains of twine and nails. A man with washers woven into his beard questioned us only briefly before starting in on a well-rehearsed status report. His beard jangled as he spoke.

An old woman sat beside him, whittling a piece of wood with a pocketknife. She was gouging out a jagged shape, like a staircase. Given the intricate carvings of raccoons and rabbits gathered around her feet, the staircase seemed a strange abstraction, a modernist leap. Finally, she interrupted.

"Where'd you get all that suiting?" she asked us.

"Come off it, Ava," the man said.

"Because Henry outlawed all that."

"How'd you get here, then?" he barked, frustrated at the interruption.

"I held my breath and swam." Ava leaned on her elbows and grinned four lingering teeth.

He swatted in her direction.

"If you swam here, why don't you swim out of our hair?"

She rubbed at her knee. "You know how my joints is."

It had the tenor of a back-and-forth many times repeated. The man went on with his status report.

Later, as we sat on the edge of the moon pool ready to leave, Ava leaned close to my ear.

"If he's coming for me, you tell him I'm ready."

AFTER THE HARDWARE STORE, we had enough air for one more stop. We followed a pipe to a single house on the far western end of Main Street, isolated from the rest by a five-minute swim. Rusted cars squatted like guard dogs around the house, which was covered all over with a dark blue velveteen of mold.

When we came up through the moon pool, the mold followed us

inside. It carpeted the floor and walls, crawled up the furniture: the afterimage of a couch, a table and two chairs—these, heaped with dark, furred tendrils.

We took a few sopping steps with the floor sinking beneath us. But when May reached up to take off her mask, I stopped her. Those chairs, swollen with chest-high knots of mold—human shapes, and those tendrils—how much like gestures.

I got us out of there quick and started toward the surface. Back up in the boat, as we finished our off-gassing, I kept rubbing my eyes against the clotted dark. When I told May we were done for the day, the color had drained from her face. She didn't fight me on it.

WHEN WE TOLD CLARK about the steel pipes we'd started following, he was positively gleeful. He led us along the lakeside path at almost a sprint, one air tank in each hand. His hip was mostly healed from his fall at the school.

"You know about the pipes?" I asked.

He wheezed with excitement. "I designed the whole compressed-air system myself."

We arrived at the bluff where, less than two weeks ago, I'd helped Clark replace the bolt. Pipes emerged from the water and connected to that hulking metal cabinet. He opened a padlock on one of the access panels. Inside, a nest of belts and gauges encircled a large tank.

"An industrial air compressor," he said. "We moved it up from the factory. Then I rebuilt it for what we needed."

He pulled a metal hose from his tool bag and fitted it to a nozzle.

I don't know why I hadn't seen it. The entire compressed-air supply for the Underlake was delivered through the pipes I'd helped Clark repair. He had been maintaining it all for decades.

"I spliced into the electric lines at the top of this hill"—he pointed up the slope—"but it's really just to power the compressor. Down there, they run everything on battery."

"They've got batteries running in every house?"

"No, just the factory," he said. "They had huge stores of lead from making paint. After it was outlawed, they couldn't get rid of it. So we stockpiled the rest of the materials there—electrodes, separators, mostly salvage. Enough to build and recycle batteries for years. Then we tapped into the valley electric grid so they could send power to council houses."

Clark fitted the other end of the hose to one of our scuba tanks and opened a valve. The roar of air made it too loud to speak. Clark puffed on his inhaler. May blinked at me, teeth dug into her stunned-white lip.

The tank gauge read full. Clark shut off the air and glanced at May, suddenly shy.

"When May showed up that first time, I was about to give up. Didn't have no way to know if they survived—not for fourteen years. Even thought about swimming down to check. Bought that scuba gear. But with my asthma, I couldn't get through the first lesson." He connected the hose to the next tank. "When May told me their lights was still coming on, I can't tell you . . ." His voice quavered. "But anything can happen. Any year, the system could fail. We didn't think they'd be down that long. Honestly, we figured the Webers or the government would give in before the flooding ever started."

He rubbed at his eyes.

"Those weeks before they started filling up the lake, I warned them. I explained how once you go down, you can't come back up. How the pressure change would kill them if they tried, how the closer you get to the surface, the more dangerous it gets. They understood the risks."

He shuddered the way a dog shakes off rain.

"But I've done my job, kept the air flowing. And look: they're alive. Biggest feat in underwater living since Sealab. A hundred times bigger."

He opened the valve.

The social contract is this: if nothing bad happened, you did nothing wrong. I believed it too, but I've seen where that leads. Next, you do something worse.

EVERY DAY, after our dives, we floated by the Chimneys and May checked the waterskin hanging inside one—still full, a sign that Daphne hadn't returned. Then, back at the dock, I usually left the tanks with Clark and May to refill and was home by midafternoon to look after my mother. Eugenia was generally fine on her own. She slept until noon, then I either took her to dialysis or joined her on the couch to watch soaps.

One day, I came home to find Allie watching TV with her. She lived in the city, an hour away, so she only visited on Mondays. I dropped my gear by the door, and Allie followed me into the kitchen. I pulled out a loaf of bread.

"Some friends and I are going to a play tonight," she said, sitting at the table. "I can get an extra ticket."

I sliced into a tomato. Mushy. "For me? You don't have to do that."

"I know I don't have to," she said. "Just seems funny that my friends have met Mom and they haven't met you."

"Oh." Shame puddled in my throat. It had been so long. I seized on the change of topic.

"God, I can't imagine Mom with your friends. She still calls you 'Alby' half the time."

"I know. But she's trying. And somehow, since my transition, it matters less to me."

"What do you mean?"

I sat down across from her. She grabbed a chip off my plate. She had Eugenia's same weakness for junk food.

"It's strange." The green of her irises went liquid, the planet churning around its axis, dragging teams of clouds. "I feel more like myself than ever. But the physical transition isn't everything. I'm still getting to know myself. Like, I'm Allie but I'm also a dozen different people, depending on the day and my mood and what hurts. Alby's a part of me too. I still love him."

Our time apart had lit a flame of dread at the back of my mind: that we might be strangers. But sitting across from Allie now extinguished it. She was still my sister, with all the microexpressions and turns of phrase that I understood instinctively, and all the things I would never understand: first and foremost, how she maintained a calmness like placid water, and what churned beneath.

"How do you know which one's the real you?"

"They're all real. They're contradictory, simultaneous truths."

I bit into my sandwich. It tasted like paper. This wealth of identities was incomprehensible. The singular picture I had of myself—of what I needed to become—was flaking away like paint.

"What's keeping you so busy, anyway?" Allie sat back in her chair, wiping the chip dust on her pants. "Mom said something about diving."

"Yeah. I'm giving lessons."

Anything else I told her would have sounded insane. Maybe I was going insane, following some absurd train of logic until a drowning was no longer a drowning, the crushing weight of water only a shove through the veil at its thinnest point.

"Mom isn't happy about it."

"She's complaining to you now?"

"Well. She's got no one else to talk to."

"I wonder why." I rolled my eyes. Allie used to side with me. Now, ignoring the joke, she started weaving a loose braid into her hair.

"At least she's being calm about it," Allie said. "You remember how she acted when you did your science project about that chimney? The one we saw out on the lake?"

That spring after the rowboat, I created a poster board for the science fair outlining how Jacques Cousteau built his underwater human habitats, and postulating that these same techniques could have been applied in Weber Lake.

The morning of the fair, a murmur passed among the teachers. By third period, I was asked to take the poster down. Soon after, my mother appeared out of nowhere and dragged me out of school by the wrist. She was muttering under her breath, a string of half sentences. Tears gathered on the back of my tongue. I swallowed them down. I'd learned long ago that crying only made things worse.

Halfway home, she pulled off the side of the road beside a yellow hiss of meadow where a single oak stood. She dragged out the poster board and started kicking holes through it, ripping across the gaps until it was shredded to bits. Her face was red, not with anger so much as an indecipherable terror.

A year later, I told my mother I was going to be a marine biologist. I awaited her response, lungs swollen behind my ribs. Somehow—absurd to think it now—I hoped she might be impressed. She undid a few stitches from her knitting, shrugged, and said she didn't see the point.

The resentment, familiar now between us, clenched my jaw. "The point is I'm leaving this shithole. Everyone here hates me."

It slipped out. The bullying, the rumors—I'd never talked to her about any of it.

Her eyes twitched across my face, searching for threats. Her lips peeled off her teeth like the lid off a piano.

"You've got it so tough," she sneered. And went back to her knitting.

"You don't know the shit I've had to shield you from," I told Allie, swallowing a dry bite of sandwich.

"I know you have." She sighed. "But that's what I'm saying. She's contradictory too. It's not black and white."

"Some things are unforgivable," I said.

"And they cancel out all the good?"

The soggy tomato, the parched bread, the paper plate: they turned my stomach. I got up and threw them in the trash. Whatever twisted way she was trying to restore our mother's innocence, after the deaths she'd caused, could only make me the bad guy.

"Yes, they do."

"So what happens when you make a mistake like that?"

I let the sunporch door slam behind me.

"I already have."

THE DEEPER WE DOVE over the course of that week of searching, the more houses were flooded. Most weren't hooked up to compressed air, but others did have pipes running to them, their seal against the lake failed. A strip of clapboard shotgun houses gaped through their doorframes. A row of shops in the first block of downtown was busted through at every window, wire and glass and shreds of cloth gnawing out into the water. May had been asking about the factory, about diving down to the caves or even the aquifer below them. But these scenes confirmed for me that, even if we could go deeper, there would be little left alive.

We swam past a pharmacy with a faded caduceus painted on the window. As we approached, I glimpsed a quick shift of light, but when I pressed my face to the glass, all I could see were sheets of plastic, stirring gently—maybe from the vents. There was no entrance that we could find.

A mile out of town, down a sloping lane, we encountered a Victorian-style house with one domed turret. We swam up through the moon pool and entered a living room with three armchairs and an eight-track player on a cart. A pipe poured air through a vent taped with cut strips of paper, fluttering now.

We called out; searched the rooms upstairs and down. No one was there. It was as though the whole scene had been interrupted midsentence: a mug on a side table, a dish towel tossed onto the counter.

When we dropped down through the moon pool of the Victorian, we were pushing our bottom time, so I set off toward the boat.

Soon, I realized that May had slipped out of my peripheral vision. I looked over my shoulder. She was gone.

Heat scrawled across my chest—flash of beach at night, the phosphorescent surf. I doubled back. The silt was thick, and sudden flicks of fin or detritus startled out of it. The image through my mask felt uncanny, a photo of a drawing of a dream.

Ahead, I spotted her flipper swipe through a churn of eelgrass. May was moving fast, and I could see now her arm outstretched, her fingers electrified and taut, desperate to catch up to a pumpkinseed perch. She was gaining depth.

The panic—panic—it clawed at my throat, ripped my breath away, as I watched unfolding a hypothetical reenactment of Ethan's disappearance. The muffled moan in his mask, drowned out by the drill. Can something happen without a single witness? Could I kill him by imagining it now?

I forgot my breath, swam at full speed, and caught May by the ankle. She turned. Her eyes were glazed. I took her wrist and started our ascent, monitoring our bubbles, making sure we never rose faster than they did.

At our safety stop, we hovered belly-down. Her eyes widened and the fog cleared. How had I almost let it happen again? No. It ended now.

Otta

Loss has many rows of teeth. Each day it devours the whole world and each day it's born again hungry. Worst of all, it swallows the one voice that could identify—among the many clashing versions of the story—the one, definitive truth.

There is one truth where Ethan takes my brief abandonment to heart and never trusts me again—not when I'm his dive partner, not when I'm his tender, not when I'm his bellman.

That abandonment took place the summer after my fourth year in the doctoral program, when I was finally awarded a grant to work on a research vessel in the Pacific. It wasn't close enough to the range of the bumphead parrotfish to support my research, but it felt like I was back on track.

The moment my feet touched asphalt in Oahu, the sun sloughed everything away. It was the pure manifestation of a feeling I'd been chasing for years: a complete erasure of myself and rebirth into a new identity. I'd experienced it when I first arrived at undergrad, when I moved for my master's and my doctorate. Each time, the illusion faded. I'd eventually discover the same cringing, small being at my core, the imposter from Steels.

But for the duration of that eight-week trip on the Pacific, the fantasy endured. I became the person I'd always wanted to be: the scientist who rose before dawn, shimmied into my wet suit's cold blubber, and slipped off the boat. By 9 a.m., I was ravenous over my monk's breakfast, then spent the rest of the day checking the trawls or hauling up and redeploying sensors through the moon pool. The wind carved bright shapes across my skin, the sea in crisp resolution and utter presence. I went to bed at nine and woke at six. I had no future and no past. The crew called me Ollie. I forgot I'd had any other name.

I CAME HOME BUZZING. Transformed.

Ethan made carbonara for my first night back. As we ate, I spouted a stream of anecdotes, shining beads of glass that, strung together, approximated the person I'd become: scientist, traveler, scholar.

Ethan asked a hundred questions. But after a few hours, his attention started to flag. He opened a bottle of cheap Riesling. I knew I was talking too much, obsessing over details that could mean nothing to him. I felt myself clinging, suddenly, to a slippery thing.

When I woke the next morning in my old bed, light sifting through the slat blinds, a crack had opened. Sleep had shifted the Pacific one pace into the realm of dreaming, and this life one pace back into the real.

Come autumn, NOAA researchers published their discovery of a critical bumphead parrotfish behavior: massive mating events where they rammed their heads together like stags. They'd observed it that very summer, on a grant I'd been turned down for. It would have been a breakthrough for my dissertation.

That winter—all fog. A turning gray mass of water. I remember only flickers: the caramel glint of whiskey, smeared globes of streetlights.

Ethan spent most weekends diving remote keys with some friends he'd met at the bar. I think he was punishing me. But one by one, those friends trickled back north as though waking from a trance. We were characters in the luminous interludes of others. When the last of them left, it was Ethan and me again, clinging to each other in a way that had teetered away from its former effervescence, and closer to the desperate.

IN FEBRUARY, our landlord raised the rent. Hoping to make some extra cash, Ethan enrolled in a commercial diving course to learn underwater welding, oil rig maintenance—everything that stood to destroy the reefs we dove.

We got into a heated argument about it. I pleaded, I yelled, I slammed pots around the kitchen. Finally, he leaned back into a cushion. His eyes went flat.

"Gotta pay the bills. When's your degree going to do that?"

The last summer grant rejection arrived soon after. Ethan stopped trying to drag me out of bed. I sank deeper into the long days, their thick dreaming.

But come the first of May, Ethan swung open the door to my room, stripped the covers off, and said, "Rent's due. I've found us jobs."

Ethan had gotten hired on an offshore oil rig—the same one we could see from the beach, an immobile mast on the horizon.

"No," I said.

"Then you're moving out."

I tried to drag up the covers. He ripped them down again.

"Fucking get out of bed."

His voice cracked.

I rolled over. His eyes thumped with desperation. Ethan had been homeless after his dad kicked him out. He was sixteen. The way he had clawed himself out of that, he took a lot of pride in—not the methods, but the fact of it. If I could do one thing right, I would help him now.

ETHAN STARTED ON the rig as a standby diver, and I was hired as a dive tender. That first summer, I barely got in the water. I just helped Ethan and the primary diver suit up and monitored the safety line. It was boring.

Ethan earned his diploma, then started on the DCBC certification, which would allow for international work. He talked about moving to Australia: the Great Barrier Reef, the men, the sunshine.

As he spoke, the path to finishing my dissertation opened up along an unexpected route. If I couldn't get the grants, then a job with good pay and ample time off could get me to the West Pacific. Meanwhile, the more time I spent on the rig, the easier the hypocrisy was to bear. I wasn't building anything, wasn't destroying habitat—I was just making sure no one died. What industries had financed Lindsay and the other trust-fund kids at school?

After a few months, Ethan moved up to primary diver and started doing some underwater welding. The new job came with a raise. The certification courses were starting to look like a good backup plan. I enrolled.

That fall, I worked as a teaching assistant, so I spent half my time talking about conservation and the rest of it learning how to support the oil industry. But somehow, I felt more driven than I had in a long time. I could see the finish line and it seemed attainable—like how I used to feel about marine biology.

Come November, nausea rippled through me as my commercial diving certification inched out of the printer. The next day, I took it to the rig and got promoted to standby diver.

We were now living and working on the rig for one-week blocks. It was almost all men, so for my safety and Ethan's, we claimed to be married. Ethan washed the magenta out of his hair and slipped into the silence of his role.

Ethan and I were always paired up, but we worked on a team of six. Dave, leathery and orange, was the other primary diver, and had his own standby and tender. Ishaan had taken my place as Ethan's tender.

One day, Ethan and Dave were on a dive, each working on a different leg of the rig, when Ishaan got a signal from Ethan—a tug on the rope—to pay out more line. Again, more line. Then Dave's tender got the signal that he was fouled.

The tenders radioed the tower. Dave was caught on something. His standby perched on the edge of the platform, waiting for the go-ahead to dive. Ishaan nudged my arm.

"Feel this." I gave Ethan's line a tug. It was slack—like there was nothing on the other end.

I felt sick, a palpitation in my throat. I shut my eyes. I wasn't going to wait for the tower's go-ahead. I would dive after five more breaths—four—three—

Dave's tender called out: "All clear. Hauling up."

I glanced at Ishaan. We froze, watching the line. Above our heads, wind yanked a flag, smacking grommets against the pole, dull metallic clangs.

Then the rope stirred: three pulls. Ishaan let out an exhale. "Hauling up!"

We learned later what had happened: Dave's line had gotten wrapped around one of the trusses. Ethan tried to swim over, but couldn't get enough slack. So, instead of following protocol and waiting for Dave's standby, Ethan hit the quick release on his safety line and swam to Dave completely untethered. He untangled Dave's line, then swam back to his own.

Ethan received a formal reprimand, but he got roars of applause when we walked into the galley that night. Suddenly everyone knew his name. A group of men invited us to sit with them. While Ethan told them the story, Dave, who was old enough to be his father, rested his hand on Ethan's shoulder.

In the spring, I requested the semester off from my doctoral program, and our whole life became the rig. The money washed over us like a warm wave, a kind of caring that neither of us had experienced for a long time—that we couldn't even give each other.

ETHAN PULLED THAT TRICK twice more. The next time was a deeper dive. He was alone and he dropped his Powermig. When it drifted out of reach, he released from his umbilical and swam out to recover it. He got a lot of back slaps for saving such an expensive piece of equipment, but I didn't speak to him for three days.

A month later, Ethan was promoted again, and me alongside him. We would start doing bell dives, working pipelines on the seafloor.

These dives were deeper than any we'd experienced, and much more dangerous. We'd be at the mercy of the diving bell, a two-ton capsule of steel and PVC that was lowered from the rig. A dome on the top held a pocket of air like a glass turned upside down. Below our chests, it was an open frame that let the water in. I was Ethan's bellman, responsible for staying inside the bell and tending his umbilical during bounce dives—quick descents where he had just forty minutes to swim out, do the job, and return.

Our first dive, my heart throbbed as the bell slid through the surface of the water. I clutched the grab bars as water poured in around our hips on the fold-out seats. But then the hum of the machinery, the gathering dark through the dome's portholes, lulled me. It was existence in the utter present, at the tip of a needle, body and mind. I had a clearly defined task and I completed it—that first job, then the next, and the next. Ethan finished every assignment in the time allotted: quick inspections, the replacement of small parts. We emerged from the bell hours later decompressed and exhausted, and I slept through the night without dreaming.

My mind had never been quieter. I was an empty vessel: clear of doubts, singular in purpose. Surrendered. It was good.

I HAVE TRIED to report the facts. I used to believe that I knew what a fact was: the reading on a gauge, the peer-reviewed assessment.

But facts can fracture.

Here, a version of the story in which Ethan believes I will have his back. He radios that he's fouled his umbilical, and we follow the protocols: I radio up to the tower; I consult; I swim out from the bell to untangle him.

Here, a version where we've switched places. Ethan is my bellman, and maybe I don't get fouled at all. Or if I do—a dozen variations branch from that.

Then there is something closer to the truth, where we each live alone inside a sealed dome. My earlier abandonment has snapped any thread of connection between us. Ethan knows this, knows that in the roiling pitch of the seafloor, there's no one better equipped to rescue him than himself. So when the accident happens, he doesn't wait for help. He lifts the crush of the entire ocean onto his back and tries to carry it.

That's what he's still doing, if I don't take the story further. If I stop myself.

Otta

May called me a dozen times the next day. Each time, I said the same thing: "I can't be responsible."

I'd explained it all clearly enough as we stood dripping on the dock: that she seemed highly susceptible to nitrogen narcosis; that she hadn't followed the safety protocols, swam away without signaling to her dive partner. She stuck out her chin, argued, stomped away.

On the phone, May was calmer, but her voice wheezed with panic. Her daughter had been missing for more than three weeks, she said, might be held hostage or starving. I could tell, even as she spoke, that this was occurring to her for the first time. We'd seen the clinging hands, the whites of Underlakers' eyes milking into their irises, the clavicles tenting translucent skin. When May talked about her daughter, my gut gnawed enough to double me over, but then, on the insides of my eyelids, I saw it replay: May's fin slipping away into the grass. We stay here, Daphne could be in danger. We dive again, I could get May killed.

"Go back to the Chimneys," I begged her. "Check there first."

But May insisted that Daphne would have drunk from the waterskin by now if she was back. "And if they see me, I'll have to explain where I've been. That I committed the worst of all crimes, coming here. I don't know what they'll do to me."

"So you want to go deeper."

"We've looked everywhere else. What about the factory? The aquifer? She wanted to find the aquifer."

Swimming in an aquifer—May refused to believe it wasn't possible. She seemed to be picturing some kind of underground lake, instead of what it was: a thousand square miles of porous rock, sixty feet below the surface of the earth. And, as I explained again, the factory was just too deep. We'd explored every part of Paintsville above a hundred and twenty feet. Any deeper and we'd need trimix instead of compressed air—especially if May was going to get narced on a dime—and in an ideal world, rebreathers to extend our bottom time. I'd brought mine home with me, but a second rebreather would cost north of eight thousand dollars.

I abandoned this line of reasoning when May asked how she could come by eight thousand dollars.

"The point is," I said, "I can't help you."

Acid down my veins. There was no right answer, but I wasn't going to kill May myself. I had to hang up on her every time.

I SPENT THAT MORNING wandering Paintsville posting missing-person signs, futile as it felt. In the afternoon, I took Eugenia to dialysis. I tried not to think. I remained, as best I could, inside the quivering sphere of now.

Eugenia had been handling the treatment well, and the dementia was only an occasional cloud passing over her eyes. The next morning, my mother marched into the kitchen decked in khakis and a plastic visor. At the sight of me hunched over my coffee, she barked: "Wake up, Ottilie."

Upstairs, autumn light slanted through the lace curtains of the spare bedroom.

Eugenia pointed. "Start moving these boxes to that other wall."

I'd learned not to ask too many questions—especially if she was in a good mood. When I was a kid, her best days were when she had a task ahead of her. She worked nights as a janitor, and during the week, she slept through breakfast and trudged through dinner, Hamburger Helper and canned beans. But on rare weekends, like a shock of electricity, some mission would bolt her awake, and she'd drive us halfway across the state for a flea market, or to the city for sundaes. She squeezed our shoulders, kissed the tops of our heads. We carried each moment carefully, a glass ornament, in both hands.

Today, she was on one of these missions. We started carving our way, stack by stack, toward the buried back wall of the room. While we worked, my mother wheeled along her normal conversational ruts.

"This was my room when I was a baby, and my daddy's before me. But when you come along, I had to have your crib in my room with me. That's what Grandma Ottilie done with me, you know, after my mom died."

Eugenia dropped a box of magazines, shook a tremor out of her left hand. "You were both good babies."

Usually, I didn't dare mention our father, but today I chanced it. "Did Dad ever look after us?"

"Him? No. He was only good for farming, and hardly even that."

"What do you mean?"

"Well, you know he lost his parents' land to the eminent domain, down there in the valley?"

I didn't know.

"He always said to me how much he wanted to get that back, that kind of life. How we was gonna build that here. Well, turns out he didn't know what he was doing. Didn't really want to learn, neither."

She lifted her visor to sop the sweat away.

"But it's always been the women in this family. Ottilie taught me everything. Allie's got a touch of the green thumb, I told you?"

"No."

"She planted those tomatoes out back."

I'd never imagined Allie gardening. More surprising, though, was that our mother included her among "the women." When we were teenagers, that would have been impossible.

At last, we unearthed a bookshelf on the far wall of the room. My mother inspected the spines and pulled out one, clothbound with gold lettering: *A Coates Family Almanac.*

"You've read it," she said.

I shook my head. Her lips pursed with disappointment.

"This is where I got Allie's name—Albion—from your great-great-something-grandfather, back to the 1780s. He was the first settler here."

An old annoyance washed through me. This pride that had consumed our lives—all built on nothing.

"The first one?" I asked. "What about the Miami settlement that used to be there? Does that book say what happened to them?"

Eugenia only flashed my annoyance back and bit her cheeks. This conversation always ended in silence.

She sat on a box and started flipping through the book. I thought I'd lost her again inside of memory. Then she smiled up at me—even a little shy.

"But your name, you know where you got it. From the best of us. You can be proud of that."

ALLIE WAS WAITING TABLES, so after dialysis we drove to the restaurant for an early dinner.

"Food isn't worth it without the discount," Eugenia whispered after the host had seated us. It was a stuffy establishment with heavy curtains and white tablecloths.

"What a surprise." Allie set down our waters.

"You know what I want, my usual." Eugenia slammed the menu shut.

"Say hi, at least," Allie said.

"Show her the kitchen, Allie." Eugenia was already out of her seat.

Allie walked us down the serving line; many of them had already met my mother. Allie introduced two servers rolling silverware, Nate and Lisa, as her roommates.

Lisa threw her arms around me. "We've heard so much about you."

She started asking about diving and the places I'd traveled, and my limbs stiffened. I could feel Eugenia observing my answers without ever laying eyes on me. She re-rolled a few of the loose setups.

Allie nudged my shoulder. "You okay?"

She walked us back to the table. Eugenia rattled on about Lisa's mother's nerve damage, about how Nate's sister contracted Lyme disease on Long Island—"It's dangerous up there, even in the country"—and then, when the food arrived, fell into silent focus on her burger.

She had spent time learning about their lives, shown a real interest. Meanwhile, she hadn't asked me more than two questions since I'd gotten home, didn't know I hadn't finished school, hardly knew Ethan existed.

It twisted at me, this profound disinterest. But if she had asked in that moment one real question, I wouldn't have told her a thing.

BY THE TIME WE GOT HOME, Eugenia was falling asleep in the passenger seat. She went to her room, and just as I was pouring myself a drink, I heard a knock from the side entrance.

The bulb above the screen door wobbled with the flutter of caught moths. May stood beneath it.

She knew the look on my face before I did.

"I'm not here to ask for anything," she said. "Can I come in?"

She sat at the kitchen table and peeled off her shoes. I topped off my drink and poured her one with extra Coke. She took a sip, made a face, took another, and settled it between her hands.

"I wanted to say thank you."

She rubbed one socked foot.

"I been so focused on Daphne, I forgot how it can't be easy for you. With what happened to your friend."

I winced through my drink.

She was wearing thick socks too long for her feet. It dawned on me that she might have walked here all the way from the lake.

"And so I been thinking." Sparrow-tilt of her head.

"What?"

"I didn't listen to Daphne about how she was feeling. But then, I told you about being a bastard, and I felt better after." Her voice cracked. "Maybe if I'd have listened, she'd have even never left."

That frothing, impossible regret—I knew it. Every day, I heaped sandbags against it, and it tore them down grain by grain.

"Look, I come to say this because—you can talk like that to me," she said. "About Ethan."

A stone down my throat. There were no words.

"Thanks."

I got up and poured another drink. May had made an impressive dent and I topped her off.

Her strained eyes, her sunken cheeks—it was clear that she hadn't been sleeping. Every day we'd known each other had been about the mission at hand. I was most effective in these conditions. In that sense, I guess, Eugenia and I had something in common. But the future haunts, its billion terrible unknowns.

"I come to see a lot of things different since I got here," she said, tilting the ice in her drink. "Like, how I thought they'd finally accepted me. But I see now they disliked me *more* after she was born. Because Daphne was mine and not theirs. Because of all people, it was my daughter who survived when—you know, none of the other children did."

The room crusted over in ice. "What?"

She nodded.

I glimpsed, for the first time, the horrors dragging along behind her. Her own seafloor, all its gaping phantoms.

"But you didn't leave."

"No." Her eyes dropped to the floor. The peach fuzz along her jaw glowed in the fluorescent light. When you see a housecat out of doors and it suddenly freezes, its eyes trained on a marvelous discovery that no one but the cat can see—she looked like that, staring at one corner of the kitchen. "I couldn't."

"Why not?"

She shrugged.

"They loved Daphne, and she loved them. The hardest thing in this world is to find home. How could I take it from her?"

Otta

You know to be suspicious of the sweet times—not to let them lull you. I know this. But for a while, I let them. Now look what I've done.

WAITING FOR ETHAN in the bell, I'd sometimes enter states of what I can only call expansion. The roar of the drill made the bell vibrate, and merged with the sound of Ethan's breathing through the comms into a single braid of static. During these interludes, my mind dilated outward, and I could almost touch the scallop shells half-buried in the seabed, the spined skins of sand stars, the milky cloud of silt that the drill kicked up.

Ethan had walked directly into that cloud. He was supposed to do a minor weld on the jacket—the four-legged tower that protected the oil well and extended from the seafloor all the way up to the rig. He'd radioed when he arrived. After that, he had fifteen minutes to complete the job.

Suddenly I shrank through the walls of the bell and back into my body. It had been twelve minutes, and Ethan hadn't spoken in three. Over the noise of the machinery, I tried to make out the sound of his breath.

Topside signaled to him. "Confirm status, diver."

No response.

"Diver, confirm status."

Then I heard a crackle, and a voice came through: pressurized, clipped. And this is where—even though I thought I understood it at the time—I doubt my senses now: Did he say *explosion* or *explode* or *load* or *tow* or *how* or *fouled*—or did I hear none of this? Was it my imagination, the way all those bell dives manufactured flicks of shade through the portholes, scents of strange flowers, unraveled singing?

The rest, I remember in clips: his umbilical when I hauled it in, the wire laid bare along one burnt length of casing, but the end of it undamaged, released as if on purpose from the diver's suit. I dropped into the water, my exhaust manifold sending up a roar of bubbles. I left behind the bell, a bolt-studded sarcophagus dangling ten feet off the seafloor. I dragged myself along the downline, whose taut rope led the way to the job site. The heave of the water against my helmet drowned out everything: my own thoughts, the signals from topside, the organ sloshing in my chest. I plunged into the fog of sand around the well.

I reached one foot of the well jacket. This was where he should have been. I pushed out into the fog again and again beneath a hundred pounds of gear and the drag of my umbilical, watching it all through my mask as though on a television screen.

I circled one jacket foot, then shoved my way to the next. I gasped and blinded. I couldn't see my own body. I believed I had lost it. I offered to trade it for his.

I found no sign of him.

It felt like hours but could not have been.

Topside signaled for me to return to the bell. I argued, but could hardly catch my breath.

I slipped out of the well's seething cloud. As I hauled my way back along the downline, there was what seemed like—after that churn—a famished silence.

Then, out of the dark, sparked a small glassine creature. Translucent, eyeless, shapeless, it floated a few paces in front of me. I trudged toward it. It lilted, leaned, coiled its hundred arms around itself, then went limp and emptied out. It seemed unaware of my presence but never strayed far from the downline. So, beneath a trillion empty tons of water, it led me along the rope and, just before I entered the dome of light that the bell cast down, did not swim off but vanished: gone, utterly. It's hard to believe in things that disappear like that.

WHICH IS WHY, LATER, I wondered was it his voice I'd heard through the comms or another being's. In recent months, Ethan had become unfamiliar to me: a new twitch in his cheek; his hypermasculine joking on the rig. I had been buoyed along by his sparkle and easy influence, and now I found myself in a strange land with a stranger.

As they hauled me up in the bell I screamed until my voice gave out. They dispatched another dive team, who found nothing. They deployed helicopters and response boats, which searched for hours.

They treated me as the panicked wife and wouldn't let me help, so that as the days passed I grew suspicious of the search itself: how hard they were trying; whether they were telling me everything; how they might weigh the intangible cost of lost morale against the tangible cost of dedicating further resources to finding him. I started to question whether we had done the dive at all; or whether, if we had, they had sent me down with someone else. The constant drone of the rig blurred days into other days, nights into other nights, men into other men, and our voices were so often not our voices—squeezed by helium or hoarse from the gases.

And so I came to feel sorry for a wife who had lost her husband but not for me, and not for Ethan. I understood that when the next crew boat came, I'd find Ethan waiting for me back at the apartment.

But when I reached the third-floor landing and saw our door, I felt a great whoosh of silence coming at me like the mouth of a whale and fled back down the stairs.

Night after night, I picked up shifts at the bar, then found someone to go home with. I spent three days on the beach, sheltering under a cluster of sea grapes and oats whispering into each other's necks.

I stopped by the apartment only once more, to check the mailbox. No paycheck yet. What I did receive was a letter with sincerest condolences, etc., etc. I stuffed it into my backpack, looked up at the building. In the windows, no stir.

That night I boarded a long-haul bus back to Steels.

Otta

I blurred into my drink, May blurred into hers. She liked the Coke, it pinched her cheeks, and we started to drift, to sway into the ease and blank, which was the drink's gift. We laughed, we played with my mother's tchotchkes, porcelain figurines and an iron horse. I told May that Ethan and I weren't married, just good friends, and she was thoroughly tickled, cackled—Ha! A boy!—and fell over on the rug, taunted the tabby with a stray string.

But then, out of nowhere, she pulled me back from it. She grabbed my hand and said, Tell me something. I tugged away, I drank more to wipe it off, but she kept asking: why did I like diving; did I sleep through the night; what type of sewing was my favorite; did my mother sing to me. She wouldn't let me disappear.

The next thing I remember, I was weeping with my cheek wedged on her shoulder and she wiped the matted hair from my eyes, saying, He hasn't stopped loving you, he hasn't stopped, he can't.

A mother, and also not—claiming no knowledge that I couldn't access, or couldn't understand. It was more like hope, the way she said it—an invocation. We were together so that we, together, could ache to believe it.

WHEN I CAME DOWNSTAIRS the next morning, May was sitting at the kitchen table. The sudden recollection of last night crawled down my neck, a flushed shame.

The kitchen was stifling—too hot to breathe in. So I made two cups of coffee and led May to the front stoop. Sprays of yellow grass shivered in a wind crusted with winter.

We sat on the steps.

"I have a question," May said.

She picked up an ochre leaf and twirled the stem in her fingers.

"Ethan. You said you never found him?"

The caffeine thudded into my skull, locking teeth with the vestiges of vodka. I'd said too much. "Right."

"Then—respectfully—how can you be sure that he really—you know. That he really died?"

I squeezed my eyes shut. "What the fuck, May."

"My daughter is lost under the water, but she's alive," May insisted. "Do you feel him gone?"

This sliced to the core of it: the sensation for the last two months that I was floating six inches above the ground. I hadn't seen a body. Whole lives don't just dissolve. I had felt little more than a crystalline numbness, like the slow ringing build from the rim of a glass—and it was the numbness that hurt.

"Look, there aren't secret fucking cabins and whole towns just living on the ocean floor. If he went down and didn't come up—that's that."

She held the leaf out. The wind tugged it into the yard, and I lost sight of it.

"But you didn't know about us," she said. "So—you don't *know*."

She tendered it. She saw it wasn't easy. I'll give her that.

"Okay, no, May, I don't know everything. That's a shocker."

"And anyway. We've seen from the Underlake that the human body can do miracles. It can adapt."

I shook my head. I saw where she was going now.

"You said with the right equipment it'd be different. We could go deeper," she pressed.

"It would *maybe* be different. But equipment's not everything. If you're prone to—"

"I'm not." She stood, looked me dead in the eye. "I know how the narcing feels now and I can control it. It won't happen again."

"Go home," I said.

And I left her outside in a coil of leaves.

May

I learned my whole life how not to steal and yet when I tried my first time to do it, I had no real trouble at all.

If Otta wasn't going to help me, I accepted that. I'd made a mistake. The shine and lure of one fish made me lose my focus. That feeling—I'm inclined to lie about it: say that I was possessed, that I went crazy. But that's not what it was. What happened really was that I felt suddenly free of all my worries.

But remembering it later felt worse than I can describe. I didn't want to be free of Daphne.

Deep into our drinks, Otta started to talk about Ethan. I had meant to give her some release, same as she'd given me. But soon she was digging her own nails into her neck. I led her upstairs, folded her into her sheets. I had witnessed the greatest griefs tear through people's chests. But I had never seen anyone sad in the same way she was sad.

I laid down to sleep on the living room couch.

Then I woke. Through the curtains, the night thinned. I crept upstairs.

I'd seen the rebreather—a backpack of tubes, pipes, and gauges—in the hall outside Otta's room. I knew it from a picture in my instruction manual.

I hoisted it by the straps and down the stairs. Crossing into the living room, a voice jumped me out of my skin and I dropped it on the rug.

"You stealing from us?"

Eugenia sat in the armchair. Morning light crossed her body in bands.

"No," I said. A lie.

I couldn't make out her face.

"Sit down."

I left the rebreather where it was and sat on the couch.

"You going to tell me finally what you and my daughter have been up to?"

I rubbed my thighs, wondering if I should run.

Instead, I told her everything. How my daughter was lost under the lake; how Otta and me had searched and searched. How time was shrinking: three and a half weeks gone. If she wasn't fishing, she might be out of food now. I could feel the thread linking me and Daphne—the way I knew she was all right—starting to strain.

Dawn filled the room. Eugenia's eyes had grown wide, and all the color was gone from her face.

"So," she said at last. Her voice was thin, like she couldn't find her breath. "You really made it."

Such a tremble passed through her that her teacup rattled on its saucer. It shivered down through her feet and disappeared.

"You don't know how long—" She exhaled, pink blots on her cheeks. "I can't believe it. Henry's plan worked."

It was the name we'd heard again and again in the Underlake.

"I don't know Henry."

She set her teacup down. "He died?"

"No—I mean, I don't know. I never met him."

She read my face careful, left to right, like lines on a page. "You're not from the factory."

"No." I was stunned. "How do you know about that?"

She squeezed her eyes shut and open, then picked up her cup and sipped.

"Who's your daughter's daddy?" she asked, out of the silt.

"What?"

"Humor me."

I'd never told it to anyone. But what had felt like a dense gem, shining in the dark of my fist, had dulled. There was no sense in keeping it now.

"He was a Vaughan. One of the highest fates. So when I had Daphne, he couldn't claim her."

The steam poured up around Eugenia's face. "Did you love him?"

Lake in my eyes. I blinked it off.

"It doesn't matter," I said, "but I did. And now I don't."

"All right, then," Eugenia said. "So you know how it is to be foolish."

And she started to tell me a story that at first I didn't understand why she told it. It was about how her family had lived here for generations and worked the land and grew food from it. Her great-greats built a town, and then another family came in and instead of food started growing paint and paper and factories, and soon no one could live making food alone. There was more that this world wanted. *Coveted* was the word she used.

By the time Eugenia was born, the farm was getting smaller, and the person buying a lot of the land was from that other family, a man named Charles Weber Jr.

"The funny part was, me and Henry bonded over hating his father." Eugenia's eyes were fixed on a painting above the mantel, a field done up in creamy browns. "Stupidest thing I could do, to fall for a Weber. But I got a flat tire one day and he stopped to change it. I couldn't believe he knew how."

"And—you loved him."

She smiled, slow-dripping and sadly.

"For all the good it did me." When she looked at me now, I believed she knew every secret I hadn't told a soul. "You understand."

She sniffed her eyes clear.

"I told him how much it hurt me, losing our land. But then he claimed that hurt, and took it too far."

"And—he was Otta's father?"

"Oh, no." She waved it away. "I always knew we weren't a match. We were from different worlds. I met someone else—a farmer. That broke Henry's heart. Last time I seen him, I knew it had."

She stood and approached the painting.

"My grandma did this. Ottilie Coates."

I joined her at the mantel. Up close, I could see details that the thick brown swirls had almost hidden: a blue bird on a branch; a black-and-white spotted cow, too small maybe for the landscape, nestled in the grass.

"When I had Otta, me and her dad was on the outs. We were off and on like that for years—it's why I didn't marry him. My grandma Ottilie come to see me in the hospital and she was wearing her ruby brooch. It was only for special occasions. Nobody else thought it was special, me giving birth out of wedlock. My daddy thought I should get married. But my grandma leaned right in and said, 'That girl's the only promise you got to keep.' "

Eugenia took my wrist.

"Your daughter needs you. So you put that machine out on the sunporch. Talk to Otta one more time, and if she still won't help, just take it with you on your way out."

WALKING BACK TO THE MARINA with the rebreather was heavy work. I had to stop many times on the roadside while the cars flashed by in their terrors. By the time I got back to the bait shop, my limbs were cringing and my breath short.

I sat down at the counter and opened my manual to the part on rebreathers. A lot of instructions didn't match the device I'd taken from Otta. An hour in, and the sun starting to wilt, I felt a whimper building in my throat. Half the words in that book didn't make any sense. But I had no choice.

I assembled the gear in the best way I could figure. I pulled on my suit and dive socks and flippers, and practiced breathing into Otta's machine.

It was surprisingly quiet. It didn't push air into my lungs like the other tanks, and felt so natural I was sure I'd gotten it right. I hauled to my feet and shuffled out the door. I reached the boat ramp and waded in, practicing first in the shallow water. I dove five feet, ten, and felt pleased and good and shining, but then all at once got turned around on myself. I discovered I was back in the shallows, breathing hard. I stood and tried to lock my knees above my feet, but my soles now were prickling, and here came a sickness and the sky folding over, then the lake, rising to take me to her.

Otta

When I picked up the phone, Clark's voice was drowned out by the roar of air through the stuck-open window of his truck. I pieced together directions and ran out the door.

I pulled up behind his truck at an urgent care on Main Street, a converted bungalow. Clark was helping May up the plywood ramp and I rushed to grab her arm. She was in her wet suit. Her eyes drooped.

A doctor held the door open; white coat, moth-eaten sweater. We followed him into a parlor and helped May onto an exam table.

I held her hand. Her eyes were a warm bronze with a single dark fleck in the left, eyelids bloated and sleep-starved. All those nights Allie lay awake in terror of what she was, until I lay down beside her . . . I had abandoned May to her suffering.

The doctor tapped each knee with a hammer. "When did this start?"

“I don’t know I don’t know—” Clark puffed on his inhaler.

“Has she been diving?” I asked Clark.

“Diving?” The doctor peered over his glasses. “Like scuba diving?”

“Yes,” Clark said. “I came home and she was face up in the shallow water.”

“Passed out?”

“Half-awake.”

The doctor flashed a penlight in May’s eyes. Her gaze was returning to the room. He checked her pulse, her heart, her lungs. “What’s your name?”

“May.”

“How do you feel?”

“Dizzy.”

“Short of breath?”

“Not now.”

“Chest pain?”

“No.”

He set his instruments aside.

“Looks like a panic attack.” He addressed his comments to Clark. “Maybe brought on by exhaustion. I’ll give her a benzodiazepine, and let’s get her hydrated. I’m just going to get fluids ready.”

The doctor left the room, and May started to cry.

“This is what I get,” she said, looking at me. “I stole your breather. I’m sorry.”

“You—what?” I dropped into a chair. There were a hundred mistakes she could have made, a thousand ways to not come back from it. I’d been trying to protect her, and what had come of it was worse. “You could have died.”

Tears streamed down her cheeks.

“You have to stop this, May, you have to—”

Clark cut me off. “You know she can’t.”

He put his arm around her shoulder.

“And if I was dead then who”—May gasped for air—“would

be here to find her? But if I have to die to find her—I'll die—but I don't—"

Watching her now, the answer was clear. It wasn't just the daughter who needed saving.

I'D SEEN IT BEFORE. May didn't change out the CO_2 pellets in the rebreather. She'd run low on air, panicked, and fainted. Thankfully, she'd fallen short of a CO_2 hit, which could have been deadly.

The doctor told us to make May rest for a couple of days, and she agreed. But the next morning, I heard a knock at my mother's door. It was Clark. He jabbed his thumb over his shoulder at the truck.

"You gotta rest her here." May sat wrapped in a towel in the passenger seat. "She keeps trying to get in the lake."

We led her upstairs. Clark and I cleaned off the bed in the spare bedroom while May watched from the corner, chin on her chest.

The floorboards groaned in the hall. By the time I turned around, Eugenia had wrapped her arms around May.

The tenderness was inexplicable. Eugenia was disinclined to emotional displays, and they'd barely met. Nevertheless, it was my mother who, for the next day and a half, brought May soup and cups of tea, and whenever she started putting on her shoes convinced her to settle back down.

When I came out of the kitchen on Monday morning, they were side by side on the couch. May stroked my mother's gray tabby, who purred in her lap.

"Morning," my mother said, straightening in her seat. "May's looking good, right?"

The color was back in May's cheeks, and her knees bounced. But I was suspicious of their alliance, which seemed intent upon swaying me to do something that neither of them knew the dangers of.

"I feel good," said May, glancing at my mother. "And I'm sorry for what I did. I'm here to learn from you, if you'll please be my teacher again."

I took a long sip of coffee, and sighed.

"We'll switch to a different gas mixture," I said. "Trimix. It'll help you keep a clear head. It's for deeper dives, so we can stay longer—not as much as with a rebreather, but we can't afford a second one."

I locked eyes with May. "You'll need to do what I say. Fucking exactly."

May clasped her hands. "Yes. I will."

I stood.

"Take my car," Eugenia said, triumphant smile on her lips. I wanted to wipe it off.

"I always do."

TRIMIX REQUIRED A DIFFERENT APPROACH, different math, and May took our three days of training seriously. Each evening, Clark and I drove an hour and a half to the nearest dive shop to refill the tanks. The second night, two of Clark's cards were declined before he found one that worked. On the drive back, I had to ask.

"You okay paying for all this?" I said. "I can cover the next one."

The next one, yes—but after that, my account would be drained.

"I'm good, getting paid on Friday."

I couldn't press the issue, so I changed the subject.

"I know you've been eager for us to find Weber," I said.

"Sure." His eyes fixed on the road. Knots of white showed through the sunburned red of his knuckles.

"So if we find him, then what?"

He hesitated, stole a glance at me. "You ever heard of Jacques Cousteau?"

That surprised me.

"Yeah, I know Cousteau." *World Without Sun* was the first underwater film I'd ever seen.

"Well, when I was a kid we had the moon landing. Everyone was floored with it. Me too." He took a sip off his Big Gulp. "Nobody around here went to college back then, but I thought I'd give it a try. Engineering. I got my degree, mailed in my résumé to Lockheed and NASA. No one took me except for Steels High. But then, I seen this headline in the newspaper one day: *Paintsville to stay put*—quote—'*even if we have to live underwater.*' And you know, I took that literally. Had a girlfriend once said I was too literal." A twinkle drifted across his face. "So I went and done all the research I could about Conshelf and Sealab, rewatched Cousteau's films. And it come to me, at some point, that underwater living made a lot more sense than space living."

"What do you mean?"

"You go to space, your body gets weaker. You come back to Earth, and you might not even be able to stand up. But underwater, it's the opposite. You build muscle, moving under all that weight. On Conshelf, their wounds healed faster. Their beards stopped growing. It was like they were aging slower, or even in reverse."

I didn't remember this from the film. What had impressed me most about Cousteau's aquanauts was that they never stopped smiling.

"I may just be a high school teacher," Clark said, "but to them under the lake, I'm Cousteau in the *Calypso*. I'm Houston down on the ground. My job is to keep them alive, and if I do that, it's us that the next generation of explorers is going to be learning from."

He tugged at his beard.

"So if you'd asked me a month ago, I'd tell you to bring back data on how they've adapted, how they've aged. How their diet's impacted their health, if eating algae was enough to keep up their vitamin C, how their eyesight is."

Clark wiped the sweat from his forehead, though a chilly night poured through the window.

"But forget about all that. You got to find that little girl. If it's not too late . . ."

CLARK HAD SUCCEEDED where even Cousteau had failed. I'd seen it with my own eyes. So the question began to gnaw: If this had been possible in a backwater town, couldn't there be someone else in the world who had quietly succeeded—who slipped through the surface of the ocean for the last time and managed to stay?

My imagination colored in the details, almost without my noticing: a ring of living quarters on the seafloor just beyond the swamp of sand that the drill kicked up; corals encrusted around the expelled oxygen from the exhaust; algae harvested daily for the vitamins. A rebreathing system recycled air, while artificial gills extracted oxygen from the water. Hydroelectric power was generated from the currents.

Take all of this, for a moment, as fact.

Then imagine, on our last dive, if Ethan had unhooked his umbilical just long enough to untangle it—if it was ripped from his hand by the water gnashing around the drill—if this had tossed him clear of those clouds of silt—if he had hooked up his bailout bottle quickly enough to stay conscious—if some aquanauts from the underwater outpost had glanced out into the swallowing dark and noticed the beam of his dive light, how unlike an abyssal fish with its slow effulgence—if they had swum toward it while he, glimpsing the glow of the portholes, swam toward them—well, it was all possible—more so than it had ever been.

This image, in the weeks since I'd seen the Chimneys, had grown more tangible than my own skin, than my hands held up before me. I rolled it up like a pillow and slept on it at night. I woke every morning sick to my stomach.

May

Those days I recovered from the accident, I was working on my mind. I had been maybe too enthralled of a new concept, which had come to me as we swam the ruins of the sunken town: that the lake had its own divineness that wasn't His and wasn't the Jewells' but was the lake's only. It had crafted every cottage in its own scheme, without His intervention; but also it could tear the throat from any plan or human conviction according to its will.

Then I nearly fainted in the shallows with the rebreather on, and when I came back to myself I saw things different. I'd been trying to mold the lake into another Him, who thought the way a man thinks. But even as the lake cradled me on my back, I knew it wasn't love—that the lake doesn't love in any way we use that word. The reverend had preached that He made the lake to serve us. But I felt now, deep inside my body, that the lake did not care for human beings because it was not *about* human beings. It existed for its own purposes, or maybe for no purpose at all.

I expected a flood of grief at this realization, at all that benevolence draining out of the world. But it didn't come. What I felt was the wrath dissolving like a fog. He no longer held me in His teeth, waiting to bite down. I wondered if someday I would mourn it—an emptier world. But for now, I felt my bones in my skin, and my skin all inside of my control.

I tried to explain this to Otta: that I wouldn't fall into worshipful reverie anymore because I was free from worship. Otta brushed it off like a reassurance made of words only. I understood that. But I was going to prove it to her. If we were going to find Daphne, I had to.

WE REACHED NEW DEPTHS in training, though all of it close to the dock. Otta quizzed me triple on every detail, since trimix training usually takes four or five days and we were doing it in three. One morning, glass-eyed and flat in her voice, she told me that, when I got to depth, I should imagine Daphne drowning in front of me, and to watch it happen and keep my breath calm.

"You're sick," I said. I had the urge even to spit at her. The reverend had relished describing the sufferings of the Overlakers in end times. This felt like that.

"We're operating at pressure," Otta snapped back, "and looking for your daughter who doesn't have any equipment or training. So you might, at some point, find yourself watching her drown. You need to be able to control yourself."

So I did it—that dive, and the next. Then Otta told me the next time, to move toward her. And then, to practice passing my mouthpiece back and forth between us, sharing our air. I saw now that Otta had a path carved out in her mind, and I wondered how, when she gave these instructions, I could have seen anything other than pain.

On the fourth morning we drove the pontoon out over Paintsville, where the lake's three arms intersected. We made our descent quick, and I could feel the gathering cold. The air grew thick through my regulator, bulged in my ears. Darkness muddled in, the sunfish replaced with tousles of silt—catfish burying themselves—and near the grocery, a silver sturgeon with razors down its sides, something I'd seen only in pictures.

We reached a hundred feet of depth near the pharmacy. A dozen plexiglass tubes stuck out of the building. We'd spotted them on our last visit, even seen them hooked up to other cottages, and the hope was that some led to houses we hadn't visited yet. Up until now, we'd been traveling from east to west, from the Chimneys near the dock down the slope and along Main Street. Now we turned southwest, following a tube that trailed off into a meadow of eelgrass.

We gained twenty-five feet of depth, thirty. The tube was matted with algae in some places, but in others, clumps of catfish were picking it clean. Up to this point, the tube had been empty. But then we reached a spot where it was plugged with a capsule like a sealed glass of water, lid at each end, full of wet paper. As we continued, there came another, and another, burst open and spilling pages like from gray books. After that came tiny discs of copper, scraps of leather pasted wetly against the tube's insides, long metal rods lashed together end to end, and finally, one metal blade like the gash of light across your vision when a candle's blown out.

WE BURST THROUGH the moon pool and pulled off our masks, inhaling a sour smell like the tip of a pencil. The only windows sent down shifts of gray light from high above our heads.

The ceilings were as tall as the Shuttle's, the whole structure one broad room. At its center was a massive cogged and piped and belt-wound machine. Stretched out between two metal rollers was a sash of paper, text blooming into wet petals. Otta studied a ream.

"Newspapers," she said. "Can't read them now."

In a dim corner, we found where the tube entered the room. Wads of paper burst out the hole, with wrenches and broomsticks scattered on the floor, like someone had been trying to force objects through.

On the wall, writing scrawled in every direction. It started with diagrams and labels for the control panel, which was busted open with wires lacing out. Then there was a list of dates, starting with when *M. plugged the tube*—BY ACCIDENT, it added, in a different hand. I searched for the kind of tiny and careful cursive we'd learned in the Chimneys. As the writing traveled along the wall, moving farther from the tube, more handwritings joined in, a chorus of voices talking back and forth, giving opinions that others disagreed on, drawing pictures that others crossed out and corrected.

At last, I reached a diagram that was different from the rest. It reminded me of what that woman in the hardware store, Ava, had been carving in a block of wood: something like a staircase. But here, on each step was a little house drawn, and for each house a mass of labels and most of these not making sense. On one step, for instance, was sketched a flashing mass of rainbow trout, eelgrass tickling their bellies, next to instructions written out: to stay low to this grass, hold your breath hold your breath, and to follow a knotted string of clothes up and in.

At the top of the stairs was a vertical dark bar, drawn over and over with pencils till they darkened the whole shape. It shone a burning exclamation as heavy and watchful as the cross above the Shuttle altar.

To the left of it on the wall was a gap where the stair steps ended. In that void just past the final stair was a single word, written in cursive. It looked like a name. My heart skipped. I stepped close.

Despair, it said.

ALL THIS TIME and not a sign of her—not a single drop. We'd visited dozens of cottages, spoke to how many strangers, and not one of them knew her name.

A thread is made of smaller threads twisted together. I imagine that each of these threads is braided of the same pattern, smaller still. And suddenly I felt, in that thread connecting me and Daphne, a single strand fray and snap.

I'd believed I could feel in my body the state of hers, because we were tied together. Now I started to doubt that I ever could. Which meant I didn't really know if she was safe or not.

"You okay?" Otta pinched my wrist to count the thumps. The sob in my chest I swallowed down.

"I'm fine," I said. "I'm controlling."

I was. Not because I hoped—because I had to. It was a gasping quiet in my head without being able to feel her there. But I could use that quiet inside to hear what was out: the lake's slosh against the walls, the things it whispered. Not to the reverend, not to Him, not to Daphne—to me. And what came next—I would decide.

–144 ft.

Once upon a time and was there a house before this house? Yes. And was there a house before that house? Yes. And before this log cabin, all its ancestors, was there shelter beneath the trees, how their branches wound into a single being, how they cast down spackles of light that warmed each nettle and vine and stalk of grass in turn? Also.

I grew up listening to stories of the trees before there were trees and the houses before there were houses. They were told by my mamaw whose mamaw told them to her. How we was Shawnee descended from Weyapiersenwah, victor of the Battle of the Wabash, betrayed by the Treaty of Greenville. How what we lived in now was the remnants of what they called a Miami town. Called this because, of those Indians back in the 1700s who'd survived the diseases and the land theft and the wars, some of them started coming together into mixed-tribe settlements. Ours, so happened, had more Miami than anyone else.

My mamaw said to keep all this a secret, never taught me the language, else they might ship us west. She and my mom was passing white, and I spent my whole life white and not making much fuss about these stories, with no kids of my own to tell them to neither.

But what else was there to keep me busy in my old age? I just thought more and more about it. I was living in the house that they passed to me and so it was all around reminding. I spent long hours refitting the stones that had fallen out of the chimney or resealing between the logs outside. This house was three hundred years old, and every log had over time been replaced with a new log, but it was still a living history standing up. There was no sign left of the Miami town except us and the burials and the water well. Still, it was put to my mamaw by hers and by theirs before hers that we should protect the house and the burials nearby, so that's what we did.

One day, two factory men come down and asked to see the house. Big white guys with wet eyes. I didn't want to unlock the screen door. But they brought along a crate of canned goods, all for me, as "a thanks for your time." That was respectful, surprising, enough that I let them in.

I showed them around and they told me how impressed they was by the sealing I'd done and how I'd maintained the place. "Ain't seen nothing like it, Mrs. Reed," they said. That was good to hear, considering how the rest of Paintsville always talked like it was an eyesore and grumbled how they had to lay the road down to the factory bending around my land instead of straight—which added, what, a minute to their drive? But now, at last, here was some appreciation.

I'd heard how they was building a lake and hadn't thought fully what I'd do. The government taped letters on my door, but my husband had been the big reader between the two of us. And so when those factory men offered that I should join their cause and said they could even hook me up to HVAC, which I'd never had before, I thought long and hard. And the more that I thought, the more it felt like my mamaw was working through them, making sure I could stay on this land, where I was supposed to be.

In exchange, the factory men asked if they could connect a pipe to pull water from my well. They said mine went deeper than any other well in the area, to the lowest pockets of the aquifer. I said all right.

Still, the day the water started rising, I was shaking like a leaf. I kept my eye all day on the two little houses that still stood to mark the burials, which I could see from the kitchen window. The water outside rose to knee height and the tops of the bark roofs lipped above it and held firm. The pipe pulling water up from the well, which run through and past my house down towards the factory, didn't budge where it was bracketed to the ground; same for the air pipe they'd drilled into my kitchen wall. When at last the water crawled past the tops of my windows, the house stayed just as rooted in the earth as ever.

Over those next weeks—with the lake weighing heavier every day over my head—I grew even joyful. I slow-danced in the kitchen all the steps I'd learned for our wedding. I sang the lyrics to every song I could recall. I started playing games with myself about different ways to mix canned foods into new dishes, and even placed bets between the cans and me about who'd be the first to go—all of it good-natured, knowing in my heart I was planning to let them win.

I heard somewhere how there used to be an ice age here. And watching out the window, it felt like I gone back in time, with the ice melting and everything flooded and Noah somewhere out there on his boat ready to start the whole Earth fresh with people that this time was going to do it right.

There was a winking pool in the middle of the floor that the factory men cut out. I was unsteady on my feet and had the bad hip, but some days I felt so good I put a pillow down to wash my face in it. I felt like I'd done what my blood assigned me, and saw even the spackle of light come down through the branches—the ancient and towering oaks, caught and remembered in that water—and those became the happiest days of my life, where a past I'd never known streamed around me and wasn't gone at all.

May

We started at dawn, with a grim mass of cloud clutching the sky. We had one tube left to follow. Otta led the way, checking the dive computer on her watch as we descended. Soon we reached a fence that had been peeled open to make way for the tube. After that was a stretch of asphalt, cracked and with algae tufting through.

I could make out a structure ahead—the largest that we'd seen so far. A brick wall three stories high, windows dark like throats.

We circled three sides of the factory trying to find an entrance. On the western side, the land dropped down into a puckering dim beneath us, and Otta signaled for us to turn back; she wasn't ready to go deeper. The asphalt was littered with metal cans and planks of wood with nails spitting out. Here and there, shards of mirror and glass threw light back on the high brick walls of the structure. It seemed like another abandoned building, with no way in.

Otta gave a thumbs-up; it was time to ascend. The factory

unfolded beneath us: long and narrow with windows along the eastward side and two Shuttle-size chambers, one at each end.

In the pontoon, Otta spat out a stream of water. She asked how I was feeling. It was the deepest dive we'd ever done. But I was steady—no dizziness, no distraction. We waited out our decompression, watching the here-there glinting sun carve up the water.

"We should try again," I said.

Otta shook her head. "Waste of time and trimix."

"But there's got to be something there," I pleaded. "Where else do we have left to search?"

Otta had no answer to this. We were running out of options. So she agreed to dive the factory one more time and, if we had to, try the back side, which according to her maps sloped down into the deepest part of the lake.

But as we were descending, we saw a strange thing. Where we'd first approached the building along the tube, there was now two red rugs laid out end to end like a tongue.

Otta blinked at me through her mask and I could feel her hesitation. Not just that we didn't know who was inside, or how many. But also that they had been watching us through the plate-white reflecting windows while we swam. I felt those eyes prickling across my skin like fingerprints. But if it frightened me, it didn't matter. We had to see if Daphne was inside.

We swam along the rugs, and found at the foot of the building a wooden pallet pushed aside to reveal a staircase, and a doorway leading into the ground.

Otta motioned I should place my hand on her leg. Then she swam down the stairs and me after, into a darkness so thick it was like swimming into the cave of my own stomach.

Otta flipped on her dive light. Objects floated in and out of the beam, angular, hard. I imagined a set of giant teeth loosed from their jaw.

A dim light cast down ahead. It was a moon pool. As we swam beneath it, I was struck by a wave of sickness: leaning over it in wavering shapes I saw the stalks of bodies, waiting for us.

Otta

In the pitch dark of that flooded basement, I discovered a too-familiar nightmare: a bell of cast-down light.

I calmed myself. I squeezed shut my heart with my mind. May's fingers brushed my calf and I remembered where I was.

We rose through the moon pool's easy lip of water and found ourselves surrounded.

Three men stood around the edge of the pool. They were beardless, skin pale as the meat of apples, and wore matching shirts, over-crisp and mottled cream.

May and I pulled ourselves onto the ledge.

We were inside a long whitewashed room. Meek sunlight dripped through the windows along one wall.

A man with straw-yellow hair cleared his throat and I stood to meet him.

"Hello," he said.

He was stiff, his eyes wide with something like terror.

"Welcome," said another man.

"Welcome," the first man corrected himself.

The air smelled like pennies, but we needed to conserve our trimix. I motioned for May to take off her mask.

"My name is David." A thin streak of hair was oiled over the dome of his head, and sweat darkened his collar. I wondered if this was the first time he'd introduced himself to anyone.

"I'm Otta."

"Hello. I am May," said May, overarticulating.

"That's Jack." David pointed at one man, then the other. "Arthur."

Jack's blond hair was shaved close to his head, and the whites of his eyes glistened like soap. Arthur gave a small nod, his face blotchy. A cut was healing on his jawline. His shoulders hunched, and he avoided our eyes.

"Nice to meet you," I said.

There was a long pause. David seemed to have forgotten his lines.

"I am your Underlake neighbor," said May. She slipped off her second flipper and stood to deliver the short speech she'd started reciting at every house we visited. "Here to wish you good catch, all trout, may the lake rise them to you. We are looking for my daughter. Her name is Daphne. She is lost in the Underlake. Have you seen her?"

David let out a shaky breath, folded his hands in front of him. "We're supposed to take you to him."

"Him?"

David approached a door at the far end of the room.

I exchanged glances with May. Our BCDs and tanks were heavy. I didn't like to let them out of my sight, but we had to keep up our strength. We piled our gear against the wall and followed David. Jack and Arthur fell in behind us.

DAVID OPENED THE DOOR, and the hum of machinery washed around us. The next room towered three stories high and half a football field across. Steel beams stretched from floor to ceiling, reinforcing the walls. I noticed now that the mirror shards we'd seen outside were tilted so that they caught the sparse light filtering down from the surface and redirected it through the windows along the eastern wall. The whole place quivered with the movement of water.

A mechanical moan emitted from the far corner, where a pipe passed down through the ceiling and fed a giant machine that was huffing out air, probably an air handler. It looked like those foot-wide pipes Clark maintained on the lakeside.

In the middle of the room, a row of tables had been set up in a makeshift assembly line. The plastic shells of two large batteries were splayed open on the floor, and one man was chiseling apart the metal plates on a third. He threw the plates into a bowl that another man—rag tied over his nose and mouth—heated from beneath with a welder. The bowl quaked with molten metal, projecting dollops of silver light onto the men's faces.

There was something hypnotic about that pool, a leisure and slow richesse. I watched the man skim the gritted slag that floated on top. As I approached, he pulled down the rag. His lips were a thin gash the same gray as his face. He squinted—not surprised, but like he was trying to remember my name.

"That's not the way," said David.

I started as though tossed awake, and turned back along the wet track of footprints my dive socks had left, back to May's side.

We followed David—his hands still folded over his belly—across the room and through a swinging door. Here, we entered a corridor lined with windows to our left. To the right was a row of shut doors.

We passed the first few, and then I heard a sudden knocking over my shoulder. It swelled and cascaded down the wall past us. Now, as we walked, the doors ahead of us began to open, some cracked into a long drip of darkness, others gaping wide. The first room I could see inside, there was a cluster of four men, half-clothed. Their ribs bolted from beneath their sunken chests. Their skin was so translucent that I could trace their veins, even—it was a strange light—glimpse the blood slither through it.

The next stretch of doors revealed groups of women. Some had rope-muscled necks that bloomed into the sharp petals of their cheekbones. Others were so round-faced that they looked like children. One old woman wore a knitted scarf that draped over both arms, then trailed behind her into the dim. She lay her cheek against the doorjamb, her toothless mouth hanging open and her tongue glistening like the meat inside a scallop. I tried to smile but couldn't muster a convincing warmth. They set their eyes upon us heavily, plates on a table.

We reached the end of the corridor. Jack, who hadn't yet said a word, spun around and barked: "Back at it."

A waterfall of doors clicked shut. Jack stalked down the hall, door by door, inspecting. His eyes flashed yellow, as though searching for something to spark a rage.

The heat was oppressive, the way it used to get in the bell—typical at high pressure. Sweat crawled down my back. But May was trembling. Arthur pulled out a towel from his canvas sack and tried to wrap it around her. May leapt back, startled. Then she let him lay it across her shoulders. Jack returned to his station behind us, and David resumed his march.

We traveled next through a series of rooms, each affecting a queasy balance between disrepair and order. In the cafeteria, the tables shone from scrubbing, but linoleum curled off the floor in brown crusts. The locker room air hung heavy and sweet with urine. Most walls were freshly whitewashed, and in many spots caked several layers deep. The last room was windowless, stocked with spools and meager remainders of thread.

David opened a door. Light poured in, and for a moment all I could see was a mote-pocked blue.

We stepped through.

Another chamber opened up before us—twice the size of the battery workshop. It was almost entirely empty, except that standing in the middle, encircled by a moat of concrete floor, was a house.

It was a two-story Federal-style farmhouse in red brick with carved moulding around the windows. The rippled glass panes yawned mutely, ink on their tongues. Next to the door was a bronze plaque. As we approached, its raised letters came into focus: *First house in Paintsville, 1789.*

Jack and Arthur fell back, Jack poised with feet apart like a soldier, Arthur shrunken into himself. David stepped up onto the concrete stoop. He smoothed down his hair and opened the door.

We entered a foyer with polished floors and a stairway that climbed to a landing, turned, and disappeared. Dangling from a long chain down the center of the stairwell, a lamp lit the room with a bronze glow. We could have been in my mother's house, or any one of the aging farmhouses that haunted the low hills around Steels. My vision jolted, like a film skipping a frame. It was disorienting.

David pointed us through a doorway to our left, but himself hung back in the foyer, the fingers in his clasped hands twisting at each other.

The illusion dilated. It was a sitting room, with twin velvet sofas pinning down a rug and a crossing of logs in the fireplace. Above the mantel, four heads—a hare, a raccoon, a coyote, a possum with exposed teeth—encircled that of a massive twelve-point buck. The buck stared through two glass eyes, each a galaxy of glinting copper. Strips of label tape, too small to read, stuck to the wall beneath each head. Shelves of porcelain figurines lined the front wall, many also labeled. The window was hung with tasseled brocade, and beneath it was a small table with a Spode blue teapot and a bowl of sugar, and beside the table was a wingback chair with a man sitting in it, steaming cup in his hand.

The violet curtains, the painting in the corner (a child in a lace ruff, with a magpie on a string) boiled with mottled shades that cast the color of his eyes in doubt, of his skin in doubt—whether it was the translucent gray of the others' or the color of bruising. He had the swollen jowls and knuckles of someone who has subsisted on organ meat, and was smoky somehow at his edges, like the soft effulgence around a still-life peach, yellow and sweating and monarchical and anointed.

"Well look, well look." He stood and approached. His frame was leaner than I had expected, and he was over six feet tall.

He folded his hands around mine. His palms were cold, despite the steaming cup. We locked eyes. Yes, violet, and like the galaxies in the eyes of that buck, carving a slow spiral. He appraised me. Then he moved on to May.

After another long moment, he released May's hands. I saw a shudder run through her. The man took a seat on one of the sofas, which faced each other at the center of the room. We sat opposite.

"Welcome you both to our community," he said.

He stretched his arms along the back of the sofa, a crane spreading its wings. A gold chain glinted through his swallowtail collar.

The place was lit by a pair of Tiffany lamps positioned behind each couch: one a stained-glass arrangement of dragonflies, the other of white lilies. These created pools of the known in a space that quickly crumbled into darkness. Behind him, the depth of the room was impossible to gauge.

"Your names?" He laughed. We had forgotten ourselves.

"I'm Otta."

May uncrossed her arms. "May."

"Well, fine to meet you, I'm sure, I'm sure. We haven't had too many visitors, I can tell you that, though I guess some of it is our fault."

He laughed again, a rich tone that quaked into his belly, which had gathered in front of him again now that he was seated.

"I got to say, though," and his smile flaked away just as quickly as it had appeared, "I might have expected Jeff to come down here himself. All due respect, but I'm not sure what you two can do about it."

His gaze moved sorghum-slow between us.

"Do about what?" I asked.

"I mean, you seem like ladies from good stock. So you wouldn't go reading other people's letters. You wouldn't do that."

"Jeff," I said. "You mean Jeffrey Clark? We know him. But we don't know anything about a letter."

His tongue picked at a canine, a glint of gold filling along the gum. "I don't figure."

May took a deep breath and recited. "I'm your Underlake neighbor, here to wish you good catch, all trout. We are looking for my daughter—"

A woman emerged from the dark room behind him carrying a rattling silver tray with a teapot and three cups. She set it down on the coffee table between us. Under the apron, her belly bulged.

She poured tea into each cup, then disappeared again into the dark over the man's shoulder. I heard a door shut.

He picked up his cup, and when he tilted it to his lips, I saw a cursive letter printed on the bottom. Familiar somehow.

"You're Henry Weber, aren't you?" I said.

"Oh oh, I didn't introduce myself, that's rude." He slapped his thigh. "You can see how I'd forget, being as there ain't a lot of people down here not knowing. Call me Henry."

There was something in the way he spoke—a Southern accent drifting in and out of his speech, like waves hitting a beach. The drawl, better said, was the foam—the decoration on a pattern more akin to newscaster English, except that even this was soft around its edges, the crispness drained out of its consonants. The result was unlocatable and unsettling.

"So Jeff didn't send you down here to help us with our water."

"He did not."

"Well. Maybe then we should color ourselves lucky that you're here at all. Jeff's never gotten any bottle I've sent up. Started to figure he must be dead. Drink, drink."

We picked up our cups, brutalist orange cylinders oddly mismatched with Weber's curlicued porcelain. It was an ensemble not unlike the rest of the room, or Weber's accent: treasured antiques interspersed with midcentury necessities.

"Look, sir—Henry." May shifted forward in her seat. "I don't know about bottles, but so the reason we're here, I'm hoping you can help."

Her voice caught in her throat. She cleared it.

"You mentioned your water. My daughter, Daphne, is missing and maybe she passed through here, looking for good water. Have you seen her?"

Weber's gaze settled onto May, a syrupy weight. For a full minute he didn't move, as though he had laid down his attention and forgotten where he put it. May shoved her hands beneath her thighs. Dark creases in green velvet.

Finally he stood, sauntered to the hearth, and picked up a blue plastic label maker from the mantel, a little gun with a wheel on it.

"I would like to put an answer to your question, Miss May. You said May?"

He selected letters one by one and punched them into the tape.

"In fact, yes, I will. She's your daughter, and I'm a man who respects property." He rested his elbow on the mantel. "We have seen Miss Daphne."

May shot to her feet—then stopped, squeezed her hands in front of her. "Is she all right, sir?"

"She come to us sickly. But I can rightfully say that we helped her as best as we could."

The drawl thickened in and out. It occurred to me that we were at the kind of depth that could alter your thinking. One martini for every thirty-three feet was the rough math. There was no precedent for the impact of living at this depth for this long. Even more pressing, I needed to watch for the symptoms in us.

He tore the newly created label off the tape roll and dropped it on the coffee table. M A Y.

"Where is she now?" May was adding some sweet twist to her voice.

"That there is the part I don't know what to do with. Because I've got an obligation to our council. I'm a servant and guide, and to them I owe my loyalty."

He moved now behind the sofa across from us and disappeared into the darkest part of the room. It was difficult to untangle—an embossed chair rail, side tables set loose in the middle of the rug, curios jangling as he stepped along the floor, and farther back, clusters of fur—mounted on what, species of what.

"When the lake filled up, we won—in every way, we won. We kept our land. We stayed alive. And the government was too afraid to come after us down here."

He chuckled from somewhere in the depths of the room. "Or that's what I tell people. They think we're dead, right?"

He didn't pause for an answer.

"There's just been one hitch: our water supply hasn't lasted like it should. I've had to limit access, and the people have suffered, the children have suffered. Our mission here, to build up a society that reflects the traditions of this country, has gotten held back all ways because of it. We can't be ready to rise up if we aren't nourished. So you might could understand my answer to your daughter's request to share our water."

At last, he reemerged from the darkness, holding a picture frame. He walked up behind the lamp so that an hourglass of light cast up onto his face.

"Otta," he said. "That's an unusual name. I'm figuring it's short for something."

May's legs trembled beneath her. I tugged at her suit and she sat down.

"Ottilie," I said.

"Well, look at us." He set the frame down on the table, came around and dropped onto the sofa. "Not even knowing who among us we got."

He reached out both hands. I didn't take them.

"What do you want me to say, Mr. Weber?"

"Henry!" He waved me away. He started fiddling with the label maker again, punching in letters. "Especially for you, young lady, with all your family's done for us. How is Eugenia?"

I felt again that jolt in my vision, as though I wasn't where I believed myself to be.

"You know Otta's mother?" May asked.

"Our savior."

His eyes glittered at my discomfort.

"Didn't you know that?"

I exhaled the unevenness from my voice. "I don't think she'd call herself a savior."

"She was always a humble woman."

May's cool hand lay over mine. Weber observed the gesture. He noticed everything—I could see that now: every movement, every twitch of emotion in our faces.

"How do you know her mother?" May asked.

"Your mother"—he addressed his answer to me—"built all of this."

So, at last, it was confirmed—something that I'd known for years but that Eugenia had never admitted out loud. She'd given the stolen money to the factory, and it had funded the infrastructure they needed to live under the lake.

Weber ripped the new label off the tape roll and grabbed the picture frame. He stuck the label to the back and handed me the frame.

It was a photo of my mother—young, with her hair bobbed around her cheeks. She was smiling at someone off camera, one corner of her mouth skewed higher than the other, which was the way—I'd almost forgotten—that she smiled when she really meant it.

I turned the frame over. The new label, stuck to the back: COATES.

A shiver ran through me.

"I see the resemblance—in more ways than one." Weber observed me, his lips curled. "You come here to save that girl, and she's not even yours? You got a hero complex, just like your mother."

"A hero doesn't get two hundred people killed." I remembered where I was. "Almost get them killed."

Weber shrugged. "That was our choice, not hers."

This response caught me off guard—most of all, because it had never once occurred to me. I'd only ever blamed her.

Weber groaned to his feet. He retrieved the first label from the coffee table and ambled over to the fireplace. In the dim light, I could just make out the labels beneath the mounted heads—all names. Coyote: JACK. Hare: JIM. Possum: AVA.

Weber scanned the collectible plates on the mantel—*Gone with the Wind,* a golden goose, Elvis—some labeled, some not. He squinted over his shoulder at us, shook his head, bent into the hearth, and pinned the label to a cross section of firewood, a long, dark scorch running along its base.

He flashed a grin at May. "Suits you."

At his whim, poised to burn.

With a click of his tongue, he crossed the room. "Come on, come on, you'll like this."

From the foyer, I glimpsed beneath the staircase the velvet erasure of a corridor—the same one the pregnant woman must have traversed to bring us our tea. It was too dark to tell how far back it went. Weber disappeared for a moment down the hall and reappeared patting his chest pocket.

He ushered us out the front door.

Light muddled the stoop. Strange that this could seem, even for a moment, bright. The concrete floor pooled out around us, and the towering brick walls of the chamber quivered with the water's dim glow. We followed Weber around the side of the house, with David skittering along behind.

Weber had a strange, pulsing energy for his age, though he must have been at least sixty. His long legs loped in one fluid motion like a spider's. We had to rush to keep up.

As we rounded the side of the house, I saw that an addition had been built onto the back of it—a windowless clapboard annex that converted the house into a T-shape.

And behind it, an expanse of green. It was a garden. It unscrolled behind the house, raised three feet off the floor and contained by concrete blocks. Like the house's interior, it seemed hewn from some other life: ideal and idyllic, with clusters of pink begonias and tendrils of rosemary shaded by saplings. The pregnant woman pushed a small child on a swing set. Mirrors were suspended from the ceiling, angled to redirect light down onto the garden.

But as we climbed the steps, I saw that the begonias were made of fabric, and the grass was plastic. The garden extended some sixty feet until it reached a wall at the far end of the chamber, and in that whole expanse there were only a few living plants: some mint; clutches of wild onion.

When we reached the swing set, the woman lifted the child into Weber's arms. He whispered into her ear, making her giggle.

Weber turned to me.

"If you don't believe about your mother, look at her." He nodded at the woman. "Tell them, tell them your name."

"Genie," the woman said. Her eyes stayed fixed on the child.

"Her parents wanted to honor what your mother did."

He handed the child back to Genie, and we continued along the garden. The chain on the swing started to squeal again.

When we were out of earshot, Weber arched his long frame down to speak to us, his voice hushed.

"She's back to her husband soon—Jack, you met him. But this is what I been telling you about the water. People been having to drink lake, and it's caused issues for the men. I've had to keep a certain ration for myself to maintain my duties, and it happens that I can still produce young. So I've had to take on this obligation."

A wet chill crawled down my spine. The drawn disgust in the corners of Genie's mouth, her nails ripped and flaking—a low hum of danger had been lingering just behind my ear, and now it crackled all around.

As we reached the end of the garden, a door at that side of the room opened up and Jack reappeared, hands locked behind his back. We descended the stairs and Weber patted Jack's shoulder.

"At ease," he laughed.

Jack glistened like a sheet of tin.

We found ourselves inside a room lit with windows on the far wall. It appeared we'd reached the end of the building and were as far from the moon pool as we could get. We were cornered behind layers of sentries, with this man whose control was complete.

It looked like a museum, hung with photographs and tacked-up newspaper clippings. Weber led us along the wall to our left and began a well-worn monologue. The first photos were in black and white: construction and ribbon cuttings and men in stiff suits. He pointed to a bow-tied child. "My grandpa, Charles Weber Sr."

Paintsville had been "perceived and platted and patronized" by the Webers from the start, he said.

"Great men. They built all this from nothing."

In the first color photo, factory workers assembled up a set of concrete steps, each in coveralls with a patch showing the Weber Corporation logo: an eagle with wings curved into a W.

"Those were the golden years. Good, honest men doing good, honest work. A real community, and no one coming in to tell us what to do."

He unrolled a sheet of newspaper so yellowed that it had curled up onto itself.

WEBERS ANNOUNCE AGREEMENT

WITH STATE FOR HISTORIC SALE

"Then they passed a law to make us take the lead out of our paint. My dad just gave in. Said costs were already too high. So he went and sold all our valley land to the government."

He shook his head.

"He had no appreciation for what we'd really built here. An identity. My grandpa showed me that."

He stood before a painting, a portrait of a gray-haired patriarch.

"He'd walk me around the factory, show me how it all worked. My dad could care less. Liked to keep his hands clean."

The next photo showed a crowd assembled at the factory entrance, watching a figure at the top of the stairs shout through a megaphone. Some held signs, others raised their fists. The man with the megaphone was Henry Weber.

"My grandpa would never have let him sell it."

I stole a glance at Weber. He was bleary-eyed—not tears, but like he was gazing at something so far distant that it exhausted his vision.

As he spoke, I'd been turning his story over in my mind. I couldn't make sense of it. I'd always thought my mother gave the money to the People's Council out of pure spite because that movement, like my mother, hated the Webers: their land deals, their inhumanity, their ruthless ambition. I didn't know that a Weber was leading the council.

"Why would my mother help you?"

His pupils contracted; he returned to the room.

"You mean a Weber? Well, she wouldn't, would she?" A smile flicked his lips. "But she supported Anti-Dam. No one in Paintsville wanted the lake, and some Steels folks like her—they joined us. When we lost that battle—well, she started to lose her way." He led us to a corner, where the chronology drew to a close. Sitting on a plinth was a duffel bag, zipped shut and stuffed, with one of Weber's labels below it: E.

"Your mother has a big heart. At one time, she might've even been rather fond of a Weber." He winked. "But I made my choice, and she made hers. I chose the council. She chose a man who sold his land the second they issued the dam permit. But that's what you Coateses do, right? Acre by acre, everything you ever stood for, sold for cash. No offense." He grinned, pointed a long-nailed finger. "In fact, by the time she came down to us with that bag, she was pregnant with you."

A slow maelstrom expanded in the pit of my stomach. I realized now where I'd seen the cursive stamp on the bottom of Weber's teacup. My mother had a favorite cup herself. The design was a blue overlay on white, and it had the same insignia on the bottom, in the shape of a *W*.

"I'll get to the point." Weber stepped up to a framed schematic. It mapped out the air and water supply systems for the factory, with air channeled down via pipes from the surface and water pumped up from an aquifer below. The water pipe emerged through some kind of well off the factory property, then ran along the ground, maybe a mile or so, until it reached the factory wall.

"We were told this would last." He pointed at the aquifer. "Local men whose families known this land for a hundred years got down on the ground with their tuning forks and promised me it would. But you can tell Jeff he was right—that it doesn't last forever. And he can gloat about it all he wants. So long as he turns the water on."

"I don't understand," I said. "What water?"

But Weber had already opened the museum door. Outside, a golf cart was waiting with David and Jack in the front seat.

Weber motioned for us to climb aboard. But I held May back. I smelled the menace on their breaths. The smile dropped off of Weber's face.

"I don't think you do understand. I need to provide for our people. So if she wants to know where her daughter is"—he gestured at May, swatting a gnat—"you'll deliver this message to Jeff Clark. And when the fresh water's running, that's when I'll tell you."

May shot forward and grabbed the collar of his shirt. "You have to tell me you have to please—"

Jack and David leapt out of the vehicle. They grabbed her shoulders and dragged her away from him, even as she clawed the air.

I tried to rip their hands off of her and Jack elbowed me in the face. For a moment, I sat on the floor, stunned. Then I leapt to my feet, struggled to find my balance.

"Stop!" Weber's voice boomed, cascading from wall to wall. The garden's empty swing quivered on its chains.

The men released May. She stood there, her pupils trembling in a way that worried me. We'd been at pressure too long.

"Ladies, I apologize for Jack's poor judgment." Weber whipped a handkerchief from his back pocket.

Jack stood by the golf cart, chin in the air.

"Trade off with Genie," Weber told him. "We need her to clean this up, anyhow." He waved the handkerchief at me. I touched my face and it came back bloody. It was from my nose.

WEBER LOPED OFF and vanished around the side of the house.

Jack, meanwhile, climbed the steps into the garden, spoke to Genie, then took the little girl inside.

Genie heaved to her feet—she must have been eight months along—and came to meet us. She motioned for me to sit on the garden steps and pinched the bridge of my nose until the bleeding stopped. David held out his hand for the handkerchief and escorted us to the golf cart.

Genie climbed into the passenger seat. David drove around the front of the house and pulled up beside Arthur, who was standing against the opposite wall, holding a watering can. A trail of drips led to where he stood, but there wasn't a single plant on that side of the chamber—only an iron door, with three padlocks.

"What are you doing?" David grimaced but didn't wait for an answer. "You can walk back." He hit the gas.

Once we left Weber's chamber, Genie pulled the ponytail out of her hair and tilted her head as though to catch wind in it. We drove back through the long chain of rooms. Every door stayed shut.

David parked the cart at the far end of the battery workshop and we entered the room with the moon pool. David gave an awkward bow, shut the door behind us, and padlocked it from the outside. We were left alone with Genie, who helped us put on our BCDs and flippers. As she tucked the hair back under my hood, she spoke for the first time.

"Does your mother want it back? Is that why you're here?"

"Does she want what back?"

"The money." Genie tightened a strap and stepped back to survey her work.

"Why would she want it back? Weber said she gave it to him."

She expelled a dry laugh. "Henry likes to tell stories."

May was sitting on the edge of the moon pool. She swiped at her eyes. She'd been crying.

"So—she didn't give him the money?"

"Not to him. And not for this." Genie gestured at the shut door. "She just knew that no one made enough money from the eminent domain that they could afford to move. My family didn't make nothing—we were renters. So there was a group—my mama was one—that snuck up to ask Steels Evangelical for help. But they wouldn't. It was a Weber church." For a second, our eyes met. Across so many kinds of distance, we both knew what this meant. "After that, Eugenia—she was secretary to the treasurer of that church—she emptied out their safe. She gave my mama that money to share with whoever wanted to leave—so we could start a new life in Steels or in the city somewhere. She did it to save our lives. But Henry got a hold of it."

Her hands settled on her hips.

"Anyway. That's why my mama named me Eugenia—not for any of the reasons my daddy or Henry think."

It happened in an instant. The image of my mother that had been crystallized in my mind for twenty years shattered into a thousand pieces. The selfishness, the obsessions, the callousness—they crumbled away, and what remained was the outline of a woman, too thin from decades of lost appetite, sick inside her memories, with flickers of suffering that passed across her face like a near-dead bulb trying to revive.

"Do you know where Daphne is?" May whispered.

Genie flushed, crossed her arms over her belly. "That—I can't. I'm sorry. If you want to know what happened—just do what Henry says."

She traversed the room, knocked on the door, and was let through. We heard the padlock fasten again behind her.

I looked at May, her blotched cheeks. "How are you feeling? Any dizziness?"

"You're still bleeding," she said, and wiped under the seal of my mask.

WE'D BEEN AT DEPTH much longer than I'd planned, so our ascent was slow. We made two stops where all we could do was hover and wait out the decompression.

As I looked out into the coils of silt, the feeling crept around my shoulders that I was staring into the eyes of something. My mother's perpetual half presence was like this: a cloud passing over her vision.

I had reflected that distance back to her. I'd done everything I could to leave this place behind—every voice that sneered and haunted at my heels. And all this time, I'd been taking their side against my own mother.

That cloud, I understood now, was never hiding anything: It was the pain. It was everything she'd tried and failed to do—not so different from what I carried now.

We urged toward the surface, foot by foot. For the first time I could remember, I wanted to be there, desperately. She'd been alone for far too long.

WE DUCKED INSIDE the bait shop just as a roil of clouds busted open. May was shivering. I peeled off her wet suit and wrapped a towel around her.

I changed my clothes and, when I picked up my phone, saw that I'd missed three calls from Allie. I called her back.

"Mom's not answering. I'm driving there now."

I PULLED UP the driveway right behind Allie. I left May in the passenger seat, grabbed an umbrella, and together Allie and I navigated the puddles up to the sunporch. We let ourselves in.

The kitchen was empty. The dishes in the built-in rattled as we crossed the front hall.

Allie called out for our mother. No response. We climbed the stairs.

A museum, this place—as though, so long ago, every story had already ended.

We found our mother in bed, breathing shallowly, with the covers thrown off. There was vomit on the floor. Allie fell to her knees and put her hands on Eugenia's cheeks, trying to wake her. Her eyes fluttered open. She mumbled something I couldn't hear.

Allie glanced at me, her face fevered with hope or desperation. I've never known how to tell the difference.

−153 ft.

Once upon a time promised a wedding and the promises that weddings make. Look at Mother's face laced over like a bride's should be, fifteen years old in her hand-me-down dress. Look at Father's lapel with the oxeye daisy picked at the foot of the hill on the way to Paintsville Church.

Look at the house Father built with his own two hands, and also with two dozen migrant workers. Mother picked the same paint color for inside and out: a coltsfoot yellow that to her evoked the earliest light of dawn.

Look at Mother cradling her firstborn, a boy, who will always be her favorite. Father will be jealous of this. He'll beat the boy and she'll blame herself and try to treat him like she doesn't love him. With the other children this is easier to do.

Look at the girls lined up in their hand-sewn Sunday best. The skirts and the boys' pants cover their legs, which is where their father belts them, as though he plans it this way, which Mother is thankful to him for, even if he was born in sin like the rest of us and not a perfect man.

Jim, Judy, Janet, Jake, Julia, Margaret. In the end, they run out of *J* names and the will to pick them. Look at Margaret playing in the yard until she sunburns a troutflesh pink. It peels for weeks. Unpresentable, even in her church clothes.

This is probably the beginning of her downfall—those few Sundays she misses services. She will become the greatest shame on a family whose children will all bring various shames upon it. By the age of thirteen, she'll be drinking in barns with boys. If she could tell her story, she would say that she didn't let them touch her. But the whole town's already got an idea in their heads.

Sure, that's what eventually happened. Sure, it was bound to, wasn't it? Blood is blood. After all, look again at the frayed wedding dress Mother inherited from her mother and couldn't even mend. Not one good seamstress among them, not a dollar for new lace. And wasn't the neckline a bit teasing, like who knows what kind of women they were, this lineage of laundresses, prolific breeders all?

Margaret every evening comes home a little later. The coltsfoot yellow is painted fresh every five years. Margaret makes a mockery of its innocence.

If she could tell her story, there'd be a sick burning cord down her throat that roils and rages at the sight of her father, and at the sight of her mother looking at her father. She would tell you that there's a plan behind all this—that she's been working her way up to the right man, and that she knows the power of her body to get him. She would say that she has, at last, found this man.

He's older but well-off, infatuated with her physically but distracted in his heart—by his all-important activism; by a woman whom he's trying to forget. Margaret doesn't mind this distraction.

Look now at her swollen belly and the contented smile on her face as he finishes his speech, descends the factory steps, and takes her hand. When her father looks at her now, his eyes spit like oil, but he doesn't dare touch her, and she loves this more than she loves anything in the world.

She's convinced Mother and Father to stay. But then the lake starts to rise. Look at her mother weeping in a puddle on the floor, as she has for a week straight. The water outside has risen halfway to the windowsills, and flecks of yellow paint sway in it like the petals of a thousand flowers.

Margaret watches from the stoop as they drive away. And when they're gone, she—all set to wade back to the factory—cannot. She feels how the water inside her belly surrounds the child, and how once the child escapes it, she'll be surrounded again by water a million times its weight, and nothing to see in every direction but these men, these men, and surely there must be something else.

Look how, setting out on a path she has never in her life chosen, she chooses the path she has taken a thousand times. She trudges through the rising water toward higher ground. In her belly, the baby turns like she doesn't want to wait. It is springtime—May—but somehow it begins to snow.

Margaret, swimming now, passes over the field where, thirty years before, Mother picked an oxeye daisy, then climbed the rest of the way to Paintsville Church, where she knew that Father stood in his best suit waiting, and knew that he wouldn't have thought to pick any flowers. Already she had forgiven him this oversight, because what is love but an endless series of forgivenesses, of choosing what to remember and what hurts too much to hold.

Otta

There are a thousand, thousand details: the way the bedding was tucked; the sweat on her brow; the droop on the left side of her mouth; how we said it again and again, *left side,* to the medics, the nurses, the doctors; how the streak of gray in her hair coiled overnight into tight curls. How tangled she spoke in the thick of it; the first words she spoke after waking up; and the words after that, how much slurred sense they made. Then the fall; the ICU; the rest. Yet all of these things that mattered so much—in the end, they don't matter at all.

A thousand branches, all of them bare:

If she hadn't been on dialysis—

If it were a different kind of stroke—

If we could prove a transplant was urgent—

If she had a lighter blanket—

If we turned down the lights—
If we could find a channel playing her soap—
If she could swallow this—
If I could tell her—

SHE SPOKE. Allie heard her first. Our mom raised her voice so we could both hear.

"Ssss—so nice of you to come."

An echo of some deep-ingrained propriety. But I could see tears in her eyes and squeezed her hand and said of course.

We took turns sitting with her through the night and the next morning, adjusting her pillows, feeding her, calling the nurse when she needed changing. Her words came slow, but they came. She spoke mostly in praise of the hospital: how good the food, how comfortable the bed, how diligent the nurses, and how one had a daughter taking the SAT and another had a son who flew planes.

That afternoon, Allie had to go to work. Eugenia and I watched all her favorite daytime shows: dramas of families betraying each other, splitting apart, reconciling. Outside the window, the stain of sunset faded. The few lamps in the parking lot cast out nets of orange light that lent a peculiar grandeur to whatever fell within their scope: a corner of dumpster, a Cavalier with four flat tires, a smattering of moths on their passages elsewhere. I realized suddenly that the television was playing some kind of cop show.

"Turn it off?" I asked.

My mother nodded.

She reached for a magazine and flipped through it.

How many times had I wished for one more moment with Ethan? I had a hundred things to ask him, a hundred things to say. The night before, Allie and I had fallen asleep in the chairs beside her bed, and I dreamed I had the chance. He was floating in front of me, a black hole of water turning around him. But all I could say, over and over, was *Don't Don't Don't Don't Don't.*

For my mother, there was no plan. So what came out of my mouth surprised me.

"I didn't know," I said. "I thought you stole that money for yourself. I didn't know."

She shut the magazine, raised her eyebrows—her right one, anyway. "What, now?"

"I didn't know you were trying to help those people evacuate the valley. To keep them from drowning."

She folded her hands on top of the magazine. One side of her mouth drooped, and I could read her even less than normal.

"I ffff—figured I deserved it," she said. Her eyes glistened. "What you thought—thought of me. What everyone thought. All this time, I believed those people died. I didn't ssss—save them. I made it worse. So what shhh—should I have done different? You can spend your wh—whole life asking."

I took her hands in mine. They were cold, the skin soft and loose. I didn't know the last time I'd held them. "Mom, I'm sorry."

She started coughing and I poured her some water. The cup trembled in her hand.

She set it down, sighed, and settled back into her pillow. For a moment, I thought that was it. Then she reached out—a gesture as clumsy for her as it was for me—and patted my arm.

"Do me a ffff—favor and don't worry about it. Don't hurt yourself anym—more. It don't make anything better, and it makes you worse."

Her hand lay on my wrist for a long time. She drifted into sleep so gently. I like to think I helped her do that.

MY MOTHER DIED of complications from a bleed that arose from complications of a fall on her way to the bathroom, a bleed exacerbated by the blood thinner they'd given her to counteract the stroke, which arose from complications of kidney disease and the dialysis that treated it. The kidney disease we never understood the cause of, as it didn't run in our family. But anecdotally, the number of cases in Steels was disproportionately high. One of the nurses told us that a hospital resident was writing a paper about it, something to do with lead exposure.

Eugenia didn't want a memorial, or a grave, or a gravestone. Her will requested cremation, then to be scattered "along the length and breadth of our land." They gave us the ashes in a twist-tied bag inside a plastic box. We dispersed them in all four corners of the yard: down near the cul-de-sac, up along the edge of the woods behind the house.

Now we stood on the stoop, Allie holding the empty box. Somewhere inside the house, a blanket thrown off the bed and a cup of cold tea.

"Want to go out?" Allie said.

We went to Bud's Diner. When we were little, our mother would take us there on special occasions. We scooted up our stools and ordered two burger combos—our birthday meals.

I ate mine so fast I hardly tasted it. My head was humming, a white noise that numbed everything and fed on feverish motion. I'd signed the forms in a blur, packed her things in a blur, driven us home from the hospital and couldn't now remember the drive. When I looked up, Allie was picking at her fries.

"So what's next?" she said.

"I don't know. Do we need to figure that out now?"

"No." She dipped a fry in ketchup. "I mean, yes, there's a lot to do. I'm leaving."

My breath caught in my throat. "What?"

"I've been deferring it for a year. But I got into a BFA program. Dramatic arts."

She met my eyes. Beneath the drawn pain, she was sparking, expansive.

"Congratulations," I said. That little girl in the tilt, taking a bow from her makeshift stage—I did now what I rarely did then: I hugged her.

“I’ve been saving up for the move,” she said. “The school’s in Vermont.”

I felt a drag at my heart, like all the blood had been sucked out of it. We’d lived apart all of our adult lives. But parting ways a second time felt off—a brick laid wrong.

We had, in our family, learned no language for such feelings. So I mustered the kind of phrase Ethan might have used.

“That’s incredible, Allie. I’m proud of you.”

“Thanks.” Her face relaxed, and now her smile was unrestrained. “It’s far.”

“It’s time you got out of here,” I said. “Leaving was the best choice I ever made.”

It was. I didn’t know what to tell her about the rest—about how to be happy. But I knew this.

“I’ll miss you,” she said.

It churned through my chest, a seasickness of terror or hope, and hope inspires terror, so terror—terror. I wanted to tell her everything, about all my failures, about Ethan, and to see at the end of it that she still loved me. There was never any guarantee, but I was so tired of not trying.

“I’ll miss you too.”

“We said it,” said Allie. She laughed and wiped her eyes, took my hand. I felt the damp between our fingers. “Let’s start there.”

“All right.”

WHERE IS THERE TO GO from here? A hallway crushed to its gills but empty, empty—not because she’s gone, but because it always was. Collections amassed in the hopes that they could, through sheer density, finally collapse into a black hole that shifts the past into the present. Scent of her father’s skin, just in from the fields; tinny music from the television; how that magazine page, fresh off the display, tasted like copper; the warm hum from the mirror when Ottilie stood inside it, pinning her brooch. Whatever our mother had built that was still alive, she could see only squinting. She had lost the thread of her story, and couldn't move forward until she found where she'd left off.

I slept that night on the couch downstairs—woke to a crusted light over all things. They had coalesced into a single beast, hulking and colossal and toothless, not an endless chain of significations but all of them together signifying one thing: Eugenia, the callous and ashamed and unknowable and also kind and too-soft Eugenia, the brokenhearted.

I could rip the beast open, roll inside its jagged pieces because only suffering could pay for what I'd done. This was my instinct. Or, instead of carving from myself one more wreckage for the world to bear—what could I mend?

I opened all the windows to their screens to let the air bite in. A green scent coiled through the house, reunited with the sills and floorboards and rafters, all harvested from the same forest that still breathed outside.

When I left, the curtains waved behind the screens, sending me off or calling me back again. Let it, for a while, be both.

III

May

The body emptied of the ghost is danger. Leave it lie too long and it turns to poison. I remember that sermon. It was a lesson in not dwelling on the before.

Still, I think the older people dwelled a lot. Mrs. Wallace with her yellow mutt; and once, mentioning that they'd had another child up there, a boy. When she told it she was half-drugged on a mixture of blood-of-Him and Peach Warren's medicine. She said his name was Walter; she said he had chestnut eyes. I looked up *chestnut* in the encyclopedia but didn't understand.

It was only certain pasts we shouldn't dwell on. Others we couldn't forget: The reverend sermoned every week about that perfect prespoiled history before the Overlake's decrepitude. Before the outsiders eeled in to steal our land, it was almost another Eden inside the walls of the valley.

I learned it from drawing maps: that walls are about making

something small enough and alone enough to fit inside of your control. When I first left the Chimneys, I discovered that the reverend had no control at all in the Overlake. I chewed at that for a long time. But when I started to dive, he flickered back into sight. Each cottage we visited haunted with a piece of him. When I stole the rebreather, I stole it not so much against Otta but against him—because I could feel what he would say. All my life, with everything I did, I heard him pronouncing judgments—him and everyone in the Chimneys. Their voices followed me around. Far outside those walls, they controlled me still.

AND SO when we rose through that veil of water into the factory, and the stalk-bodies became the bodies of men, and those men recited the decrees of their leader and locked formation around us to restrict our movements, I fell into step with them. My body obeyed quicker than I could stop it.

Then my mind clicked awake. I let my body follow, but my brain paid attention: roved around the rooms, studied their layouts and exits.

When we reached the chamber with Henry Weber's house, it was not so strange to me as it should have been. I saw another reverend's cottage; the room that held it, another Shuttle. But when David told us to go inside, my body fought back. My knees locked and for a moment I couldn't step over the threshold. The menace hummed. The closer any shepherd-of-men lets you get to their skin, the less likely you'll slip away scatheless.

I knew at the sight of that shrine to himself—the corner where he sat, the shelves packed with figurines and idols, mysteries of his legend and holy vision—that this was a game. I took a breath and resolved to play it. Dug something loose from myself and puppeted it around, as though it was his to command.

To read that shrine—for me it was easy. What a mystery is is a story whose telling would drain it of all magic. That's why the reverends—and Weber, I saw him for what he was—leave it a mystery, stoppered and behind glass.

I let him drone into his vanity. I spoke only the question I had to ask.

"Miss May. You said May?"

I knew what he was doing, knew the sticky sweet of his tone. Benevolence always takes more than it gives.

So I gave him what he wanted: desperation. I jumped to my feet when he told us he'd seen her. I trembled at his labeling game. When he meandered into his own sufferings, the quiver in my limbs was more anger than fear. I used it. I let him think me weakly. I kept demure, like I trusted him to guide me, which was the only way he would guide me, even if he was doing it despite himself.

All the while, a new power coursed through me. This man, who thought he knew me enough to hold my name in his hand, knew nothing. I would not let him. I'd learned from watching Otta: how she didn't try to please that woman in the diner; how, instead, she'd left the whole town behind and gone in search of a world only she could imagine. She showed me how to be brave in myself.

In the conversations with Weber, I let the words lilt around me while I observed the room, scanned every surface, under every piece of furniture, searching for signs of Daphne.

The mention of Otta's mother drew me back to attention. It had the scent of truth, and it felt like a mistake to dangle it in front of us, a yarn I could follow to more truths.

So when Weber led Otta into the foyer, I hung back. I crept behind the sofa and picked up the photo. It was Eugenia: recognizable not so much for her features as for the twinkle of defiance in her eye the same as when she'd told me to take the rebreather.

In the far corner, where a door led back behind the stairs and down a hall, I heard the floorboards groan. Now I saw Weber pass into the hallway, snatch a key off a nail, and put it in his shirt pocket. I rushed to where Otta waited in the foyer.

Across the garden, through all the museum, Otta's eyes were flat, her lips a line. I think she believed this to look like no emotion. But I could see a knot spasming in her throat. I stayed close. I listened most of all to the story of the aquifer, memorized the map where his finger traced it. This is what would have interested Daphne. This was the yarn.

I used my silence. I disappeared. I watched Weber's fingers twitch on his knuckles, pick his teeth, fidget at his rings. He was a man who could see most clearly his own aims. So even when he spoke of Daphne again, he spoke to himself, he droned and marveled at his own droning—and I leapt.

I grabbed his collar and started to hit him, to scratch his neck, his arms, his chest, and—just before they dragged me off—snatched the key from his shirt pocket. I balled it in my fist, and when Jack knocked Otta down, I swung and hit him in the jaw before he pinned my arms behind me.

As we rode back to the moon pool I completed in my head a map—not the whole factory, but enough to start. I would try to get Weber what he wanted, because I didn't know all his strengths. But I'd seen where that tray of tea came from—that is to say, the tray of water clean enough for Henry Weber to drink: from down the hallway beneath the stairs and behind a locked door. I had to follow that water.

OTTA AND HER SISTER came out the front door carrying Eugenia between them. I rushed to meet them, tried to cool her sweat with my palms, tried to get in the car with them to the doctor's.

"Stay," Otta said.

When I woke the next day and they were still gone, I called Mr. Clark to pick me up.

As we bumped down the slope-road to the marina, the air was crisp and misted with a new chill.

"We found the factory," I said.

Mr. Clark sucked in his breath. He spat out a laugh—once, sharp. He slammed the steering wheel. "Goddamn."

I let him glow in it a minute.

"Are they doing okay? Is Henry alive?"

He saw it in my face.

"What about Daphne?"

I THOUGHT THAT IT would be hard to say out loud. That the panic would choke me. But I explained what Henry Weber wanted and the trade he'd proposed. Daphne itched through my skin, like the time for her was fleeting. We needed to act.

By the time I finished, Mr. Clark had pulled off onto the side of the road. His hands on the wheel shook.

"I wouldn't have thought that of him," he muttered. "I wouldn't have thought that."

He puffed on his inhaler. He unclipped his tie and put it on the dash.

"Fool," he grunted. "All we worked for, come down to what? Anyway."

He put the truck back into gear and U-turned up the slope. Then he started to explain. Years ago, as they prepared for the Rise, the factory needed to find a new source of fresh water. The valley's water treatment plant was going to be submerged. Even though everyone else was happy to drink lake, Henry Weber had insisted he needed water from somewhere else. That's why a white PVC pipe was installed alongside the two steel air pipes by the water's edge.

"Before the valley filled up, I was trying to convince the city to lay a water line along the shore of the lake. The plan was to hook it up to that PVC pipe," he said. "Then one day, Henry come to me and said he found another solution."

There was a well near the factory that was already drilled down into the aquifer. They'd asked the old lady, Mrs. Reed, whose property it was, if they could draw water from the well and she said yes.

"We capped the PVC pipe, and there's still no city water running along that shore," Mr. Clark said. "But I might know another way."

THREE MORNINGS LATER, I stepped outside into the frost, and there was Otta.

I knew what had happened. She'd called last night and explained it to Mr. Clark. When he told me, I searched the air, smelled and tasted for a difference—if I could feel Eugenia gone out of the world.

I could not.

Same as I could not feel Daphne.

When I reached the end of the dock, Otta's face was pale, splotched, like Daphne when she was a toddler those mornings she woke to the world slow.

I folded around her.

She softened beneath it. The child inside her skin was so different from the child that Daphne had been. I felt it in the thinness of her limbs, the contour of her bones and how her clothes fell around them. I wondered if my own small self was still sealed inside that cave of desire and shame inside my belly. Fog of breath as signal.

Otta took my shoulders and stood us apart, eye to eye. It felt like we'd been a dozen years apart.

"So tell me," she said. "What's the plan?"

I ASKED IF SHE WAS READY, even as the words scraped my throat—because what would I do if she wasn't? I would fall on my knees and beg.

But Otta nodded, took a slim breath, and said, "Let me be useful."

We were on the boat within the hour. Our pockets were zipped up with protein bars wrapped in plastic—Mr. Clark had insisted. "Five days," he'd said. "Five days and I'm calling in the National Guard." We knew it would take that long to bring Daphne up safely outfitted in the extra gear we were taking down. What he didn't say, but that I understood by now, was how many more days it might take to convince the National Guard that he wasn't crazy.

The lake branched out in three directions. To the south, toward the dam, was a whole arm that we hadn't much explored. According to the maps, it was mostly empty, except for some scattered houses. To the east were the marina and the Chimneys, with Paintsville in the middle, and to the west was the arm (utter quiet, even of birdsong) where the factory was. The steep shoreline of that western branch was overgrown with trees and ivy. Fingers of land drew secret coves, folding the route in ways the map didn't show. But as we approached the spot above the factory, I knew it. A disc of still water hovered on the lake's surface, like a massive hull had sunk and left behind an absence.

The water churned in tall spirals that ushered us downward. Soon the silt swept apart and we were in the factory yard.

Otta and me carried an extra tank each, and a rented BCD and wet suit for Daphne. Wherever she was, we'd have to take her up slowly. Our plan was to stop along the way in the empty newspaper plant and the Victorian cottage to decompress.

We passed into the basement, no carpet now to greet us.

Swimming through the dark, I glimpsed movement. My heart buckled. Otta shone her light and caught the whited-out eyes of two people: swimmers, with no masks. They returned our gaze, then went back to collecting scraps of metal from the floor.

The moon pool room was empty. We started removing our gear, and soon the two swimmers broke through the pool, wheezing and tossing their items through the breach. One was a woman. The other was Arthur.

They pulled themselves out. Thin shirts clung to their bodies. The moment Arthur got to his feet and glanced at us, his shoulders hunched up around his neck, a kind of defense.

The woman raised her hand in greeting. Her eyes were two thrumming tunnels through her skin.

"I'm Joan," she said. "You know Arthur."

Arthur kept his distance, dabbing the cut on his jaw with a towel.

"Hi." I introduced us. "We're here for my daughter."

Her coal eyes burned on us. She crossed the room and rapped on the door.

"Henry said you come, we should take you to him." She leant against the doorjamb.

We waited. Not a sound from the other side.

"They forget about us," Joan said. She sounded annoyed, and rattled the door, which we'd seen padlocked from the other side.

"What were you doing down there?" I asked.

Her mouth twitched. She was measuring us, I think, with more interest than she wanted us to know.

"They used that basement for storage," she said. "You can find all sort of things. Arthur's dad once found a whole crate of lead nitrate cans, full sealed. Easy to extract the battery lead from that stuff."

"You can really hold your breath," said Otta.

"Three minutes twenty. But I don't push it."

"Do you ever go outside the basement?"

Joan looked past us at Arthur. I don't know what message passed between them, but when she spoke next, her voice lowered.

"We have," she said.

"How far can you get on three minutes twenty?" I said.

"You'd be surprised." This was Arthur. His voice was gravelly, thick with gunk from his chest. He'd lowered his shoulders, stretched out his neck. He seemed dazed, like the conversation drained a great lot of energy from him.

"Find anything interesting?"

I was pressing. I knew I was.

Joan crossed her arms but seemed again to get some signal from Arthur.

"Sure," she said, "you know where to look."

Arthur cleared his throat. "Can't go too far, though."

Joan nodded. "Gotta follow the rule: not-down, not-up, or the pressure change gets you."

"You don't come back." Arthur tapped one of our tanks with his nail, releasing a dull echo. "But you can do it with them things."

"If you know how," Otta said. She picked up her BCD with the tanks attached, cradling the heavy gear in both arms. I did the same.

Arthur retreated a few steps.

Joan banged her fist on the door. Finally, we heard a key turn.

DAVID WASN'T PREPARED for us this time. He was dressed in coveralls like what the battery men wore. At the sight of us, sweat sprung up on his lip, and he tried to slick the wisps of hair across his scalp.

He didn't say a word to Joan, but pointed at Arthur—"You"—indicating he should climb into the passenger seat of the driving cart.

Otta and I loaded the extra tanks into the back and climbed on, holding more gear on our laps.

David drove fast, whisking us across the factory like to keep us from looking. The battery men were nowhere in sight. Baited hooks, one with a fish caught, drifted inside the window boxes near the cafeteria. In the locker room we saw two men, one on a bench with his head in his hands, the other staring at a wall, stark naked. I'd never seen a man full naked like that, not even Jonas. He was completely hairless, with a drooping belly above his parts.

As we passed into his chamber, Weber came loping around the side of the house. The mirrors outside seemed to be tossing in some current, and the beams of pale light through the windows nodded up and down the walls. It was dizzying. Weber opened his arms, gangling-broad as Him on the altar. Me and Otta exchanged looks. We hoisted our gear and two tanks each onto our backs—the most we could carry, leaving Daphne's extras on the cart.

"How was your trip, good?" Weber said.

He didn't wait for an answer. Instead, he took us each by the shoulder and led us toward the garden. He rambled through pleasantries: complimenting us on our swiftness, our navigation of the lake, our knowledge of diving, "a great skill."

"And Jeff—he was glad to hear we're well, of course?"

"Not glad to hear how you're holding my daughter hostage."

Weber didn't react. I felt his hand grip tighter for a second—that was all. "But we have what you want."

I explained it to him as clear as I was able. There was no way to get a city water line laid on that side of the lake. For starters, Mr. Clark couldn't explain to the city why he needed it. So he had sold his pontoon. They were coming to pick it up next week, but he'd already got the down payment and we'd gone to buy a plastic tank, big as half a room, for the back of his truck. He would fill up the tank, then drive his truck down the path—it was rocky, but he'd done it before—and start channeling water through the PVC pipe that he'd installed decades ago, running down to the factory alongside the air pipes. The water from this tank would supply them for a while, and then we'd have to refill it.

Weber led us along the outside of the garden, giving Genie and Jack up by the swings a wide berth. His hands were still on our shoulders, not friendly so much as a way to control our movements.

"He'll start the water," I said, "when we have Daphne."

Weber stopped and turned to face us.

"Hm." He let it rumble in his chest. "Strange to come to me with demands."

"We need to know she's all right."

He paced a few steps off, sucking his teeth.

"I never figured," he said at last, "that Jeff wouldn't help however he could. This is his legacy, not true? Shame-shame if we should all die off."

Weber clapped his hands. David drove around with the cart and stopped at the museum door. Jack tromped down the garden stairs. Together, they started unloading Daphne's tanks and carrying them into the museum. Then they approached us.

Jack tried to take Otta's BCD, but she held on. The dive light swung and clanked against the tanks where it was hooked to the vest. Jack kneed her in the ribs, and when she still wouldn't let go, he headbutted her. I saw a smile twinge his mouth as he turned away, BCD in hand. I felt a moment of blank, like waiting for my brain to catch up with my body. Then my chest boiled over, and as he came back for more gear, I lunged. He shoved me off, elbowed me in the throat, and I fell to the floor. David and Jack grabbed the last set of equipment—my BCD and tanks, our masks. They set them all inside the museum and locked the door, then stood at attention on either side of it.

"What are you doing?" I gasped at Weber. "Mr. Clark won't start the water until he knows we're safe."

He stared down at me, shadows blotting out his eyes. "Why don't we wait and see?"

Then he turned his back and left us, cast into dust, outside the garden wall.

OTTA'S BREATH, jagged and wet, sucked back inside her chest. Her nose was bleeding again. She looked for a moment like she was going to cry.

"We're trapped. Without our gear . . ."

Arthur trotted around the side of the house, splotched and huffing.

"Are you all right?" When he reached us, he dropped his hands to his knees, trying to catch his breath.

Otta didn't speak. She was rubbing her forehead.

"Yes," I said.

Arthur peered up at David, who waved his hand, sweeping us away.

"You're supposed to come with me," said Arthur.

ARTHUR LED US back the way we came until we reached the passageway with the row of doors. The first one on the left, he opened and motioned we should go inside.

Otta stared at the knob.

"It doesn't lock," he said, swinging the door to show both sides.

There were two mattresses on the floor with yellowed sheets but clean. Between them was a vase with a plastic flower.

"We're not staying here," Otta said, staring Arthur down.

He shrunk away, sinking into the protective huddle of his shoulders.

"I—" Shyness sputtered his words, and the blotches on his face grew even redder. I felt almost bad for him. "I'm sorry about your daughter."

A flood of sick washed through me. "Sorry? For what?"

He shook his head, shook and shook it.

"What happened to Daphne?" I insisted, stepping toward him.

He backed in the direction of the door.

"I was watering the garden the other day," he stammered. "Beautiful, beautiful. With the watering can."

"Please tell me." It was pulsing in my ears. I'd meant to control myself.

"You want to know, you don't want to know, like Joan when her mom went diving and . . ." He reached the doorway and expelled a shaky breath. He straightened up and, for a second, looked me in the face. "I c— I can't say. But you follow the water, it won't steer you wrong."

He pulled an extra blanket from his canvas sack and tossed it on the floor.

"Let me know if you need . . ." His voice trailed down the hall and was gone.

"We're not staying here," Otta repeated. Panic flecked her eyes.

"I know," I said. "But until the night comes, yes."

I STRETCHED OUT on the mattress and picked the flower out of its vase. I'd never seen anything like it: yellow petals spiraled around a cup. I wondered if somewhere in the hundred towns all across the Overlake there were some who drank from flowers, or slept on petal-sewn sheets, or pinned up their altars with so many blooms that they worshipped blooms, all their Hims forgotten.

Otta dragged me up by the armpits. "Let's look around."

We walked in the direction of the moon pool. Every door stayed shut against us now. It was an utter quiet.

We reentered the battery workshop, still empty. Otta rattled the padlock on the moon pool room. At the opposite corner of the workshop, sunlight poured through an open door.

Inside, we found Joan sitting on a bench. She was picking at her toenail with a fork. "Still here, huh?"

No surprise in her voice.

The room had windows facing north. Reading the map in my head, I knew this meant we'd reached the building's farthest other end—the farthest from Weber's museum—with no more rooms beyond.

It seemed like they prepared for their dives here. There was a pile of nets in one corner and towels on a coatrack. The walls were caked with whitewash.

Joan had changed out of her wet clothes. Her hair was drying into curls.

"Done fishing?" I asked. We'd seen in the mansion and grocery how fishers swam out with their bag-nets or spears. When I'd asked an old woman in the mansion why they didn't have window boxes, she'd pinched her lips into a hundred wrinkles, like trying to remember. *Ran out of time to put them in, I think,* she'd said. *We make do.*

Joan shook her head. "Our job is salvage. For catching fish, the cooks just use the window boxes."

"So if you're going in and out," Otta said, "you don't happen to have a key to that padlock?"

Joan smirked. "They don't trust me with that one."

I sat on a bench. I was drowsy still. I counted the towels on the rack. "Are you and Arthur the only divers?"

"Last ones standing." She started to drape her wet clothes on a line along the north wall. In the Chimneys, we hung them along our windows too, but the light here was so meager. I wondered how long they took to dry.

"What happened to the rest?" Otta asked.

For a minute, Joan occupied herself pinning clothes with her back to us.

"Well," she said. "The moist gets in their lungs, they cough too much. Plenty of headaches. Most people just get sick of it."

"You said some of them don't come back."

She froze, shirt dangling from her hand. "Arthur said that."

"Is it true?"

When she turned around, her face had gone to concrete. Not walled against us. More like she'd made a decision. "Sure."

"What do you think happens to them?"

Joan's skin hung loose from her neck. She was bone-thin.

"They go as far as they can. Push past their limits. Not-down, not-up: that's the first rule. Another one is to not dive too many times in one day. But that's what they did, tried to swim to other houses and took it too far. My mom didn't come back. Arthur's dad came back good as dead."

A clot of tiny bubbles rose past the window behind her, catching the light.

"I'm sorry," said Otta.

"We don't pull stunts like that now."

Joan turned back and threw a shirt over the line. Her hand reached out to trace a spot on the wall where a drawing showed faintly through the whitewash.

It was a zigzag, a stairway climbing up. Like the drawing in the newspaper plant.

"What is that?" I asked.

Joan blinked at the wall. She dropped her hand. "Conspiracies. Stories. Divers dream up all sort of things. Go looking for them, get dead or disappeared for it."

"What's this story?"

She shrugged.

"Same as all of them," she said. "A way out."

THE LIGHTS FLICKED ON right after dusk. We laid on our mattresses to wait. I pulled a protein bar from my hip pocket, peeled off the plastic and wrapper, and split it between us. Otta started whispering, mostly to herself, that she wondered how many of them wanted to leave—that we'd have to be careful who we spoke to, but if we could help . . .

I nodded off. The yellow flower slipped into my dream, burning like a bulb.

Otta shook me awake. The velvet of lights-out unraveled through my lashes. Her voice was pitched low, tamping down a panic. "How are we supposed to see?"

I realized then that she couldn't see what I did: the faint shine on the knob, the hallway through the door with its chair rail like a guide. A skill I'd maybe gained growing up in the dim myself. I put her hand on my shoulder. "It's okay. I can take us."

By the little light, I led us along the passageway's glowing whitewash, through the cafeteria's metallic pings, its toe taps of roaches, through the locker room with its dripping shower—the lake, testing its seal.

All the bulbs were off in Weber's chamber, but through the tall windows, the water sheened. The moon was out. Otta released my shoulder.

We crept first behind the house to where a long extra room was tacked onto the back. The key that I'd stolen from Weber, I slipped now from my pocket. But it didn't work in the door. We snuck around front.

I already knew that the front door didn't groan on its hinges. That the foyer swallowed sound instead of echoing it. That I hadn't seen any bedrooms on the first floor, whose doors had all stood open, so we could cross our fingers that Weber and anyone else was asleep upstairs. I'd mapped this all in my head. I only hoped that the key would unlock the front door. But when I tested the handle it opened without help.

The pitch-dark of the foyer challenged even me. Otta took my shoulder again and I felt for the wall. We passed under the coiling stairs and into the hallway where I'd seen Weber grab the key from its nail and where, a few feet farther, there was a door that I believed the key would open.

I felt the knob, the keyhole's grooves. The key slid in smooth, and the door released into a socket of dark. We passed into the room and shut the door behind us.

We couldn't see even our own hands.

Otta patted the wall. She sucked in her breath, and flipped a switch.

Blinding. I shaded my eyes.

At my feet, a chipping linoleum. It was a kitchen. Stiff yellow light.

I'd half expected to find Daphne inside: seated at a table, waiting.

There was no one.

The kitchen had orange counters and wallpaper of brown flowers. It had a metal table and a chair.

"Why does he keep it locked?" Otta asked, opening one cabinet, then the next. Two teacups. A plate.

Lake welled my eyes, and all at once I could barely breathe. I'd failed. And I could feel her all the more distant now, and more urgent, begging me to find her, a whimper to her voice that I had never heard before.

I noticed a dented faucet bowed over the sink. *Gone for water.* I pulled up the handle.

Water trickled out.

As it hit the basin, it rang crashing-loud. I cut it off.

"Waste not."

I spun around. Henry Weber stood in the doorway.

From behind him, David and Jack streamed into the room.

"Like mother, like daughter." Weber whistled through his teeth. "It's a special instinct, is it, Miss May? It sounds exhausting."

The men grabbed our shoulders. The back door opened, and there was Arthur, haloed in the garden's glinting plastic grass. David and Jack shoved us outside. The whole chamber was lit up now with fluorescent bulbs—long tubes like the ones that lined the passageways and the Shuttle, that yellowed and hummed and spat but almost never went out. Their gold light melted down, colossal, ancient. The chamber groaned with the same holy strangeness as the Shuttle, with this time Henry Weber presiding.

Weber marched us past the front of the house as we struggled against the hands on our shoulders, shouted what were hardly words. We approached the opposite wall, where we'd seen the dripping path of Arthur's watering can lead to the iron door that, now, David trotted ahead to unlock. Arthur took David's place at my shoulder, with a softer grip.

Weber observed from a safe distance as David opened one padlock, then the next.

"Silly to think I wouldn't notice my favorite key gone," Weber said.

His voice was cool, but it trembled the room, curdled the light. Two battery men rushed in, sweat on their brows. David opened the third padlock.

"When you steal from us, you steal against a broader mission. There's so much history here we are charged to preserve," Weber said. I could tell how it electrified him, his own voice rattling the air. "For instance, if you can believe it, we're on a hill right now. My grandfather installed this chute to move coal uphill in winter. Steps on one side, train track for the bins on the other. There's a network of caves below, so the chute was half-cut already."

A hill. He must be talking about that slope down into the darkness that we'd spotted swimming around the factory, on the westward side. I had seen no windows anywhere that looked out in that direction.

The battery men took hold of the door handle, a vertical iron bar. David removed the padlocks.

"Recall those years of winter, the cringing snow in your eyebrows, piling up in your collar, filling your shoes." Weber blinked with wet distance. "One year, my great-uncle slipped on the ice and cracked his head open. After that he couldn't tell dreams from life."

His gaze wandered among the bulbs.

"Now look at this paradise." He lifted his arms, then—seeming to remember us—dropped them to his sides. "I told myself I wouldn't make it a funeral. But here I go pontificating. Habit."

He smiled. He waved his hand. David and the two men leaned back against the handle, pulling with all their weight.

There was a great release of air, and now they were dragging against a powerful suction that was pulling the door to shut again.

Jack and Arthur started pushing us toward it. Otta's eyes surged with panic, and it shot down my limbs. We fought back. Arthur was stronger than I'd imagined and closed around me like a spider. I struggled to escape, but he kept moving me forward, step by step. I bit into his arm, but he didn't pull away; I tasted blood, and still he didn't. Jack wrapped his arm around Otta's neck and started to drag her.

The mouth of the door was a few feet wide now. Henry Weber watched it all from one side, looking even a little mournful. And then it clicked in my mind, what he'd said: *like daughter.*

Locked in Arthur's grip, I peered over my shoulder and spoke to him:

"You did this to Daphne?"

He grunted. I met his eyes and they flared sorrow and yes.

I stopped resisting. The next moment, Arthur shoved me into the pit.

Otta

The utter dark; the seafloor.

The grind of sand beneath my palms, roar of the drill in my skull. I'd never left—and he was still out in the crush, waiting.

In the pitch, I glimpsed that fish from my dreams. She was Ethan searching for shelter. She was my mother, this time asking me to follow. Maybe she was always asking, if I had listened. Depth of the sea, pit of my throat: passing all into the unanswerable.

I swept my arm against the silt. Is love a container.

My fist shut around only air.

Blood thumped in my ears. My mind was returning.

Jack had locked his arm around my throat. I sucked through one needle of breath before he tightened his grip. I tried to kick, elbow, drag, but the lack of air, so quiet about itself, expanded like water through cloth.

When I saw May pass through the breach, I went limp. It was a decision my body made, in my mind's absence. Just before they shut the door behind us, I heard a clatter, like an object thrown in after us, and then I felt the seal in my ears. I didn't even hear the locks snap shut again on the other side.

We were for a long moment frozen in darkness. The only sound was our own breaths—first heaving, then slowing toward an even pace.

I heard, like a leaf falling, May's hand pass along the floor and find mine. I was still clutching air.

"You okay?" she said.

"Yes."

She started to stand. I was blind, and let her lead.

We traced the door with our hands. There was no handle, no way to grip where it laid flush inside the wall. When we slammed our fists against it, the thuds returned dull, mute. I put my ear against the iron. We might as well have been on the moon.

We felt around all sides and found ourselves to be in a narrow space, no more than eight feet wide, like a tunnel. Just as Weber had described it, I felt two rods of cold steel, railroad tracks, sloping down from one side. On the other side, running along them, was a stairway. We stood at the wall and, with my hand on May's shoulder, started to descend the stairs.

I tripped on something. It went knocking down some steps, struck a rail, and stopped.

I had been locked into a pitch-dark panic since I woke in the factory—a seafloor haunting. It was hard even to bend my limbs. But now, oddly, one image floated to the surface: that flick of pride in May's eye when she told me how she'd stolen the key. It seemed to surprise even her—her own strength.

"Wait here," I said.

I got down on my hands and knees and felt around on the floor until I found it. It was cold to the touch, a familiar heft. I pushed the switch.

The beam splashed down the coal chute.

My dive light. It had been hooked to my BCD when they shut it in the museum.

"How is this here?" I said. The surreality was magnified by the dark or depths or both. I felt dizzy. Narcosis testing my edges.

May studied the dive light, tilted her head.

"Arthur threw it in," she said.

I blinked, trying to clear my head. The delirium, maybe, was stalking around her too.

"Arthur? How do you know?"

"They sent Daphne down here too. He told me." I searched her face, but she seemed lucid. "With the watering can and the trail of water—I think he was trying to show us."

I shined the light around us, illuminating a concrete chute sloping down inside the body of the hill.

"Is it safe to go deeper?" May squinted down the throat of it.

"The air pressure shouldn't change as we descend—not like water. Where things could go wrong is if we actually made it back through this door."

The coal chute had to be at a higher pressure than the factory—hence the heavy tow of air that had dragged us in and sealed the door behind, the pop in my ears when it shut.

"We'd get sick?"

I nodded. It wouldn't be safe to stay here for any length of time, then try to return to the factory. The pressure difference might trigger the bends. If the factory residents understood this—and they seemed to: *not-down, not-up,* Joan had said—it was possible that they'd never been down here themselves. And that they had no intention of letting us out.

When May spoke again, it was faint, like her voice was traversing a great distance. "Arthur said some people don't come back. He said, *I'm sorry.*"

She propped herself against the wall. The condensation dripped down her fingers. If Daphne had been locked down here—

I squeezed her shoulder.

"We don't know what he meant." Reassurance by reflex. I wasn't sure I believed it.

She squeezed her eyes shut briefly. She wiped her hand on her shirt.

"We have to find out," she said.

I led the way down the slope, dive light cast out ahead. Every step forward, every foot of ground the beam illuminated, I felt a leap in my throat. The question dilated, multiplied, smothered, but neither of us spoke it: how few ways such a trail can end.

DESCENDING ALONG THE COAL CHUTE was careful work. The floor was slick with moss, and our neoprene dive socks could hardly grip it. We stuck to the stairs, keeping one hand on the wall.

The ground was scattered with refuse. It appeared to have been thrown in from the factory before sliding various distances down the ramp. There were sopping books; a wreckage of rusted machine parts. Several chunks of whitewash were so thick they'd pulled off bits of concrete wall with them. These were drawn over with graffiti, which someone had tried to paint over, making it impossible to read.

"We have a chute in the Chimneys," May whispered over my shoulder, her voice cracking. "It does the same—traps you under pressure. It's for trash, and the dead."

The dead. The shudder traveled through us both. We didn't know how long ago Daphne had been locked down here. It could have been only days—but she'd been missing more than four weeks. As we descended, I searched the air for a scent. Every pool of floor illuminated was a gasp—a relief. All we found was more refuse, which seemed to accumulate around a particular category: words and tools (there was even—I dropped to my knees—a broken mouthpiece for scuba, no tank or hose to accompany it) that needed censoring.

After fifty yards of descent, the walls began to take on a more organic form, like a cave. Soon we reached a landing where the slope leveled out and met a door. When this was a coal chute, the door must have led outside, to the foot of the hill Weber had described. It was bricked over now.

To our right, the chute intersected, as if by accident, with a narrow cave. Stalactites dripped from the ceiling. The floor glittered with slick. We slipped through a hip-wide channel of rock, stepping over a cave cricket's motionless hull, legs like tent poles.

Then a massive cavern opened up before us. I cast up the flashlight's beam. It was at least three stories tall and round like a dome.

"Hello," May called.

The sound bounced around the cavern, rattling the pebbles beneath our feet. She cupped her hands over her mouth and we waited for the echo to dissipate. In a puddle at my feet, a cluster of milky fish wriggled around the husk of an insect.

I shined my dive light ahead. The puddle was, in fact, the edge of a pool that spanned about eighty feet across, filling the center of the chamber. It sat still as a pupil, swallowing up the beam of light, returning nothing. The only sound was the occasional drip, plinking as it hit the water.

"Maybe she's not here," May whispered.

It was far too dark to see the cavern's full expanse. I didn't bring up the other option, wafting like a hole in my heart: that Daphne could be here in the cave with us—not answering.

I led the way clockwise along the cavern's edge, casting the dive light around. Soon, the pool met the wall and blocked our path. We started counterclockwise, searching between the boulders and piles of rubble for exits. If Daphne really wasn't here, there must be a shaft or a passage out. Crevices gnashed away into the dark: a snake-wide crawl space through a heap of stones; a hole big enough for a person, but too high to reach. We could find no way out, nor any sign of human activity.

On the far side of the cavern, we reached a spot where, again, the pool met the wall. It lapped ever so slightly against the stone.

"No sign of her." May's voice was thin as paper.

"We're not finished." I dipped my toe into the pool. Ice. Wading across this edge of the pool along the wall would complete our picture of the cavern—and maybe somehow yield a clue. "Stay close."

I looped the dive light strap over my wrist and waded in. The cold seized my ankles, my calves, my thighs. I felt the jelly-slip of mold—salamanders—what—beneath my feet. May followed. I kept hold of the cavern wall and cast the light across the pool's brittle expanse.

May yelped. She took a few staggering steps.

"Shine it there," she said, took my hand and pointed the dive light at the wall between us. Drawn just above the lip of water, in white chalk, was a stairway.

It was the same pattern we'd seen at the newspaper plant and on the factory wall with Joan. But this rendering had a new detail. At the foot of the stairs was a circle—drawn over and over in heavy chalk—and, extending from its center, an arrow pointing straight down.

May swallowed, and I saw in her face a new kind of terror.

"Into the mantle?" she said.

Then her eyes lilted, and she dropped into the pool.

I DRAGGED HER UP, water spouting from her mouth, the beam of the dive light swaying wildly where it dangled from my wrist. She gasped: "No, I just—no, I just—," got her feet back under her, leaned against the wall as the water tilted around our waists.

"Are you okay?" My voice was strange to me, pitched high and threaded.

"Yes." She caught her breath, held on to my wrist. "I got—I don't know—dizzy."

We were deeper than ever. We were both guaranteed to get narced. The impending panic (which I was shoving with all my might into the surrounding darkness) would only make it worse.

"This is a trick," said May at last, "a trap. Daphne couldn't have gone to the mantle. She wouldn't."

She was shivering. I had to calm her.

"You good to move now?"

She nodded.

"Let's get on dry land."

We'd made it more than halfway across where the pool met the wall. We started wading forward again. The water rose above our waists. May's fingers dug into my shoulder.

I heard a splash; my heart leapt. I spun the beam of the flashlight out toward the water. A ripple spread and settled—another drop of condensation from above. But as the water stilled, the light caught something shining, small, reflective, submerged at the center of the pool.

I passed the beam back and forth. It wasn't a fish, didn't dart away, and it tossed the light back so brightly I thought it must be glass—something made by human hands.

I turned to May.

"I need you to wait here."

"Don't," she rasped. Her irises twitched.

"I'll be thirty seconds." I planted her hand on a shelf of rock. "I promise. Count."

She nodded. I tightened the strap on the dive light and dove.

The silt stung my open eyes, but as I surged forward, the cold felt bright, cleared the fog from my mind. I shined the light ahead. The bottom of the pool sank away beneath me, until at last a pit opened, a hole with no bottom to it.

I swam to the far side of the pit, where, on a mound of broken stalactites, a shining palm-sized disc was wedged between two rocks. My hair coiled around me and I pointed the dive light down, its beam fogged with floating bits of plant matter and sand. With my other hand, I gripped the disc—not sharp, no bite—and tugged it free.

It was a mirror on a keychain. I turned it over. The image had been scratched away, but I recognized the lettering along the top. The Grand Canyon.

I GASPED THROUGH THE POOL'S SURFACE. Water crawled down my nape, crept under the neoprene of my wet suit.

May pulled me to my feet.

"Twenty-nine seconds," she said. Relief quivered through her.

I held out the mirror, but before I could catch my breath, she snatched it away. She held it up in the light. She clutched it to her chest.

"Daphne"—her voice cracked—"she was here."

The flash of recognition in her eyes, the sudden swell of hope—I didn't understand.

"That's—" I coughed out some water. "You've seen that before?"

She nodded. "I gave it to Daphne."

I wiped the blear from my eyes as she turned it over in her palm.

It was unmistakable: the Grand Hope that our father would come home so we could be at last a happy family, a hope tossed away so long ago, swallowed up by the depths—now, somehow, returned. Reborn into another life. And shining just as brightly as when he placed it in my hand.

May

How we decided was there was nothing to decide. How we knew where to go was there was nowhere else. Whether a mantle really boiled beneath our feet—the swallowing punishment at the end of life—I didn't know. My belief was not a practice but a haunting. For Daphne, I would face that phantom.

Otta dove over and over into the void—looking for what, neither of us knew. I waited at the edge of the pool, dripping on the stone.

Otta took the dive light with her, so when I was alone, the cave blanked into darkness. It froze—listened. Then it stirred awake: chirrups and small shifts along the floor; sudden flutters of air. Time spilled out an unraveling thread, and no matter how I tried to count the seconds, I lost track. I wondered had Daphne stood in this spot, scrubbing at her blindness like it might come off. I wondered was I in the mantle already, not-living not-dying for the sins I'd done.

Each dive was no more than three minutes—Otta promised, and

I counted as best I could. But the fourth time unspooled into an eternity. The crickets started to gather, hundreds of them, their flecked wings glowing, and when they rubbed them together the song was Daphne's name. They climbed onto each other's backs, they built up tall as a person, they took her shape. She reached out.

Then the dive light's beam—from the pool's pit, a warbling strand. The shape collapsed into nothing.

Otta coughed and treaded water. She swam over and climbed out of the pool, sloughing lake. "I figured it out."

Her chest heaved, her eyes electric and wide open.

"Junk, trash, barrels. Braids of rope. Arranged. Like on purpose. Laid out in a line."

I wondered if I was still inside my hallucination. "What do you mean?"

"I found a trail," she said, panting. "Followed it. There's a house. Three minutes' swim. Moon pool. Air inside. And it's a small elevation gain."

Still I wasn't understanding. "Was Daphne there?"

Otta shook her head. "But she might be in the next house. I think there are more. Stops along the ascent. Decompression stops. It's a stairway."

I DOVE, and the world turned ink. The only air was the breath I held inside me.

Five times, we'd practiced it. Me holding my breath for as long as I could count and kicking hard.

Now I followed the beam of light that Otta shone ahead. We kicked straight down through the pit's mouth. A ragged throat of rock, pale creatures darting into hiding, and still we kicked, down, down, until at last we met earth—and then opening out ahead, a sand-path glittering: a tunnel.

We seethed forward along the bottom of the world.

We passed through an archway. We came out the cave. Not the mantle—release. Moon sputtered down.

My lungs burned. I followed Otta away from the west side of the factory, a brick wall of few windows, toward a metal rod with a cloth flagging off. Then I saw the trail: rusted metal pipes laid end to end, the frame of a window broken into bits, a trophy. After that, a television, a radio, a saw, a clear plastic box swimming with nails. These were laid along a slow ascent, just far enough apart that, in the dim and silt, you couldn't see the next object until you were hovering over the last. Each time, I felt a flash of panic, the slivers of remaining air about to burst from my lips—and then there it was: the next signpost.

My lungs boiled, flames and flecks of terror. They started to spasm against my ribs. As we climbed, the air expanded in my chest. I focused on the dive light's beam ahead—candle down a passageway.

The light paused, hovered.

Then I felt a hand catch my wrist and drag me up, and all at once I was gasping air. Water poured down my face. I pulled myself over the edge of the pool. For a minute, I lay heaving breaths and, thread returning to its spool, my mind cleared. Runnels of water trailed off my skin, like after a sermon, how its spell drains away.

Moonlight prickled the ceiling.

We were inside a cottage. Empty, but for one chair. The walls and baseboards and ceiling were all painted the same pale yellow. It was like being born into sunshine.

I rested inside it. I let it warm me. I would move sunward. All the rest of my days.

A SINGLE PEARL tells one kind of story. It tells about the soft meat of the mussel that made it; and before that, the years of irritation; and before that, the grain of sand; the stone that the sand flaked from; the beast that died and wasted down to stone; the body of the mother of that beast; and the body of the mother of that one; and on back in a chain without end, until at last the beginning of the world.

A string of pearls tells a different story, one that's threaded by human beings, and we don't make the same kind of sense as the earth. At the root of it all is a fear of the dark, which makes us do horrible things—and beautiful things also. Also beautiful.

What came next for Otta and me was a string of pearls: one cottage after the next. None of them were places we had visited before. All of them were empty of people. This one was full up with almanacs ending at the year 1979, that one with so many posters and models of trucks that somehow the air smelled like gasoline. Each was its own world, complete, and if you erased for a minute everything outside its walls, you could see the sense in it.

We understood now, from the compass on Otta's watch, that we were heading south, into the third arm of the lake toward the dam. We swam hard and shoved into the delirium, what Otta had tried so hard to avoid—the strange skips in our hearts, the kicking too fast, the blots of dark from the corners of our eyes crawling in. But the swims were almost always less than two minutes, and I began to see what this feeling was: not so much suffocation as it was fear. I learned to press it down, remembered my training from Otta—how to keep calm, even in the face of drowning.

Between swims, we stayed several hours in each cottage. With how deep the cave beneath the factory had been, according to Otta's dive watch, the plan was that we should take three days to make our way back to the surface. Any faster was too dangerous.

In one cottage, the walls had been pasted over with the pages from a book. They were reordered with drawn arrows, and also the words and sentences revised, and exclamation points and circles in red crayon, and finally three arrows drawn over and over again for emphasis, pointing straight down. In another, a collection of dolls lined every wall, blue eyes all, round and wide and baubled with lashes and their faces watchful on our rest.

Otta and I took turns sleeping. But she needed it more. She seemed absent-minded, chuckled at odd things. Or she might be timing our stop, then forget what she was timing. So after the fourth cottage, I let her be the one to sleep.

I spent this time seeking signs of Daphne. In the first and second house, none. But then, in the chaos of the house of pages, I found a message scrawled in a different hand.

Did you find it?

My heart skipped. The text was wobbly, uncomfortable with its own largeness. But I'd taught her to write myself, before she even went to school, and I made the *D* special, copied off an ancient page—handwritten all in reverse, like in a mirror—from the *Renaissance* book where I'd found her name.

The more cottages we visited, the more signs I saw of her. She had left them everywhere. If there were pens, she wrote on paper. If crayons, she scrawled on the wall. If knives, she carved it in the floor.

Mom, are you coming?

X

This marks the path out

D

This marks the path back

X

J + A said when you think it will never end, you are near the end

D. C.

The last one was a name only I called her, only when we were alone, though she never knew why: Daphne Clark. In honor of who kept her safe, like a father should.

I could feel her humming in the walls; I could taste her breath on the air. She was closer than she had been in weeks, what felt like a lifetime gone. And all this time of unknowing—now that she was close, I felt it shuddering through my skin, a surging excitement and also dread, that the next cottage could take those million branching paths and shut the door to all of them, save one.

−165 ft.

Once upon a time laid plans for a future so brilliant could replace even sunshine. But that was a fantasy.

The water rose, and the light filtering down through the lake was dim and sickly. The panic seized me. I could barely pull my breath around my heart. I woke up gasping from dreams, sure that the HVAC had given out. Jeff Clark had warned us how, once we let the lake rise, the pressure would make it impossible to leave. He'd laid out the mechanics to anyone that would listen: how even a short ascent too fast could kill a person. This played out now a hundred different ways in my nightmares. I did my best to hide it all from Arthur. I couldn't let my son catch on what I'd gotten us into: how his mother was right not to stay; how trapped we were.

I was supposed to work battery assembly, but even the walls of that huge chamber felt suffocating. So one day, I volunteered to dive the basement to search for supplies. The moment I slipped into the water was a release, like my lungs was in a box and the box opened.

Over time, I collected dozens of cans of lead oxide for making batteries, thousands of nails and screws and bolts. I got good at it, finding my way with a flashlight sealed inside a plastic bag.

I started to test the distance I could go on a breath. I swam out to salvage windshields and broken mirrors, tilted them to direct light at our windows. This eased the gloom. I pushed farther each dive, until one day I reached all the way to the fence. From there, I could just make out the log house we'd outfitted for Mrs. Reed as a trade for pulling from her water well. I'd helped cut the moon pool for her.

There was only four of us that dove: me, two other fellas, and one of their wives, Ava. Me and Ava was the best by far. I got to where I could hold my breath for four minutes, but Ava could do almost six, then pop up through the moon pool not even heaving in her chest.

I got it in my head one day that I should go check on Mrs. Reed. If I was being honest, I had another question stewing. Wondering how far we could go, really. How, if we wanted to leave, could we get out alive?

I knew I shouldn't. I had a son to take care of. Arthur was always a quiet kid, but after his mother left, he got even quieter, spoke only to me and to Ava's daughter, Joan. He needed me.

But it tugged at my mind—begged, whispered, promised.

So one morning, I did the dive.

I swum faster than I'd ever done and reached the log cabin right when my lungs was about to burst. I come up through the moon pool dizzy. I grabbed the edge of the floor and turned around.

And come face-to-face with her. Wide-open eyes.

I never described it to no one and I won't now. Only to say I think she died peaceful, probably of old age, not long before I come.

I had to float there, water at my neck, until I had the breath to leave.

What I saw in that house—it replaced the dreams of drowning.

The new dreams were worse: that we didn't drown. That things stayed exactly like they was, and we all died of old age. Like that.

Paintsville was uphill with a few moon pool houses, but I knew the closest one was too far to reach. To the south, though, in the direction of where the dam was now, was a slow-sloping road with a string of brick farmhouses. I'd drove that slope a thousand times. It could make for a steady climb.

I turned it over in my head for months. We'd hooked up air pipes to some of those farmhouses. A lot of them had cellars with access from the outside, and we'd used the opening for the interior staircase into the cellar as a built-in moon pool. For the ones without cellars but with two stories, air might be squeezed and trapped on the second floor.

The two men who dived with us wouldn't do it. They knew if anyone found out, we'd be in deep shit. Anyway, they weren't good enough swimmers, and Ava's husband was getting joint problems and headaches like so many other people in the factory. But me and Ava started swimming farther out, to the closest houses we knew, being careful to keep half a lungful of breath for the return trip. We took note of the ones that wasn't flooded and left trash from the basement as markers for the way there. Piece by piece, we started laying a trail. *Not-down, not-up*—or up slowly: that was our version of the rule. And the farther we got, the more the surface felt within our reach.

Ava, when she swum like that, it wiped her out. We tried to keep the up-down to a minimum, but really, there was no way for us to know what was too much. After a twenty-dive day Ava could forget her own daughter's name. We all told her to stop pushing her breath the way she did, but she wouldn't stop.

Some nights they invited me and Arthur for dinner. We'd shut the door, and Ava would feed us all on steamed bass. In whispers, we would fantasize about what we'd eat when we got out: steak with A.1. Sauce, green beans stewed with bacon. Arthur and Joan were too young to remember that stuff.

One day, me and Ava was bobbing in the moon pool of the old Victorian house on Maple Road. The three old maids, who we'd come to check on, were gone—just an eight-track player in the corner, three pairs of shoes on the hearth. We'd found no sign of their bodies, no hint to how they left. And Ava said, out of the blue, "I'm fed up."

I asked what she meant.

She shook her head, shook her head, like there was water in her ears. I could tell there was something off, the dives twisting her thinking. She said: "If them old ladies can do it, so can I."

Then, before I knew it, she was gone. By the time I made it out of the cellar, there was no sign of her. I dove from house to house to house, searching, and did it all too quick. I went up and down, not paying attention to my depths. I was in a panic. All truth, I was a little stuck on Ava. I needed her to be all right.

After a while, my head started thumping and my skin itched. I had to get back home. So my last swim, I made it all the way from the newspaper plant to the factory wall. Seven and a half minutes before I lost count. I remember the basement door, black clouds closing in around it. Arthur dove out himself to collect me. I learned that later.

Anyway, after that, there's not much else to tell. So stiff in my joints I can't walk, much less swim. At least I sleep better with my hearing this bad. I only wake up when Ava throws the door open, drops onto the stool beside my bed, and, picking at her teeth with the rib of a bass, raises her eyebrow like I'm an old man.

"I made it," she says. "What you waiting for?"

Otta

A mystery is a lie of attraction. You see in it a grand revelation of your own story. You miss the other stories it tells.

As we waited out our decompressions—at least two hours in each house—sometimes I nodded into a crushing dream, where I lived out the rest of my life as one version of myself: the thief's daughter in Steels, the impostor at college, the washed-out diving instructor, the drunk at the bar, Ethan's friend, my mother's child, the killer, killer, killer all alone on the ocean floor.

Then water started to crack the walls, and my mother's voice leapt out of the collapse, a memory from every Sunday morning of my childhood: *Wake up.* I startled upright.

Now, half-narced in the dim light, I felt them crowding: what Allie had called contradictory, simultaneous truths. I didn't want to become what each of these sunken houses was: a snapshot, paralyzed inside its frame. It's what happened to my mother.

So every time May said my name, I rose to my feet. I cleared the sleep from my eyes. I took stock of where I'd laid my dive light, always pointed along the forward trail. And just before I slid back into the water, I took one last breath of that particular air. As we swam I pushed the bubbles out of my nose at a steady rate, expelled everything about that place that claimed it was the only possible world. And on to the next.

OVER THE COURSE of the first night and into the next morning, we passed through four structures. With each one, we only gained a small elevation. It really was a stairway, laid out in the only way that could keep us alive: on a gradual ascent.

We followed as best we could the decompression tables I'd studied in my commercial diving courses. After more than a day at depth, we were fully saturated, with helium and nitrogen having fully dissolved into our bloodstreams and tissues. Coming up too quickly would cause them to surge with bubbles—like a fizzing Coke, I told May—and block our blood vessels, tear our muscles, choke our lungs.

The first houses were hooked up to air pipes, and inside kept an even pressure. By now we'd practiced plenty: keeping our hearts steady, blowing out air as we swam to keep it from popping our lungs, modeled after an old navy technique for escaping submarines called the "blow and go" that Ethan had told me about.

But as the sunrise trickled down and we swam toward the fifth structure, I saw there were no pipes running to it. A terror melted through my chest. We had fifteen seconds before we needed to turn back. But the stairway hadn't yet led us astray. I made the choice. We swam down into the cellar, and at the top of the stairs found the living room flooded halfway up the walls with air trapped against the ceiling. We burst through the surface, both of us wheezing.

It followed the same principle as any open-bottom diving bell or upside-down glass: when pressed into the water, it retains air because that air has nowhere else to go. We floated there more than two hours before moving on.

The entire rest of the day and into the night, we stair-stepped through almost a dozen houses, most of them in a similar state. We had to decompress bobbing in the slush of shredded carpet, coffee grounds, curls of wallpaper, the black mold throttling our airways and planting its spores in our hair and lungs. Sometimes I glimpsed tears in May's eyes at the thought—the hope—that Daphne had done the same. That night, we found five hours of sleep in a damp attic, wisps of insulation tickling our hair, a disassembled plastic Christmas tree stuffed into the corner.

The next afternoon, we reached a structure from which there was no clear path forward. We emerged through the moon pool to find ourselves in a large, dry space with a corrugated metal roof, a loft, and one end of it converted into a kitchen and living room. According to my watch, we were at about twenty-two feet of depth—still many hours away from safe decompression, the slowest part being the closest to the surface.

I could tell that the place had been built for underwater living—if maybe never used. There was sealant on all the seams, steel-beam reinforcement, and flashing around the windows. Crates were stacked along the walls and spilled over with machine parts and rope.

"I'm guessing they converted this from a barn," I said.

A row of stalls at the far end retained the stale scent of manure and mash, and were outfitted with long metal stock tanks standing at thigh height.

May leaned over one of these and wrinkled her nose.

"What were they doing with this?"

"They'd fill it with drinking water. It's for livestock."

"Hm. We use them for breeding minnows."

Night fell. We split a protein bar, our second to last. I curled up inside a blanket on the floor, and sleep thudded down in an instant. I woke to a meek light puckering through a window.

With May still fast asleep in an armchair, I pulled my neoprene up over my now-dry swimsuit. When I dropped through the pool into the barn's root cellar, the cold water shocked my legs stiff. Dozens of jars floated around me, pallid globes of preserves suspended inside them.

I dove again and again, swimming out each time in a different direction, searching for where the trail picked up. But the lake floor was barren. No railroad spikes or broken-down bicycles or birdcages. Other than the trail we'd followed to get here, it may as well have been raked clean.

When I resurfaced through the moon pool after my seventh dive, the sun was starting to tilt across the barn. May was awake and watching from the armchair, her chest red and mottled beneath her half-zipped suit.

"You need to let me try," she said.

At first I refused. I was the stronger swimmer, and even after a full night's sleep, dark circles pitted her eyes.

"I'll find the trail," she insisted. "I know I will."

My heart was giving odd skips. If this was the end of the path—if Daphne had swum too far out, searching—I couldn't complete the thought.

"You can lead," I told May, "but I'm going with you."

May pulled on her hood.

As she swam ahead of me, her legs pinched together, swaying from side to side like a fish's tail. This method had come naturally to her from the start. It propelled her so quickly, it was hard for me to keep pace.

She started off in one direction, where a beam of pale light filtered down. After fifteen seconds searching the lake bed and no sign of a trail, she turned sharply, then another fifteen seconds, and again, again. I needed to catch up to her now; it was time to go back. Each movement she made seemed decisive, but there was no reason behind it. Exhaustion was driving her; desperation. Blood thumped in my ears.

I caught hold of her wrist. She looked up.

In the corners of our eyes, a glint. We both caught it, and turned to look.

It was a fishhook, bobbing on a nylon yellow cord that trailed away along the lake floor.

May reached out and tugged the hook. Our eyes met. The silt turned around her body like silk, a coil of regalia.

The hook tugged back.

May shot off swimming along the cord, and I after her. It carved a long, slow arc through the water. May was kicking up billows of sediment, and I lost sight of her. I kept along the line, but my vision was spotting. We'd been out too long—my mind was starting to blur. Just ahead, a shape rose out of the lake bed, a two-story concrete structure with an open door on the lower level. I swam through the door and up the staircase, and the lake at last slipped down my cheeks. I gasped for air, clutched for a handhold, choked out the water in my lungs. My vision prickled back. Light poured in from all sides.

May was standing above me, soaked through and wheezing, her arms wrapped around her daughter.

Daphne

I ached my time away from home—every second of it, from the moment I wedged open that chute. Mrs. Wallace used it to send our dead to the core of the Earth. I hoped, since I wasn't dead, I wouldn't go that far.

I felt I had a responsibility on myself. I knew, through what my mother told me, something that no one else did: that there were caves below us, and underneath those, an aquifer full of the same clean water I'd been drinking from the waterskin all my life—what had kept me healthy. I felt guilty for that. All those children dead, the reverend dead, and me still living.

I didn't have a plan. How could I? I had to believe that when I saw the aquifer myself, I would understand how to bring some water home. The reverend spoke a lot about blind faith, and what was more blind than the tunnels of the earth?

So I took the only way down I knew. I propped open the chute with a trash can lid and started to climb through, but the suck of air was so strong it dragged me downward and my foot slipped. I heard the door slam above me, and then I was sliding into forever, into the core and before my time.

I hit my head, I think. I woke to a sliver of blue light. I wiped a crust from my eyes just as that light snaked away into the dark.

My school sack was twisted around my arm. Inside it: seven strips of trout jerky in a glass jar, miraculously intact; a lighter gifted to me by Mrs. Partridge from the stockroom; the little mirror keychain from my mother; and four fat candles. I lit one and lifted the flame above my head.

The room was large, like the Shuttle, but not at all like it. The ceiling dripped, and not far from where I landed were heaps on heaps of the burlap we used to tie up our dead. I shrunk to the other side of the cave.

I could just make out the hole that I'd fallen through: dark mouth gaping from the ceiling ten feet up. It was too high, and no way to climb to it to get back home. My head thrummed from the fall and my ears felt pressured, like wanting to pop. It made me dizzy. Mrs. Wallace had told me that if you go down, the heavy air wraps around you, and you can't come back up. That was why no one had ever tried. But I knew this must be wrong. I knew it because my mother's friend, Mr. Clark, must have done it to fill up our waterskin.

I leaned on the wall, steadied myself. I was in the cave already that my mom had mentioned, and if I was searching for water, the drips from the ceiling meant I was on the right path. So I followed the sounds.

I passed through tunnels and caves cobwebbed together, listening always for the next plink of water. I squeezed through narrow passageways, scrambled over mounds of rock, backtracked from dead ends. The water dripped now from all sides. I caught it in my palms and licked it, and it tasted of sour and teeth. In the past weeks, I'd snuck drinks of lake water, away from my mother's eyes, to understand better what to look for. But this didn't taste like lake. It had to be aquifer.

I explored for a long time. I got so far from where I started that I wasn't sure I could get back if I tried. After many hours, sleep seized me, and when I woke, hunger. I opened the jar to eat a strip of jerky, and at the smell, felt a twinge of sorry. My mother had made it. She must be wondering about me now. Still, I'd left a note. And just like Mr. Clark must have come down for water and returned to the surface, again and again, I would figure out how to do that too. I stood, brushed the dust from my bag and jacket, and continued on my search.

A few more days passed like this. Two, if you judged by when I wanted to sleep; by when my hunger came; by my first candle burned down. It was longer already than I'd believed it would take, and I stuffed the nerves down beneath that faith, blindly. I found myself with three strips of jerky left, and wondered did I need to ration them now.

The next day I got hungrier, and that feeling made me fluttery in my chest. I'd seen no glimpse of what I'd imagined was a grand golden gate, like the passage to the core, glimmering pool of aquifer beyond: because didn't He want us to have it? Was it not the reward for the Earth's chosen people, if we only put our minds to finding it?

Two candles gone, and next time I awoke I felt a strange shift: opening my eyes to find them closed. For a few long minutes I couldn't remember where I was. Then I fumbled for the jar, and found my last strips gone—disappeared.

I groped around on the ground for them, thinking them spilled. I dragged my bag along with me but, in my panic, didn't stop to light a wick. Then I crawled onto a patch of slick ground, sloping downward. I tried to stand, and my feet slipped from under me. I landed hard and started to slide.

And kept sliding. It was like the chute again—less steep, but so wet that when I tried to grip it, it escaped me. As I dragged my nails along, my shriek came out dull and unechoing, like the space was tight. I was moving all at once too fast, and then I was falling through air—then through water, water all-around swallowing, and I clawed against it toward what I thought was up.

I burst through the surface. I gulped air. Once I caught my breath, I held it, and found that it floated me. I swum myself sideways, and finally dragged onto a stone shore.

The pool I had escaped, I could taste on my lips: lake.

I laid there a while. My ears felt suctioned and dull. I think I slept again.

Then I started upright. I felt for my bag. There on my arm. The jar inside, still empty. I pulled out a candle and the lighter and spent a while lighting the damp wick.

When I could see, I stood and walked all the way around the pool, even wading, trying to find where I had come in. I found it, above me: another hole too high to reach.

I tried to climb to it. I could barely get a foothold and the rock was slipping wet.

Fell at last against the wall, exhausted. Maybe slept again. Dreamed about the zigzag I'd seen chalked on the wall above the pool. Dreamed I drew a bigger one, then climbed it back up to the hole. When I woke, my head was throbbing, my stomach turning over itself.

I circled the cavern again, this time along the wall, and found on the far side an opening. Relief wobbled through me. I realized that, for a moment, my belief had wavered. But there was a way out.

I passed through the opening, through a little passageway of stone, and on the other side found what used to be a door, bricked over. I saw a ramp to my left, stairs running up one side of it and smooth on the other. I started to climb. At the top of the ramp was a door of heavy iron. When I knocked, it thudded dull with no return.

No handle. No way anyone could have heard me knocking—and anyway, who would have been there to hear it? Flutter of seasick in my gut. It kept sawing and rising, sawing and rising, until I had to sit down. The exhaustion tumbled over me, and I fell asleep against the iron door.

Then, through a dream, I heard its insides wheeze. The door opened, and pouring air tried to shove me down the tunnel. I clung to the open threshold until hands reached in and pulled me through.

AT FIRST, I WAS PETRIFIED. A whole settlement of living, unanointed people in the Underlake—it stamped onto my vision like flipping through Mrs. Wallace's illumined manuscript book: plate after plate of bright colors, each nothing to do with the last. I thought I might be dead.

Right away, I fell ill. It struck me the moment I was pulled through that door and the pressure in my ears cracked. They carried me to a room with a real mattress and a yellow flower. I slept for days. Women brought me steamed fish in broth. They tsked and held cold cloths to the bruise on my head. I was itching, exhausted, aching in my elbows and knees. I lost track of time, for the sleeping I did.

When after a few days I was well enough to walk, they took me to a grand house, all brick-made. The man there was like the reverend but warm, curious. He asked me questions, wanted to know how I reached the cavern. I told him about the hole in the ceiling, how I could not get back out but for the luck that they were throwing—what? Trash?—through that iron door a day or two after I arrived.

At this, he licked his teeth and his eyes went velvet and wide.

"Does anyone else from . . . your parts . . . know how to reach our refuge?"

"Oh no," I said, rubbing at my aching knees. "No one's been even to the caves."

He nodded, satisfied. "Rash thing to do. Around here, we know that going down in those caves, there's no coming back up. The pressure change can kill a person. You got lucky. Poor thing."

He cooed this last bit. He put more cushions on my seat, had a woman bring me smoked cheek and a cup of water.

Good water.

I asked where it came from. He did not like that. The face on him changed. When I said I wanted to bring water back with me, he said he had given it to me as a gift. He said even if I lived here the rest of my life I couldn't earn more, because I hadn't worked for it, and he called me a greedy child.

I WENT TO HIM AGAIN many times, but they wouldn't let me even into the wing.

The women who had nursed me heard what I had said and soured on me. The word spread and soon no one wanted to cross my path. They left me the scraps on their plates only. They put me last in line for lake water, and wouldn't let me fish in their window boxes, which they said was the fate of just a few.

Not since the last year of the reverend's life had I stood before a person that, if I smiled, I could not soften them against me. I was used to people telling me their secrets, feeling relieved in the telling, and then feeling bound to me after. Making them trust and adore me is how I kept safe, and kept my mother safe through me.

I was small when I first noticed the looks people sent in her direction. How she curled around me like a shell, curled around herself, lost her appetite, gave me the rest of her portion. I wanted her to eat and be glad. And I found that being small made me easier to love. So I used it. It was a pencil I shaved over many years to make the sharpest possible point. A performance, yes, but what else was there? The reverend, day in and out, performed for us, and all of us for him, and whoever did it well was rewarded. I was lonely locked inside that suit, all the time. This is not to say I was not most times sincere. But I became the best of any of us at my craft.

Yet, in the factory, it failed me. The people, I could not read. Their eyes were flat, untrusting even of the walls around their bodies. They were, more than any other word I can think, threadbare.

I spent my days pacing the passageways, trying to recover the movement in my joints, and mapping out each face I saw. I listened for names and slices of conversation. They talked about an alchemy for repairing fabrics. They talked about the well-being of "the child" and if her mother could birth another healthy one. They talked about reprocessing, which I come to understand was about making batteries—not just building them, but all the steps leading up: sanding grit off the tables, rinsing it from their clothes, breaking up old batteries, diving for supplies. This last bit I paid attention to most, because I needed to get home somehow, and diving seemed like the only way anyone left.

So I hung around in the corner of the battery workshop, outside the divers' changing room. They would slip past with a peek aside at me, go to their work, and come back hours later soaked and their eyes gnashing sparks.

One evening, when the cafeteria had mostly emptied out, I sat across from one of them. Her name I'd overheard was Joan.

She was picking at the bones of her fish. Her eyes were dark like tunnels through her head. Her hair was damp still. It took longer here for things to dry.

"Who taught you diving?" I said.

She tried not to meet my eyes. "What?"

I repeated my question.

She shrugged. "My mother taught me."

"My mother likes to swim too," I said. She'd only just told that to me. The way she had described the water on her lips and wrapping around her body—it made me understand why she moved that way when she was dreaming. She was in love with something, though she would never tell me what.

"People swim there?" Joan asked.

She had heard by now I was from the Chimneys. They knew more of us than we knew of them, since the reverend had said they drowned with the rest of the unchosen. What had really happened, it seemed, was some sort of falling-out. Weber sneered with glinted teeth to say the reverend's name—Jewell—without his title. I had never heard anyone do that.

In secret blaspheme, I believed the reverend to be just a man, but I felt sad for him more than I feared him. And I believed that he did receive His messages—in sparks, like a power surge bursts a bulb. Who, in those conditions, could know without flaw how to read them?

"We don't swim," I told Joan. I spoke in a low voice. I wanted to give us a secret together. "But my mother does."

"It's her job, then?"

I shook my head. "She is an explorer."

Joan now stared openly across the table. She didn't ask any questions, just listened to me for the rest of the meal telling confidences that I should have never shared. I told about how my mother saw a person still living in the Overlake. And I told about the water there—that it was clean and good.

She slurped the last meat off a pin bone.

"Hm. Your reverend told you there was no one left up top?"

"Yes."

"Smart."

"They didn't tell you that?"

"I hear it's a bunch of Communists and thieves. But alive, far as I know."

I leaned in. "Have you been there?"

She stood from the table. She left the tray behind, with half her fish.

JOAN WAS CAREFUL to talk only about diving. She told me the rule: that you couldn't go up or down in the water more than twenty feet. A few had tried, and come back deathly sick.

"Sick like you been." She gestured to where I was rubbing my knees.

The worst was a man who blurted through the moon pool one day, babbling about a stairway to the Up. Started spasming, vomiting, and talking gibberish—"talking *more* gibberish," Joan said—and died a few weeks later.

"That was Arthur's father," she said, her voice hushed. It was the first secret she had shared with me back.

The clean water, I learned, was real. They gave out allotments twice a month.

"It was every day when I was little." We stood in the door of the changing room as Joan pulled on her gloves. A battery man nearby was scraping down the walls with a wire brush.

"What happened?" I asked.

"The aquifer is drying up," Joan said.

"It's not," the man interrupted. His blue eyes flicked like the tips of flames. "They're trying to smoke us out."

Joan didn't respond. He put down his brush. Every movement the man made came in jerks, like oil was spitting in his veins.

"What do you mean?" I asked him.

"They're draining our aquifer and taking it for themselves."

"Who?"

He shot his eyes up at the ceiling. "Them up top."

"The aquifer is yours?" I asked.

He slammed his bucket on the floor, grabbed his towel, and marched off.

"It ain't fucking yours."

I WON'T explain all the ins and outs, the manipulations—because as I look back on them now, I know that's what they were. The little smiles we shared, the whispered confidences, how I endeared them to me.

Joan introduced me to Arthur, and they told me things I knew were dangerous to tell. They took me with them to collect their water allotments—the only time I could sneak back into Weber's chamber unnoticed for the crowd—and pointed out the room where the faucet was locked inside. They told how Arthur's father tried to build a trail that rose like a stairway to the surface. They said also that he'd failed in his mission, that people had died or disappeared trying. How Joan's mom was one that vanished.

"How do you know she didn't make it to the surface?" I asked.

Joan flung a towel over the line that hung along the divers' changing room wall.

"Because she would have come back for us," she said. Her voice quavered.

"We don't mess with any of that now," said Arthur. He looked always to Joan for approval when he spoke. She didn't notice how he gleamed at her. How everything she touched, he afterwards touched.

I told them about the Chimneys too. They wanted to know how we got our air, and did the electric still run. I learned the factory had tapped into electric lines in the ground and pushed power to everyone that wanted it, including us. "When the reverend and Henry fell out, the lake was about to fill up," Joan said. "Story is that Henry could have cut the lines to the church, but was too benevolent. I think he just ran out of time." Another secret.

All this was new to me. I'd believed what the reverend told us: that our lights were powered by charges from the core, glimmers sent up of our promised paradise. But Joan and Arthur were patient with my ignorances. They let me sit with them to eat, and if anyone spoke harsh they stood beside me till it was done. In the end, we became friends.

They even taught me to swim. They convinced the key-keeper, David, to let me help them salvage in the basement. I was terrified at first to see that hole in the floor quaking with water—an enchantment. But they taught me the ways of kicking and moving my arms, and over the next days and weeks I learned to move fast, to hold my breath. They even swam me once out of the basement and around the back side of the factory, which no windows looked down on. There, we saw a metal rod down the slope with a little flag on it. They said that's where the stairway to the Up was supposed to start. "Good way to get yourself killed," said Joan, toweling off after, "if it's even real." Later, when she was in the showers, Arthur whispered to me that the stairway *was* real, and told me how it worked, how to climb it, the rules to follow.

But all this time that I spent with them, a few weeks in total, I could feel the people of the Chimneys like a pulse across the water—their thirst, their grief. My whole world had only ever been them. So maybe I placed their suffering above the factory's. I don't know if that was right.

When I think back on my time there, I wonder: the way that I leaned close, the secret telling and the eyes so wide and steady to meet theirs—was this the way I have always been? It had never felt wrong before. When people feel like the center of all your adorations, it gives them strength. What was the difference now with Joan and Arthur, the soft in my voice and the hands tended to their shoulders? In my actions, nothing. In my intentions, it was very different. Still, I didn't tell even myself what I was going to do—until I did it.

THEY WOULD CALL ME a thief now. I maybe am. But it feels strange to call it stealing when it's what you need to live.

I tried to steal the water because I thought it was my purpose. I believed if I followed the water to its source, I could find a way to channel some of it—they used to call these rivers—back home.

I didn't have a plan yet. I wanted to see it for myself first. So I snuck inside Weber's cottage in the deep night. I followed where I knew the faucet was, found a key on the wall, and went in. But one of Weber's men caught me there, studying the pipes under the sink. They dragged me outside, and called in some battery men and Arthur to open the iron door. When Arthur wouldn't help, they beat him till his face was bleeding. I bawled while they did it and felt more sorry than I had ever felt. Then they threw me back down the tunnel and sealed the door behind.

Crushed. Returned into the pit. But now my face felt like a mask. Deceptive—not the face I thought I had.

I felt around on the ground for my bag. I hadn't thought to grab it before they pulled me, half sleeping, through the breach. It was still there where I'd left it. I lit one of my candles, tucked the lighter in my pocket, and made my way down the ramp.

At last, I knew where the aquifer was. I had seen how we could use pipes to pull water up. The pipes, I didn't know how they worked, but it was a start. Now I needed to get back to the Chimneys and share what I'd learned.

But that hole in the ceiling: impossible to reach as ever. I stood beneath it, begging Him to drag it down to my feet. He did not. And as I waited, I felt the dark closing around me like a sack, and wondered how long could I breathe in here, how could I find an exit when there was no exit. I dropped to my knees at the pool's edge and splashed my face, trying to wipe clear the fog from my mind.

When I looked up, I glimpsed on the edge of the candlelight that zigzag chalked on the wall. From all that Joan and Arthur had told me, I realized now what it meant.

A passage out.

So I accustomed myself. I swum back and forth across the pool, tried the different kicks and paddles that I'd learned, and dove deeper and deeper until I felt ready. It had come to me quick, swimming. I wondered if I got it from my mother.

When I dove at last into the tunnel at the pool's navel, I carried my last lit candle inside the upturned jerky jar. I managed to dive down twenty feet before I lost my grip on it. Then my sack slipped off my shoulder and I was left with nothing but myself in the utter drowning pitch.

But in that moment, a miracle occurred. Spackles of blue light surged up to meet me. It was the same as what I seen when I woke beneath the chute. They slithered in and out of the crags. They spiraled like the snake that churned the lake back into the originary garden. I followed them down, forgot the breath burning in my lungs. We dove so deep, and now along a sandy tunnel, and passed finally through a rock arch, into wide-open lake. They shied from the moondrip and left me at the cave's mouth.

I saw I was on the far end of the factory from where I'd dived with Joan and Arthur. I could just make out the flag that they had showed me: the trail's start.

My lungs hummed with heat. I swam along the trail of broken things, thudding in my head, biting my lips shut, swam and swam until the first cottage opened up its mouth to me and swallowed me into its full stomach.

I followed the trail how Arthur said. With each dive, the panic seized me halfway through—and then I imagined the ball of air in my lungs like a baby I was cradling. I got better with each swim, and stuck to the instructions he had whispered to me, waiting at least four hours, as best I could guess, in each cottage. This went on for days.

Each time I fell asleep, I dreamed my mom was swimming toward the core of the Earth, and woke up sick to my stomach. Strange to learn about myself, who I believed was such a mirror to other people's feelings: how could I not guess the way my own mother would suffer from me disappearing? So I left signs for her along the route: carvings in the floors, drawings on the walls. But it felt like a weak offering. I wasn't sure anymore I could trust myself to do what was right.

Then I reached a vast cottage with rooms of empty minnow troughs and crates of puzzling collections. The light by now was ample and poured down like in the Chimneys, but the walls of that place groaned. I could see them bulging. So I slept in the loft above the main room, sure the flood was coming. The next morning, with the light tipping in, I discovered on the wall beside me a kind of chart: a circle with arrows drawn out from the center, and each of these arrows in turn crossed out. Over that day, as I swum out searching for the trail and couldn't find it, I come to see its meaning.

I was trapped—could not go down, since it would only take me back to the factory, and could not find the next step up in the ladder. Arthur had warned me to take the shallow parts the slowest—that here was where you could get really sick. So if I was going to the surface—and now it seemed I had to—I needed another step.

In the cabinets there were cans with pictures of fish on them. I spent half a day smashing one open with a brick. The fish inside was sour and covered with slime. I tried to cook it with the lighter in my pocket, which burnt only small bits. I managed to choke down a little before I decided to try it as bait. I searched through the crates and found some wire and rope, a thin yellow nylon. I molded my hook, sent it out the pool, and it worked—I caught a warmouth. There was no electric, so I found a knife, scaled and gutted the fish, and after cooking it how I could with the lighter, ate it mostly raw. After the first bite, I was too hungry to mind.

My third day there, I did not swim at all. I was sick to my stomach and sick of trying. I drowsed on the floor by the pool, scooping up water with a glass or playing Upside-Down.

Though I had started drinking lake weeks ago, just before I left the Chimneys, it still surprised me every time it touched my tongue: green, tinny, with an unsettling sweet. Everyone else had always drunk it, even my mother, to leave more waterskin for me. I knew the Chimneys like it was a part of my body, yet the most essential piece—I was a stranger to it.

The next morning, I opened my eyes and the light through the windows quaked. The fish darted nervously. I had seen this before, many times. The reverend used to call it the Tears of Him falling. I decided to swim out again and learn, if nothing else, how it felt on my skin.

When I slipped under the water, a pitch of silt hit me in the eyes. I had to gasp back out of the pool and wipe my vision clear. But the churn and surge of that water also sparked more life in my limbs than what I'd felt in weeks.

I swam out and back. The lake prickled along my skin. It was speaking something.

For the next dive, I wound the yellow rope and hook around my arm. I wanted to leave the hook farther out, instead of dangling it under the cottage. I figured I could catch more fish that way.

I was swimming only half a minute when I felt, more than I heard it, a groan so deep like the turning stomach of the Earth. The silt shivered up from its seating, and the water started dragging me forward, away from the cottage, ripping all the fish along beside me. I felt the breath draining out my nose. I could see a dark turret looming ahead, and me hurtling toward it. Before I could swim clear, I slammed into it.

The air was knocked from my chest, my shoulder crushed. I choked against the urge to breathe. As I slipped down the wall, I spotted an open door. I kicked into a dark room with a set of stairs and a square of light above. I swam up and into the glow.

THIS IS, EVER SINCE, MY HOME: a concrete cube with a window in each wall. The room below me is filled with water.

When I arrived, I found a blanket and sheet folded on a cot. Above it, a shelf held two plates and two glasses and two forks. There was a table and one chair, and on the table a big cloth book with gold letters on the front: ARMY CORPS OF ENGINEERS. Inside it was page after page of what, after studying them a while, I decided might be maps. They looked like ripples in a trough when you've dropped a stone.

My shoulder felt out of place, and I couldn't swim. The pain made the sick in my stomach worse. I slept the first full day and night, and woke to the same rumbling sound beneath my feet. It was as loud as if the house were plugged into the source of it, tooth in the mouth of a beast.

I used the rope and hook again. Thank lake, the first time it caught a fish without bait. I used the scraps off that fish to hook another, and so on. I cut them to strips and tried to dry them in the window. I ate them raw when I got hungry enough to do it.

I could see through the windows the shifting light above as though it moved across a surface. Mornings were even brighter than the Chimneys, and I thought I must be very shallow now. But the days were shorter than ever, sliced down the middle, and I spent all but maybe five hours in shade. Sometimes, if I pressed my cheek to the pane, I could just glimpse the reason for it: a towering structure, blocking out the light.

I passed the dim afternoons studying that book—and slowly, I come to understand what that structure was. One map showed a wall like from the side, with a slope of earth down from each flank of it. The label said it was the dam: His final creation, that sprung the lake from itself. I'd imagined a stone rampart closed around us to calm the waters, and outside it a gnashing flood that went on forever.

The strangest part was that the map showed a tunnel passing beneath the dam. Labels pointed to gates that could open and shut, and I wondered if the deep-earth rumbling that had dragged me here had been the dam opening up. This tunnel swallowed lake through an open gate, stair-stepped up through a room, surged forward down a long passageway, and finally released out the other side into a stream of water.

I've been here for days now. I've lost track. And it's surprising what, more than anything else, has obsessed my mind. It's there when I wake, gnaws at me for hours: the half-formed image of that mythology, that relic, drawn on the far side of the dam like a fact. A river. The lake tattered into ribbons and carried off—I don't know to where.

May

Lakes, the deluge of her, her same smell of morning as the sleep sheds off, the clots in her lashes, the shift of her hair against my cheek, the bones in her shoulders lifting up her shirt—they were here, all of them, and her heart thumping beneath, and her breath rampant like the strings they played in the Shuttle all of them strummed at once all of them singing. She was alive.

Daphne loosened her arms around me. I held her cheeks in my palms to see was it her face—it was. Thinner; a little dark beneath the eyes. I stroked her hair, a tangle it would take long to brush out. I lifted her hands to my lips and she winced, which was how I found out about her shoulder.

We sat on the cot and she told us all about what she'd done, where she'd been, what she'd seen. I couldn't look away, the miracle of every piece of her.

Otta stood to one side. At first, they seemed shy of each other. But finally, she saw Otta across the room ruffling the pages of a book, and my Daphne—sensitive even to the shape of a person's mouth—stood and joined her. Otta asked some questions about the book and Daphne answered them. Daphne pointed out her confusions, and Otta started to explain the maps inside.

It turned out that the dam was very close to us now. When I was a child, the reverend used to teach it as the gate to heaven. Then a boy, my age and only nine, vanished. He left behind a note with a list of words—which was how we were taught to write, in lists—that led most people to believe that he'd gone to find heaven and that he would let us know when he got there by sending signals through the minnows. The reverend after that stopped preaching where the gate was. He said it was not a place but a time you reached. Still, for years after, a lot of us kids went searching for messages in the minnow troughs. None of them ever formed a shape we could agree on.

"These are depths," Otta was saying, pointing to a row of numbers on a chart. "We're at just over fifteen feet. Still deeper than I'd like."

"We went up and down from fifteen lots of times," I said. I half knew the answer, but was distracted by Daphne's profile in the dappling light. She looked all at once unfamiliar, angular and stretched, not like my child.

"Those were just bounce dives—now we've been at pressure for days," Otta said. "We need to take at least two hours to ascend."

"But I've been here—I don't know. A week, at least." A fog passed over Daphne's eyes, and she wrinkled her brow. "There aren't notes or instructions like in the last cottages. Like no one's ever made it this far. I don't think there is a next stop."

Soon the light was clotting into shade, earlier in the day than it should. Otta, who had been leaning over the book of maps, sighed and sat back in her chair.

"Daphne's right." She looked over to where me and Daphne sat cross-legged by the pool, waiting for the fishing line to tug. "Every structure, every single house we traveled through, is mapped out here. There's no stop shallower than this."

It landed in my head like a thump of blood—shifted the world out of focus with itself.

Otta dropped her elbows to her knees and rubbed her temples hard. But then she sensed me watching, looked up, and set her face softer.

"Rest," she said. "I'll think of something."

IN THE SPACKLING DIM, Daphne seemed all at once exhausted, sat holding her shoulder and not saying much. So I talked. I had so much to tell her: about all the cottages we'd visited, how Otta had learned me to dive, what had happened with Weber. But the more I talked, the more I returned to the Overlake—the way wind carved through the curves of your body, how it made the grass speak; the blush of a thousand different kinds of light; how the clouds uttered across the sky and were never one shape long enough before they became something else; and how the trees looked like the rafters of the Shuttle—but not that, how they towered without trying to tell you, how they sent down shade and leaves like mercies without asking you to thank them, because it was not for you, and how good this was somehow.

While she listened, Daphne drained her glass. I cringed to see her drink lake. When the glass was empty, she played with it in the pool, turning it upside down and pressing it into the water, like that old game. The air stayed whole inside the glass. A dome of water raised up inside it, pushing against the air, but could not fill it.

Otta grabbed my arm. She leapt to her feet.

"I know what to do," she said, pointing at the glass.

"What do you mean?"

"This is the same line we followed in?" Otta tugged the fishing rope.

Daphne nodded.

"And all morning, has the current changed?"

"I don't think so."

"Feed the line out farther—as far as it'll go," Otta said. "I'm going back to the barn."

Then she dove through the moon pool and was gone.

SITTING THERE ALONE with Daphne, I lost my words. The shadows were sunken around her eyes. She was thin, and bent to one side where her shoulder hung. I hadn't noticed. I hadn't wanted to. But she felt only half there, and more than just tired.

I scooted close, put my arm around her waist. She leaned her head on my shoulder. My little girl. She felt like, smelled like mine, as though nothing had changed—with my eyes shut.

The minutes sprawled. Twenty, thirty maybe. The bone in my chest felt tight, and I pressed away the worst images of what might be happening to Otta.

Then, Otta's face—sudden moon, spouting water up through the pool—and I understood now what the clouds were for: beauty is everywhere, needs even sometimes shade for its brightness. I grabbed Otta's hand.

She tossed up a sack wrapped in plastic and untied it from her waist.

"Got to swim out"—she breathed heavy—"a few more times. Wait here."

Over the next minutes, she disappeared and reappeared, diving again and again, until at last I heard a metal banging in the room below. Otta splashed up through the breach, spitting lake. In one hand, still below the water, was a minnow trough from the last cottage—the barn, she'd called it.

She climbed through the hole and we helped her drag the clanking trough up the stairs. The three of us together managed to tilt it on its side and pour out the water back into the pool. Finally, we set it down on the soaked floor. It was as long as a person and stood to the tops of our thighs.

"I've done this before, more or less," Otta said. "We have to do it again."

Otta

Daphne looked pale, and when May wasn't watching, pain washed across her face. I saw it as she hunched over the map: how she rested on one elbow and exhaled a few shaky breaths. She was injured, and I wondered whether she also had decompression sickness—how bad it might be. We needed to get her out.

On the swim back to the barn, the surface tossed down sheaves of blue light—tempting. I could be there in seconds, drowning in air. But I'd learned in commercial diving training how long it takes to traverse these last, tortuous feet, where the pressure change is most drastic—and most perilous. For this knowledge, I could thank Ethan.

In the barn, I collected a knot of clothes, sealed them in three layers of plastic bags, and tied them to my waist with rope. Daphne had been shivering, even in the heat of the engineers' office.

The trough proved harder to move than I'd hoped. At first, I dragged it into the barn's moon pool upside down, trying to create an air pocket that would float it along behind me, but it kept toppling to the side or tugging upward, trying to float to the surface. Finally, I flipped it over to let the lake water fill and weight it down and left it outside the root cellar door.

Over the next half hour, I swam out over and over, leaving it each time farther along the distance to the engineers' office. Finally, at the halfway point, I swam the rest of the way along the yellow cord, recovered my breath inside the bubble of the office, then went back three more times, moving the trough closer in increments, until I finally managed to drag it up the stairs.

Back inside, I laid out the plan for May and Daphne: a makeshift diving bell. We'd ascend slowly over the course of two and a half hours.

"I've done this." I was repeating myself, but it didn't sound assured. I felt the air in my chest chilling into stone. All the cracks in the plan were revealing themselves to me now. "But it's dangerous. Very. At some point, we'll start running short on air. It'll last longer if we don't exert ourselves. And then the buildup of CO_2 in the trough—just—let me know if your head hurts, or you feel dizzy."

What I couldn't articulate was the gnawing dread that the dam instilled in me—its long shadow, its shut teeth. I strained to remember what we'd learned on that field trip long ago—that the gates only opened when it rained.

"I don't know." May, seated on the floor, stroked Daphne's arm where it was looped through hers. "Is there another way?"

"There are no more places to stop between here and the surface. We have to try it. And I think—it's getting urgent now." I didn't want to panic her, but my gaze flicked over Daphne, and May followed it.

May stared a long moment, her bronze eyes wide as though not comprehending—trying not to comprehend. Daphne barely seemed to hear us. She was slumped and staring into the pool.

May's body stiffened, and she turned to me.

"I see," she said. "Let's go now."

MAY AND I DOVE FOR SAND, scooping it into the blanket and then the sheet and tying them up into heavy sacks, ballast to weight down the trough. We tied one to each end with the nylon fishing cord.

I took off my wet suit and zipped Daphne into it. A shiver ran through her—first the wet of the suit, then the warmth of it. "Thank you," she said. Her voice was brittle as a leaf. For myself, I layered on the clothes I'd brought from the barn.

We lined up along the moon pool and lifted the trough upside down over our heads, May at one end and me at the other, with Daphne between us, her arms around our waists. I lashed May's hand to one handle with rope and mine to the other.

We started down the stairs, keeping the rim of the trough level. We submerged to our knees, our waists, our chests. The water stopped just above the lip of the trough and held. No drips from the seams. But May and I had to pull hard to keep the edges down. We sat Daphne back up on the side of the moon pool while we filled the sacks with more sand and anything heavy we could find—bricks, paint cans. We adjusted the rope so they would hang near our waists.

The three of us descended again. This time, the ballast was heavy enough to keep the trough down without too much exertion.

At the bottom of the stairs, I ducked my face into the water and shined out the dive light to gauge our direction. I let it drop and dangle from my wrist, and we moved toward the door. The lip of lake tilted around our shoulders, blade of a knife.

In the gloom of that flooded house, the dive light's scattered beam poured down around our feet. And my scientist's brain, which had engineered this plan, which could fend off feeling, started to fracture.

This glow—like the pyramid of light cast down from that other bell.

A nightmare sliced into the waking world. I saw Ethan's face—blue, bloated, eyes gazing up—and here I was again, on the brink of that mistake. May's face, Daphne's, drained and bobbing on the lake's surface. I was dangerous—and now I had their lives in my hands. Darkness oiled across my vision.

There, suspended under a million pounds of water, May saw me starting to drift and stopped us short.

I couldn't hear her over the thrum of blood in my ears, over my own voice that I found it saying *I can't I can't I can't*.

Then I felt the lightest tremor, Daphne's palm on the back of my neck. Cool water dripped down.

"When I was lost, you brought my mother to me," Daphne said. "You can. You already have."

May

Daphne, worker of miracles, more than I ever saw Him do or the reverend or anyone. And she did it just by being kind.

Otta calmed under Daphne's touch. Her features—the set of her jaw, her drawn lips—softened. It's hard to put into words, but it was like the arrival of unknowing. A certainty crumbling.

From the flooded first story of the engineer's cottage, walking sideways along the sandy floor, we exited.

Sun rippled down. It spooled around our feet and tossed up laces into the silver of the trough.

"All right," Otta said. We were a dozen paces clear of the cottage. We took three good breaths. "Let's try a short ascent. Gentle, now."

Together, Otta and me wedged our shoulders beneath the trough's sides, bent our knees, and pushed off the ground. The water around our collarbones dropped an inch along our shoulders, pressing back against us, and then we were hovering two feet off the lake bed.

"Good," Otta said. "Now we wait."

With her watch, she started to keep time. For every two feet, twenty minutes, she'd told us. That first stop, we floated there, and talked little to conserve our breath. The light around us was an enchantment, a swirl of minnows returned to their trough. It was easy to get lost in it.

For the next ascent, we had to kick.

"As little as you can," Otta said. "The higher we go, the more the bubble pulls us up."

It took a few tries, though, to kick hard enough to move us the next few feet. Halting there, we wobbled, and I felt needles through the muscles in my arm where I pulled down on the trough handle.

On the third stop, the light around our feet all at once began to change. It flecked and shifted, shot off in all directions. An anxious knot of pumpkinseed perch drew a spiral around our legs and darted off. Daphne, who had been drowsing, started awake.

"It's raining," she said.

"Shit shit shit," Otta said, and checked her watch. "It's only a little longer, but—we might have to go back—"

"We can't," I said. I sickened even as I said it, but I could feel Daphne breathing faster, little too-quick heaves. "We might not be strong enough to do this again."

Otta nodded and noted the time. Soon, I felt it too: a throb in my head and a nagging need for air, small, but a thirst I couldn't slake.

The next ascent, we shot up farther than we meant—five feet.

Otta groaned, dragging down on her handle. The trough was trying to upend itself. The rope cut into my hand, and I felt it start to slip.

Suddenly, I heard a beast-wide groan of metal, and a shock of water passed over us. An all-around rumbling. The sand on the lake floor quivered, lifted, fogged. It went on for what felt like a whole minute, then stopped.

"I heard that before," Daphne whispered.

Just beneath the trough's edge and off to our left, I could see a churn of silt coiling up. The loose end of the rope that tied me to the handle lifted and flagged in that direction.

The whole water started to drag us toward the dam.

"Kick!" Otta yelped, and we swum against the current. The pumpkinseed whipped past, their top fins twinged a sickly orange.

"Steady," said Otta, but we were ripped along sideways, and it was all we could do to keep the trough over our heads. The water sloshed up and sprayed into our noses. I saw Daphne gasping like she couldn't catch her breath. Otta tried to lift her by the waist, to keep her face out of the water—and then something slammed into the top of the trough.

I was tossed so hard that I almost let the barrel lift above our heads. But the water all at once calmed and grew warmer, and we rose a few feet into a pitch darkness.

Otta smacked Daphne's back and she finally wheezed in a breath.

The jostling had stopped, and we seemed now not to be moving at all. Otta switched on her dive light.

The water churned by below us, thick rip of velvet. Twenty feet down was a slab of concrete. Otta reached her arm around the outside of the trough.

"I think—" She knocked, and the barrel echoed tinny and hollow. "I think we're inside the dam."

And she lifted the trough up off our heads.

WHAT IS THE DIFFERENCE between a trap and a trap? I spent most of my life inside a chain of rooms.

The scent of the air: metallic and chalk. That was new. But the suffocation, the stale fear—my oldest companions—I knew them by the taste on my tongue.

I slipped free of the rope that tied me to the trough handle. I stroked Daphne's hair, rested my hand on her good shoulder. Otta floated the trough mouth-up beside us, shone the light around the chamber. It was a concrete box, filled three-quarters with water, and us bobbing at the surface.

Daphne was pale in her cheeks. I could feel her heart beneath my palm fluttering, but she could breathe now, better than in the trough. I *shhh*ed in her ear like when she was a baby.

Otta gnawed the inside of her cheek. I could see she was debating with herself.

"As far as I can figure," she said at last, "there's only one way out."

Otta explained what she'd seen in the book of maps: that under the dam there were two gates, one after another, and a room between them. We were inside that room. Here, the different temperatures of water stirred and mixed, while the gates controlled the volume of water. We'd lost another few feet of depth, according to Otta's watch, and needed to decompress here for twenty minutes. After that was a tunnel, two hundred feet long, that barreled beneath the entire width of the dam, spitting out on the far side.

"We have to go through," Otta said.

I could hear the terror stain her voice. I should have felt it too. But I was not afraid. I could protect us. I could survive a trap.

Otta

Floating inside that concrete hull, there was no way to stop the flashback. It flooded all around me. The air itched with salt. The water shuddered with the merciless chill of the deep sea, the cringe and coil of the colossus.

But, this time, I didn't resist. I sank into that abyss, the drill and its kicked silt wailing, the earth boiling out of itself. And somewhere beyond the reach of my dive light, alone, Ethan took his last breath.

I could see his face, frozen into stone. That body had so little to do with him. The crinkle in his brow while he leaned over a drawing; the crooked grin, holding up a live whelk he'd found in the shallows; the sleep he spent hours every morning trying to wipe from his eyes—these were Ethan. And the way he tucked one corner of his mouth, lowered his voice when he was about to say something I didn't want to hear: I heard it now.

I love you.

Ever-burning ember.

Get out of bed now.

May, her lips to Daphne's ear, saw something in my face that made her reach out. She put her hand to my forehead. The color was returning to Daphne's cheeks. We could all breathe again.

When it was time, May and I bound our palms again to the handles and turned the trough upside down over our heads. The ballast had been ripped off, so there was only one way to descend into the stream churning below our feet: we had to let the lake in. I lifted one edge of the trough just an inch and a bubble escaped, replaced by a surge of water. The water level rose to our collarbones, and we sank.

Every instinct in my body told me to stop. I let the panic wash across me, breakers on a beach. Then I raised the edge again, and the water rose to our necks.

Daphne kissed my cheek, then her mother's. A tear spilled down May's face, pure glad. We all took a deep breath.

I lifted the edge of the trough. A sheaf of cold water rose to our chins. We sank. And the current caught us.

I clung to the handle and kept a tight grip on Daphne's waist. The top of the trough smashed into what I guessed was the bottom of the next gate. It upset the side, and more water sloshed in, rising to our lips. We scraped past the gate, and suddenly tore forward, and I knew now we must be in the tunnel, hurtling along with the rain. My dive light hung from my wrist, tossing beams down through the frothing current. Duckweed snarled around our legs, and somehow, a school of golden fish, moving at the same speed we were, darted between the weedy fronds as though foraging in some peaceful inlet, with maybe a moon shining down, and the hush of it all like midnight, and wasn't it good to have food to eat, and shelter, and someone alongside.

THEN A FLOOD OF LIGHT, and we slammed so hard into something that it ripped my hand from its binding. Daphne's waist slipped my grip. I opened my mouth to call out and it filled with water. Sand clouded my eyes. The current pelted me with gravel, dragged me over a succession of stones, and spit me out.

Then settled.

I floated face down. The golden fish were still there, picking at a clump of moss. Each sent up a stream of bubbles. Breath without end—for a while, without end—over and over—a celebration.

I STIRRED.

When I told my arms to move, they moved. When I told my legs to kick, they kicked. I burst through the surface of the water.

Abundance.

Air in all directions. The trees tossed in a lifting wind, ochre and verdant and flaxen, and the sibilance of insects and dry leaves stirring: a world that had been waiting just outside my field of vision for as long as I could remember, all these aching years.

The tunnel had expelled us onto a crash of baffle blocks and spume. The water then calmed into a channel lined with concrete. On each side, a rubble of stones sloped up until it met the woods.

I looked around me. May and Daphne were nowhere in sight. I called out. The words bounced up the slopes and disappeared.

The surface was thick with foam. I swam back and forth, diving and feeling through the red silt for them, returning to the surface each time farther downstream, with nothing in my hands.

I couldn't let the idea come, even as it haunted the edge of my mind. I called their names again and again. As the current carried me, the concrete raveled away. Trees climbed down the slope until at last it was a river, banks caked with mud. The canopy caught my shouts and tossed them from bough to bough, asking for me, *have you seen—have you seen—have you seen—*

And this time, a response.

"Otta!"

All my life all my life had I wanted to hear someone call my name like that.

Around a bend in the river and there they were, laid out side by side on a broad boulder, their palms locked together and their chests heaving.

May raised a hand in greeting. I climbed onto the boulder, where Daphne's eyes overflowed with the canopy above. I collapsed by May's side, wove my fingers into hers. She let out a laugh, an expulsion of relief, and it passed through her fingers until we were all laughing, laughed until our breath ran out, then heaved in another, and another, and another.

May

There is for a while after the simple sweetness of being alive.

You believe that this will last forever.

That walk through the forest with the sun winking down and puffs of seeds bursting beneath our steps; that violet flower Otta plucked from the clover; a song trickling from the canopy that no human voice can sing; Daphne's face of pure enthrall, like when she was a toddler and everything was new; how we burst from a wall of trees into a green field; how we trundled down that slope weaving and spinning; the bait shop below us opening its mouth; how a figure emerged and, when a twig snapped beneath my feet, turned toward us, its posture transformed; how it came running until we could see him: Mr. Clark, with the kind of eyes my mother had when I fantasized her receiving me into her living arms; how when he saw Daphne for the first time, he melted around us both—that none of these moments really ended—that, in a way, is true.

We slept long into the evening: Otta on my cot in the boathouse, and Mr. Clark having given over his bed to Daphne and me. We woke to the first stars prickling through the dome. Mr. Clark was at the end of the dock with a small grill. The smoke smelled of oil and salt. He handed us paper plates, and it was a fish we had never tasted. Otta joined us, rubbing her eyes clear. We spent the next many hours swinging our feet off the dock while Mr. Clark pointed out shapes the stars made, and told us a story about each one.

Daphne's shoulder needed treatment, so after a day of eating and rest, we piled into the truck. It was like observing myself from the outside, to see Daphne experience it all: first ride in a truck; first time with the wind tearing through the window; flipping through the radio; seeing the houses intact and starting to cluster; ducking as another truck hurtled past; and inside the next one, glimpsing a person—and who, and how, and all the thrill and terror of it.

The reactions flickering over her face, the wind tangling her hair, the questions she asked—it all felt electric. But then, as I told her the names for things I'd just weeks ago learned—the truck's shining hubcaps, the mailboxes, the traffic light—I realized that already, the newness of these had dulled. I'd started not to notice them. And I saw that this sweetness was not going to be the rest of life—but that maybe draining away was part of what the sweetness was.

OTTA INVITED US to stay with her while Daphne's shoulder healed from the dislocation. We all needed rest—were dehydrated and hungry, our stomachs turning and sickly from what we'd eaten or not eaten. The doctor told me my eardrum had burst, which was why noises from far away sounded close, and noises close sounded far. Otta's wrist was sprained and her finger broken where they were wrenched from the rope.

After the doctor, Mr. Clark dropped us all at Otta's house. As we trailed up the front walk, the curtains through the window shifted with the breeze through the screen.

Otta unlocked the front door but wouldn't step over the threshold.

"I need a minute," she said.

Daphne and me went in and sat on the couch. The curtains followed us inside, the wind tossing them between the boxes.

I found myself speaking too fast, like I had many times in the last two days since we'd been Over. I could already picture our new life together: the trunks of trees and red soil and the quivering heat off asphalt—roads that could take us anywhere. Daphne listened but kept quiet. Small washes of I don't know what—confusion, pain—passed across her face.

I could see that she was tired. I stopped talking. Instead, I did what Eugenia would do: I went into the kitchen and filled the teapot.

After digging through the cabinets, turning the knobs on the stove, watching the second hand tick in the belly of a cat-faced clock looking left-right, left-right, I managed to make three cups of tea. I took them all on a tray out to the living room.

Otta came in through the sunporch door. I heard her stamp her feet on the rug, and she walked into the living room, pricks of pink in her cheeks.

"You comfortable?" she asked.

"Yes, thank you," I said.

Daphne managed a smile—even at half strength warmer than you could believe.

Otta dropped into an armchair. She noticed her cup of tea steaming on the table.

"This one." She raised it above her head. It was white overlaid with a blue scene, and some design or letter was scrawled on the bottom. "This one we'll keep."

OTTA HAD A ROOM and a bed for each of us, both larger and softer than we'd ever felt. But an hour into the first night, Daphne came crawling into bed with me. I was happy for it. She had been quieter, less sure, and I'd felt between us a distance that I couldn't cross.

I could say this distance was new. But the more I thought about it, the more I knew it wasn't. I'd buried a whole side of myself when she was born and never let her see it: the ashamed and crooked self, the frightened girl. And at the same time, in her, I'd only seen my daughter. When she'd tried to show me who else she was, I wouldn't hear.

So during the weeks that followed, I listened. I held ice packs to her shoulder; I leaned in close with my good ear; and I let her speak. She talked first of why she left, next of how, next of her time in the factory and the cottages. She talked about how worried she was for the Chimneys, for what would happen to them now. She said the world had been shifting before her eyes like pictures from different books. I wanted to let her tell her story, this time, all the way through.

IN THE AFTERNOONS, I'd help Otta load up boxes in the car, which she took to the New-2-You in town. The physical labor made me sleep deep, and I liked the ache in my limbs the next morning, my body carved inside my own control.

One day, Otta came home and set a bottle on the counter.

"Look what I got," she sang. "Coke."

I laughed. She had witnessed my enchantment, and was gentle with it.

She poured us each a glass. I heard the bubbles fizz; my ear was mostly healed now. We pulled up to the kitchen table, an ease to our limbs, like sitting there together had become old habit.

"So. How's Daphne doing?"

"She's good. Healing."

Otta must have heard my doubtfulness. "But?"

"I don't know. I'm not sure she's happy here."

Otta studied me over the rim of her glass. "She's worried about everyone down in the Underlake?"

"Yes."

"Are you?"

It was a strange question, but she'd seen it in my face before I knew it was there: how the answer was stranger. I hesitated. "Yes, and no. Joan and Arthur, yes, because I think they want to leave. But the Chimneys, I—even if I told them, they wouldn't believe me. And I'm done trying to belong where I don't."

"You want to stay."

"Yes." I'd never said it aloud, but now it twisted my chest, how much I wanted it—painfully much.

"And what comes after that?"

I shook my head, shook my head. In a world so vast, there was no answer to it.

Then something occurred to me. I felt in my pocket the yellow plastic flower I'd stolen from our room in the factory. The sheets of petals, lakes of petals, clouds of petals I'd envisioned when I first held that bright bloom—they all surged into my mind fully formed.

"Ha!" I showed it to Otta. "I want to go where they have these flowers—the real ones."

"Daffodils."

My mouth dropped open. World of all worlds.

"Daphne-dil?"

"Daff-o-dil," Otta laughed, almost spitting Coke out her nose. I giggled a giddy release.

"Well, I've got news for you," Otta said. "We have those around here. Come springtime, they'll be everywhere."

Everywhere. I couldn't imagine it. I tried to picture a field of daffodils. I could wander that field for a long time, and not need to know where I was going. I liked the idea of that.

Even as she smiled across the table, I could see the weight on Otta's eyes, the bad sleep, the phantoms that trail behind forever.

"What about you?" I asked. "What are you going to do?"

Otta shrugged, peered around the kitchen. We'd cleared every cabinet, and the sunporch was now completely empty.

"I have some things to finish up here," she said. "Not just the house. But after that—I don't know. Go visit Allie in Vermont? They've got a lake there so huge you wouldn't believe."

She raised an eyebrow and grinned.

"Don't forget me," I said. It felt all at once like a straw sucking from my heart. "You got to visit me too."

"I'll visit," she said. "Where will you be?"

"Everywhere."

ONE NIGHT, as I was drifting off, Daphne started to speak.

She talked about the cave under the factory, but she described it strangely—like it was made of different colors than I'd seen, and lit in its deepest waters with glowing animals, mapping her the way out.

"I always had a secret question in my mind." She studied me from the corner of her eye. "I wondered did He feel sorry for it—ending all the world but us. Because I felt His regret, smothering us all like a blanket. The babies—they couldn't breathe beneath it."

She sighed out a shaky release.

"But now I seen the truth. He didn't drown anyone. So it has me wondering—does He visit us at all? I never seen Him step in to save those little babies, or to make anyone be good. Maybe He lives way up on that hill, sitting under a tree. Maybe it's not His sorrow weighing us down—it's disappointment. Because we're getting it all wrong."

The moon was a sliver in the window, a thread clipped loose from its seam.

"Then how do we get it right?" I said.

She rolled over on her side to face me. "Did you ever meet Arthur?"

That surprised me. "In the factory—Arthur?"

She nodded.

"Yes."

"Wasn't he wonderful?"

Her eyes swam, green pools and creased at the corners, and I saw in them something of myself. "Wonderful how?"

"I mean how in love he was with Joan."

"Was he?"

"He never said it, but you could see. Easy. When he looked at her."

I hadn't seen. I had been possessed of my own aims—maybe blinded by them. "They were in love?"

"Oh, I don't know if they were. But he loved her. I never seen anything like it."

She rolled onto her back and crossed her good arm on her chest. She dozed off smiling.

No one in the Chimneys had this kind of love, that twinkled even in its telling brighter than any bulb. Even Caleb's, over years of losses, had faded to match Mary's.

But I had felt it once. I knew that I had. I'd just never realized it could be beautiful without anything to reflect it back.

OVER THOSE WEEKS, Daphne was working out something in her mind. She talked about the different types of sleep at different depths, about reading the shapes and shifts of water, and knowing the mood of it by taste. She talked about finding more sources of it in the caves, traveling down the chute again—that the core of the Earth must be water, since how could heaven not be made of it? She wondered, if she found it, would people start trying to have babies again.

During the day, we took walks in the woods. I'd follow what Otta called "deer trails," tread quiet as I could, afraid of what we might see but burning in my chest to see it.

Sometimes I stopped us in our tracks. We'd look up and see the tops of the trees nudging each other gently, holding up the wind as it passed. They changed color every day, shifting from red to orange to gold to the crisp brown beneath our feet—crunching and much and unashamed. There was a moment, alone in the cavern, when I'd remembered these trees, and my terror had drained away. I realized I had found my way without anyone to tell me right or wrong. And I could do it again.

I believed Daphne would marvel at all this beauty the same way I did. But the glisten seemed to be wearing off. She asked questions, nodded at their answers, then turned back up the path. She started asking could we go to the marina. A few times, Mr. Clark or Otta drove us down to the lake and Daphne sat by the water, stretching her toes to touch.

Her arm was still in a sling but healing. She started doing her exercises without me, even lifting light boxes out to the car to get her strength back.

One morning, I woke and she wasn't beside me. I went downstairs and found her sitting on the front stoop. Bursts of ice patched the earth. I sat down and wrapped my arm around her against the cold. Her sling was on the grass.

"You don't have to go back," I said.

My voice cracked into bits. We had never talked about it. But all at once, it was here.

"I want to."

"So." A word caught in my throat—something I couldn't swallow, and couldn't say. "You'll tell them the truth, then," I managed. "You'll bring them up."

"I'll tell them. But it will take time for them to understand. And leaving or staying—that will be their choice."

A shrivel of wind carved between my lips and down my throat, gouging the thing free—not a word, but a sob.

"They can't stay." What I meant, and she knew I meant, was *You can't*. She took my hand.

"Trust me," she said. "Wait for a sign from me. And refill the waterskin."

Her lashes were coiled and crisp, like the brown leaves at her feet. She was so young, but with a wisdom I couldn't fathom its source.

"All right."

I pressed my lips to her temple, smelled from her hair. Salt, sulfur, stone.

Mounds of leaves heaped the yard and still were falling. The house groaned inside its footings. Birds, so many birds, sang from somewhere near, and under all this I heard the musk and hush of something growing, a burst seed, just below my feet.

Daphne

This world has more beauty than even He can measure. But if all we did was chase it, we might forget what else we need to do.

So we receive a gift. The gift is all the things we don't have. We twist, we stretch, we suffer. We reach out together. Togetherness is the second gift.

The third—and there are many, and there is no order—is water. The lake in all its forms. I had my doubts. I felt, in the middle of my mission, abandoned. My shoulder swelled and purpled. My focus flaked. I grew more and more hungry. Those blue sparks that guided me, I started to think were just fantasies, made-up hopes in the absence of hope. Alone in the cottages, alone with myself, I wondered if the threads of that togetherness could snap, so that when it came time, no one would even feel me gone.

Then the rain. It came the moment we needed it. It placed the answer in our hands. And it carried us the rest of our route, through the perilous and plummeting, it drowned and shook us awake, delivered us onto a shore so beautiful that my breath—I could not reclaim it.

Not at first.

Everything my mother said about the Overlake was true. Its sighing winds, the land yawning out in all directions, more possibilities than you could count branching from every step you took. The tastes, the smells, the sounds—they were overwhelming. Such things await us in the core.

In the factory, I learned that togetherness does not include the whole world. I should have known that sooner, I think. It never included my mother, though I tried so hard to make it. In reality, it is many smaller webs that sometimes overlap and sometimes don't.

I know where my web is. It is clearer to me now than ever. In the Overlake there may be a thousand more people, ten thousand, but I wouldn't choose any of them over those—even if I do not always love them—who are my home.

They have not been perfect. Who ever has? But untruths can make people do wrong, and so I believe that truth can do the opposite. I have so much to tell them—I'll climb to the pulpit if I have to—about all the people still living, all the delicate and strange and entire worlds, and about how maybe His grace is broader than we thought.

Otta

A hundred times, I'd come home from school and walked straight up the stairs without a word. A hundred times, skipped the dinner my mother made. I believed I was punishing her for a crime she'd committed before I was born. But all I really wanted was for her to sit beside me, ask me questions, stroke my hair.

Now, returning up the front walk, those years swarmed my senses: the sweet rot of leaves, the soft wood groaning in the rafters, and, seeping through the screens, the scent of cardboard and polymer and perfume samples: the walls of a fortress that my mother had built for herself—but also for Allie, and for me. Her pain was so clear to me now. Why couldn't I see it then?

I unlocked the door for May and Daphne and walked around the side of the house, past the sunporch and across the yard, trying to catch my breath. I found myself swinging beneath that low branch at the woods' edge. The smell of decay gave way to something crisp. The half-bare branches shook their last ochre tufts, and I remembered how we carved this path: by dragging the heaviest boughs we could find, one by one, to a clearing. I made Allie stand clear while I leaned them against the sprawling arm of a live oak and lashed them together. Then we wove twigs between them to form a roof.

I reached the tilt. I swept the plastic rug with a loose pine branch. When I thought of this place, I usually remembered our plays, for which I was often a spectator, cheering Allie on. Now, out of habit, I inspected the weaving in the roof. Keeping the structure solid had required constant maintenance. While Allie gathered her costumes and props, I'd arrive early, repair any leaks, sweep the rug and polish it with puddle water. Over the years, I scavenged rope and tarps and plastic place mats from the house to patch the roof. I brought out electric lanterns for stage lights, and once a jar of lightning bugs collected through a long dusk.

I'd cycled through the same memories like a habit: rowing Allie out onto the lake in defiance of all warnings; and, the second I could escape, abandoning her in Steels. But I'd taken care of her too. And I'd followed Ethan wherever he needed me: his friend, his roommate, his tender, his bellman, to make him happy, to keep him safe—and many times, I did.

There was another night I'd almost forgotten: my small legs crossed on the rug, clapping and hooting as Allie took her bows. I grabbed up the jar of fireflies. We marched back to the house still buzzing, trying out accents and skips and flipping our hair. When we stomped through the kitchen door, our mother spun around with affected surprise, wielded her spatula like a scepter, and dropped into a curtsy. She laid out her best china, and as we pulled up our chairs, dished out our favorite but rarest dinner: pancakes with whipped cream and blueberries from the bushes out back. This was before the city councils, before the hoarding, before the revelation of what I thought our mother had done, when the forest roiled with cicadas and birdsong and somewhere buried inside it was a treasure. And it was already ours.

IN THE WEEKS AFTER we found Daphne, I spent several nights in the city, helping Allie pack for the move and getting to know her friends. She exuded a warmth that made everyone around her feel safe, seen. When I saw her perform on closing night, a chill gripped my skin that I had trouble shaking. She was brilliant. If the MFA took her nowhere—she would still be brilliant.

As for Eugenia's boxes, I went through every single one. I took most of their contents down to the dump, and the rest I sold at the consignment store in town. But the work was quick, because I'd shaved the question down to a simple one: did this box contain anything to do with those versions of Eugenia who picked blueberries and flipped pancakes, who drove to the city for sundaes, who dug flower beds with Ottilie's shovel, who could be—sometimes—happy?

I had one finger in a splint and my left wrist was sprained from where the rope on the trough handle had twisted free. But May helped with the heavier boxes and, when Daphne's shoulder started to recover, she helped too.

One day, on my way back from the dump, I drove to the lake and stripped down to my swimsuit. The water shivered up my skin, and I swam out as far as I could, fueled mostly by the one hand. After that, I swam almost every day. In my mind, a plan was forming. I could feel Ethan now—somehow—below me, legs crossed on the lake floor with algae grown over every inch of his body. Fish pecked all around it, glad, and fed, and sheltered.

I squinted down into the water, my breaststroke surer by the day, and listened to the lake slice and settle around my arms. Impossible to save him. And possible every day to try. Joan and Arthur were still trapped down there, with dozens of others.

I was building up my strength.

THE FIRST SNOW fell in late November, early and out of season with the leaves still spiraling off the trees. I drove home that day clutching the wheel, the flakes sticking to the road and sudden gusts kicking into the windshield.

When I went inside, May was asleep on the couch, the gray tabby curled up beside her and a green sweater knotted beneath her head. Daphne had been wearing it—an oversized cardigan that never seemed to keep her warm. May's galoshes sat by the door, dripping lake.

That night, I sorted through the last boxes and stacked them by the front door. Room by room, I'd stripped down the house to its most essential items: the furniture Eugenia's grandfather had built, framed photos, Ottilie's china, and the planters that my mother bought to grow herbs—the reason she'd built the sunporch in the first place.

I sat down at the kitchen table, where I'd laid out a stack of photo albums, a teapot, two cups, a music box, a velvet pouch of Allie's baby teeth, and a ruby brooch. With the house emptied out, I could feel her coming into sharper focus: Eugenia, in all her complexities, cold spells and kindnesses, and a wave of pain rolled toward me now, the whitewater cresting above my head. I took a breath—held it. I dove beneath the break.

TWO DAYS AFTER OUR RETURN, Clark filled the tank, drove it along the narrow lakeside path, and hooked it up, starting the flow of water down to the factory. Within a few weeks, it was running low. I'd made enough cash from the consignment store to fill the tank one more time, but Clark and I between us didn't have the money to keep buying water.

That winter soon revealed itself to be the snowiest on record. It was too cold to dive again as soon as I'd hoped; we would have to wait for spring. The flurries piled up, and after successive plowings stood six feet high along the road into town, refusing to melt for months.

The surface of the lake froze over completely. May went out sometimes on foot to refill the waterskin she'd hung in the chimney.

So, with the tank almost dried out again, we got the idea one day to unscrew the lid and start shoveling snow inside. We left the cap open for the snow and runoff to collect. To keep it from freezing solid, I'd walk out sometimes along the lakeshore, teapot steaming in my hands, and pour it into the tank.

The snows lasted into March, then came heavy rains and, day after day, week after week, month after month, it was always enough. The lake teemed with bluegill and sauger and trout, and the Earth remained as ever indiscriminate in what we call its punishments, and its mercies.

Acknowledgments

It's difficult to count how many people have supported and believed in me along the way, but I'll try.

To my first readers for this novel, Meagan Arthur, E. Briskin, and Amanda Baker: I cannot thank you enough for your generosity in sitting down with this work in its roughest form, and making it in every way better. Thank you also to Brent Schaeffer, Maureen McCoy, and Paula McCoy for being early readers.

Marya Spence, I will be forever grateful for how you've believed in and championed this novel from the very beginning. Thank you for your edits, which greatly improved the book.

Lee Boudreaux, I am awed and humbled by your support, and your brilliance. This book would not be what it is without your sensitive eye, your attention to detail, and your deep connection to this story.

Thank you a million times over to the teams at Doubleday and Janklow & Nesbit, including Mackenzie Williams, Bill Thomas, Sarah Perrin, Laura Cherkas, Anna Knighton, Vimi Santokhi, Kirsten Eggart, Emily Mahon, Julie Ertl, Kayla Steinorth, Maya Pasic, and Anne Jaconette. You made my dream come true.

Thanks to Bradford Morrow at *Conjunctions* for publishing my very first work of fiction.

Gratitude to my first writing group, the Tygrrs of Seattle—E. Briskin, Amanda Baker, Brent Schaeffer, and Billie Swift—for your incredible writing and friendship.

To my professors and cohort at the University of Washington, I will never forget your support. David Bosworth, thanks for letting this poet sign up for your fiction classes. Linda Bierds, Pimone Triplett, Andrew Feld, and Richard Kenney, you helped me refine my music and fine-tune my language.

Many thanks to my colleagues at the University of Houston. Stephanie Pushaw, Tayyba Kanwal, Lisa Wartenberg Vélez, Jennifer L. Julian, and Pritha Bhattacharyya—thanks for your companionship while I became a fiction writer.

To my dear friends, for all your support along the way, thank you: Brooke Herbert, Megan Metté, Rebecca Monen, Kassie Alderson, Mike Ward, Nate Sanders, Alexa Stamets Sanders, Merv Huber, Knox Gardner, and Victor Chudnovsky.

All my gratitude to Noemi Press, *Best New Poets, Beloit Poetry Journal, Bennington Review, Seventh Wave, The American Poetry Review, Nimrod, Pleiades, Poet Lore, West Branch, The Missouri Review, Virginia Quarterly Review,* and so many others for publishing my work. Thank you to Community of Writers for the scholarship and fellowship.

Thank you to my father, Doug, for teaching me to care about the environment and to ask questions. Thank you to my mother, Paula, for inspiring my love of reading and literature, and for being the best mom anyone's ever had. Maureen, you're brilliant, brave, kind—it's an honor to be your sister. All my love to my grandmother, Doris; my uncle, John; and my aunts, Claudia, Debbie, and Diane. Thank you, Gisela Carpio, Liduvina Llanos, and Benito Llanos for welcoming me into your family. Los quiero mucho—y a Benito, te recuerdo con cariño. This book is in loving memory of my grandfather, David Cyphert Fitch.

Anthony: None of this would exist without you. Every day, you give me strength. You make this world a better place for everyone who knows you. Thank you for spending your life with me.

ABOUT THE AUTHOR

Erin L. McCoy is the author of *Wrecks,* a finalist for the Noemi Press Book Award. Her work has appeared in *Narrative, Conjunctions, The American Poetry Review,* and *Best New Poets,* among other publications. Born and raised in Louisville, Kentucky, McCoy has lived in Seattle, Malaysia, Spain, and two St. Petersburgs.